SPIN DOCTOR

M.C. Lewis

Key Bridge Books
an imprint of
Saundersport Publishing

ISBN: 978-0-9851850-1-5
Copyright © 2012 by M.C. Lewis

Published by Saundersport Publishing
www.MCLewisBooks.com

For Randy

"You know, I hate, detest, and can't bear a lie. Not because I'm straighter than the rest of us, but simply because it appalls me. There is a taint of death, a flavor of mortality in lies which is exactly what I hate and detest in the world."

Joseph Conrad
Heart of Darkness

Chapter One

The radio was as loud as I could stand it. I sipped a Coke that had gone warm between my legs. I was already late. I had waited until this morning to leave to miss the traffic. The fog had slowed me down and now I was at a dead stop just before the bridge. What could be the problem? Construction? Again? An accident? A jumper? We started moving and when I got to the steel guardrails of the bridge, I locked my gaze straight, only four miles to go. As I drew close to the square arch, looming in the low clouds at the highest point of the bridge, I slurped my Coke again to soothe my tight throat. Before my father's death, I liked driving across the bridge, crossing to the western shore and Washington, looking up the Chesapeake to see the sailboats or the sun on the water. I began to descend through the fog just as my cell phone started to ring.

I had to steady myself. I swallowed hard and sucked some slow, quivery gulps of air. "Jack Abbott," I said, voice thick. I wedged the phone on my shoulder and twisted the radio off.

"My God, Jack, where are you? The Congressman is going nuts. Have you seen the paper?" It was Martin Moroney, technically my boss. Congressman Greg Harrow's chief of staff.

"No. I'm outside Annapolis." I hit the western shore of the Bay and shot past the line of tollbooths in the eastbound lanes and the exit for the state park.

"Oh. That's right. Your father's ashes . . . Did everything go okay?"

"Yeah. I didn't fall in." It just slipped out. I didn't mean to sound so flippant. Although my father had died about a year ago, I had put off spreading his ashes. I knew what Martin was getting at—what he really wanted to know: *Are you finally going to be able to get beyond this, pull yourself together?*

"Okay. Listen . . ." Martin was whispering now. "He's freaking out. Front page of the *Post* . . . an awful picture."

Three eighteen wheelers had me closed in and I couldn't see ahead. I pushed up in my seat, watching for an exit, some place that might have a *Washington Post.* I probably could have gotten a digital version on my phone, but I wanted to see what Harrow saw. "I'll get a copy and call you back as soon as I have it."

The other side of the highway had a strip mall, a McDonalds and a WaWa. But on my side, almost nothing visible from the road. Finally I spotted a 7-11 and took the exit. I got a cola Slurpee and a suburban edition of the paper. While I waited to pay, I skimmed the front page. Above the fold, several columns wide, was a flattering picture of President Dexter in the Oval Office with the Secretary of State in the background. Dexter was a flack's dream. How hard could it be to work for a guy like Dexter? At this point in my life, I would have worked in the White House for Satan, I think. Well, maybe not Satan. But President Dexter was never more popular or respected and he was going to sail into his second term. Although everyone needs a flack.

Unfortunately, I had to turn the paper over and sure enough, Harrow's picture was right there, one eye half-closed, mouth crooked. Unmistakably, characteristically drunk. The story was on the speech he had given to a trade group. I slid some coins to the cashier and went back to my car.

The Dexter headline caught my eye: *Dexter Reelection Questions Persist.* How could that be possible? Dexter was a lock. A shoo-in. It was unthinkable that Dexter would not run. My eyes raced over the first few paragraphs. The story was actually about campaign infighting and strategy. All speculation. Would he dump the Vice President? Everyone knew Dexter couldn't stand him. Dexter was so far ahead of all possible rivals in the poll, it didn't matter who won the primaries. Dexter could "go fishing" until after Labor Day. But upheaval and uncertainty could mean opportunity. I couldn't stop myself from reading the whole long article, continued inside on page 17. Did I see a name there that I knew, or that I had a way of knowing, through a friend? Or a friend of a friend? I thought about calling Bob Carson, one of my closest friends, who was somehow always wired in, full of gossip. If the players were going to change, they would need to staff up. This could be my big chance to get back to the White House.

But first I had to take care of the business at hand. I had to flip back to the front page and read the story on Harrow.

I couldn't believe Harrow made the front page of the *Post*. For Washington PR, a bad story on the front page of the *Post* was like a nuclear disaster: There would be fallout for weeks and nobody would forget it. I was still skimming it and speed-dialed the office. "This is Jack. Put him on." I could hear Harrow in the background ask where the hell I was. Shout, actually. Then he grabbed the phone and breathed into it. "Have you seen it?"

I thought for a moment about reminding him that there was no such thing as bad publicity, but read his tone and instead came out with a firm, "Yes, sir. What happened?"

"What do you mean, what happened? You weren't around to do your job and the press fucked me AGAIN." After he said the word, "again" I heard a loud crash.

"Mr. Harrow?" I didn't get any answer. I heard more muffled talking, and he came back on the line.

"Fix it." Slam.

I called Martin back. "What happened, for Christ sake? This isn't the speech I wrote. I don't even know where the hell Lixubistan is. Where did he get all that?"

"Over dinner. He sat next to a woman from one of those groups. You know, Whackos International or something."

"Great. Blonde?"

"No. A redhead, actually." Martin breathed a long, tired sigh. "She got him all pumped up. By dinner, she probably could have gotten him to say the Pope was his father, that he likes to eat babies for breakfast. I had no idea he was going to do it. Then the reporter from the *Post* got to him before I could."

"Okay." I switched the car on and eased out of the parking lot toward the exit, missed the light and cruised to a stop. "I'll make some calls. I'll try to turn it off."

"Wait a sec, Jack," Martin said in a low voice, exasperated, like I wasn't getting it. "He isn't actually mad about the *story* . . ." He drew in a breath. "He doesn't like that picture. Says it is deliberately unflattering."

I closed my eyes. "Don't tell me."

"Let's just low-profile it on the issue. Maybe he will, you know, forget about it in a couple of days. If we try to talk him out of it, he'll just . . ."

"I know." There was no point in arguing with Martin. He had a wife and kids. He was scared to death of Harrow, lived on the knife's edge of Washington. He wasn't the first AA Harrow had and almost certainly wouldn't be the last. No doubt he had come to Washington with dreams of "doing good." He could occasionally influence Harrow, but more often let himself be the cat's paw.

A horn behind me sounded and I realized the light was green. I got back on Route 50, still waiting for Martin to answer. He went on like he hadn't heard me: "You can soft pedal it . . . You know how to do that without going over the line. If anybody can fix this, you can, Jack."

Of course there was no way to "fix it." But I could offer some explanations to the press back home, try to smooth things over. Get into his calendar and cancel any speeches for the next six months or so.

By the time I got to the office, just after noon, Harrow

was gone for the day, thank God. Esquita, his secretary, stood in his private office and rubbed her fingers along a gash in the plaster wall. She heard me at the door and looked up. "Hi Jack. He's gone." Almost to herself she went on, "What am I going to tell them about this?"

I stepped toward her and saw the hole, cracked through the outer layer of plaster down to the wood lath wall underneath. "What'd he throw?"

"The phone," she whispered.

I inspected the phone on Harrow's desk and could see a small outline of white dust on one corner. "Does it work?" I pulled the receiver up to my ear.

"Sure." Esquita shrugged. "I don't think you can break that thing."

"I guess if you could, we'd know by now, wouldn't we?" I looked at her but she didn't smile at the crack. "Just say we were trying to rearrange the furniture and pushed a little too hard."

At my desk I flicked the computer on and tried to sit down, but there were three grocery bags stuffed with dirty laundry lined up behind my chair. So everyone could see, of course. My girlfriend, Marguerite, must have dropped by. Still mad at me. I had moved to her place six months ago. She asked me. I was crazy about her, too. I saw the corner of a note sticking out of one of the Safeway bags. "*Call before you come over to get the rest of your stuff. —M.*" I knew why she was mad. She had never been to the cabin. She wanted to go with me to spread my father's ashes and I said no. I knew she was probably right but I just couldn't do it. I had to be alone. I guess I hoped she would cool off. She had definitely cooled off on me. I stuffed the clothes in the kneehole of my desk. One crisis at a time.

I thumbed through my mail and clicked through my emails. Caffeine, cola, tea. Lots of it. Then I made some calls. It wasn't hard. I put out a statement correcting any mistaken impressions that the Congressman had left. He had not, of course, misspoken. He was misquoted and misunderstood.

When you have such an in-depth understanding of the problem, and profound sympathy for those unfortunate Lixubians . . . Is that what we call them? Okay, it was hard. Hard to do with a straight face. Everyone understood I was just doing my job.

While I made my calls, Dexter smiled at me from the front page. I tormented myself with what might have been—having no idea of course, what the future would bring. I thought about the past, on where I might be if things had gone a little differently. Working in his White House, not for this creep Harrow. Maybe would have been inside the Oval myself, once in a while. I thought about the article in the Post. I should call Bob Carson. The most connected of my inner circle. Of course he was going to tell me to shoot him a copy of my résumé. Which I would do—as soon as I could figure out how to spin Harrow on it.

The day plodded by and at about six, I started worrying about where I was going to sleep, since Marguerite had probably changed the locks. I tried to call her. I tried the home number, her mobile. She didn't—or wouldn't—answer. I didn't bother to leave a message. It was clear we were through. No point dwelling on it. She wasn't changing her mind.

I thought of calling Bob Carson again. Bob might get a drink with me and let me know if he knew anything about the Dexter campaign. Bob went one better and invited me to a reception at the Greene. It was a no-brainer. Free food and drink. I wondered if Bob just needed a ride and considering the front page with my boss's pathetic face on it, already had thought of calling me. Bob was a good guy. He probably figured I was going to need a drink, too.

I had forgotten how much Bob liked to drink. We won't use the A-word, because he is a friend. I picked him up in front of his office on Capitol Hill, a converted brick town house. While he came down the walk, I dumped out the rest of the Slurpee, grabbed the other travel trash rolling around on the passenger side and tossed it in the back seat. Bob was very neat.

Before he got in, he swept the seat with his left hand, picked up a straw wrapper I missed and handed it to me like he found a twenty dollar bill. He asked if I minded if he closed his eyes for a few minutes.

At the first light, the latch on the glove compartment decided to relax and the door flopped open. Bob jumped, jolted awake. He gave the door a gentle push and it clicked closed. His eyes were open now and before he could rip me about my car, I made preemptive small talk: "So what have you heard about the Dexter campaign? Did the Post have it right?"

Bob stretched out his legs a little. "Not really. I heard he's thinking of dropping out."

I wasn't sure if he was joking. We stopped at another light on Independence Ave. "Is there a punch line?" I finally asked.

He felt around for the controls on his seat and managed to recline it a few inches. "No. I'm serious. Since his daughter died, then his wife, he just doesn't give a shit."

The light changed but some tourists were waddling across directly in front of us. "Damn. Then who's going to run?"

"Duh. Cunningham of course."

"Oh my God. Please tell me there is someone else."

"I don't know. How about your old boss? John Cook?"

"Very funny. Cunningham won't have a chance without Dexter's coattails. So I guess this would be a bad time to ask you if you've heard about anything in the administration."

"Hmmm. Let me think. I don't think I know about any press opportunities."

"Wow. Cunningham. I wasn't ready for that."

"I know. But it's just a rumor. Remember, most of them are wrong. In the end, I'm not sure he could do it. I mean, Dexter won't drop out now. Everybody knows how he feels about Cunningham. If he was going to drop out, he would have done it earlier so there could be primaries."

"I hope you're right. So who is in line for the campaign, assuming he does run?"

He didn't answer so I looked over. His eyes were closed again. We went the rest of the way in silence. When we got to the reception, he popped out of his seat and you never would have known, for a while at least, that he'd had a drop. He was buoyant. His face glowed pinkish and his eyes reminded me of a hunting dog. We had to walk a couple of blocks, since I wasn't about to pay for valet parking. An obscure group that had nothing to do with Bob's work was paying for the reception. Somehow he had a couple of tickets. When we came into the lobby, the soft notes of a jazz trio led us to the ballroom. From the doorway, I could smell the chocolate from the dessert table in the far corner. But seafood was the specialty at the Greene. The usual mountain of shrimp was flanked by raw oysters and silver bowls of cocktail sauce and lemons. I could see what appeared to be roast beef and lamb on the other side, but I followed Bob's sure steps to the bar and got a beer.

The crowd was mostly gray or dark blue suited, almost colorless. Typical Washington. Youngish, probably a lot of Hill people like me, just a few gray heads, and a lot of politicals from the Dexter administration. Bob planted himself near the bar while I made the rounds at the buffet tables. I was contemplating dessert when I bumped into Bob again. He introduced me to the best looking woman at the party. At life's great buffet of women, she was the shrimp. I would say the caviar, but I've never gotten to a party early enough to taste caviar. Gorgeous. I had noticed her as soon as we got there, of course, then lost track of her. Bob introduced me. "Sarah Gorrell." She smiled and shook my hand.

"Jack Abbott." I said. God, I must be good at this because I could hear myself talking and joking but all I could really see was those incredible blue eyes. Yes. I know. A blue-eyed blonde. She stood under a gold wall sconce and the glow on her hair, the way she stood, almost made me wonder if she had placed herself there on purpose. She glittered. Bob had eased away from us, probably back to the bar, and she asked me where I worked. What was I going to say? I work for that clown Harrow, and hope she is one of the three people in town who don't know what's on the front page of the *Washington Post*. "Up on the Hill," I shrugged.

"House or Senate?"

Uh-oh. She was going to get it out of me. "House."

"Who do you work for?"

"I'm a press secretary. You know. Anyone who needs press. It's a booming business." I flashed a confident, casual smile, like, *who cares?*

"So you work for one of the committees? Which one?"

Let's change the subject. "What?" I squinted and pretended not to hear. "Listen, can I get you another drink?"

"Sure. I'll go with you."

Her glass still had a slurp of white wine in it. "White wine?" I nodded toward the glass.

"Wow. You're good."

I smiled back. I love smart-ass women. It was a good plan, but Bob was standing by the bar.

"So, did you two straighten everything out?" He steadied himself with his elbow.

We looked at each other. "Gee, I guess so, Bob." I watched him, hoped he wasn't going to lose his balance. "What were we supposed to straighten out?"

Bob cackled. "Oh my God, Abbott, if you can smooth things over with her, you are good." Bob stared at our puzzled faces. "You know. Harrow. Lixubistan. The front page of the *Post*. Hello. Hello."

That's when I found out she was from the State Department. And of all the little countries I never heard of before today, she handled Lixubistan. When she discovered I worked for Harrow, let's just say she was underwhelmed. I went from being a fun guy to a tiny bug trying to crawl down the front of her dress.

"So what possessed you to write a speech like that?" she asked with an icy smile. "Does he even know what he said?"

I swallowed. "I didn't write it and I'm not sure."

"Oh, right. So where were you while your boss is out creating international incidents?"

"Out of town." Good answer, I thought. Not my fault.

"Out of town?" She shook her head left-right-left and on the last left, she kept going, walked away from me without even telling me see you later, call me or fuck you.

Bob was still standing there, smirking. "Thanks, Bob," I breathed into my glass.

"Don't mention it, Jack. God, she's gorgeous, isn't she. You two would have had beautiful children. "

"Bob, why did you do that?"

"What do you mean? You were going to have to tell her, for Christ sake. And I wanted to see how far being tall and good looking could get you. Not that far, after all." He shrugged. "And now you have a reason to call her tomorrow. Business. I bet she remembers you, too. Don't sweat it." Then he leaned in closer and whispered. "Come on, Jack, it's not like she was going to take you home with her tonight."

I remembered the sacks of clothes in my car. I stepped around to the side of Bob, and whispered, "Shit. Bob. You knew Marguerite kicked me out, right?"

Bob frowned at me, which I took as no.

A line had formed on the other side of the bar. "Last week. It's a long story." I didn't really want to get into it there. "I guess I could get a motel room or something tonight." I eyed him over the top of my glass.

"Sure. Motel 6. Very nice."

"Or you could let me sleep on your couch."

"Jack, you forget. *I* sleep on my couch."

I just looked at him.

"Okay, just kidding. Sure. You can sleep on a corner of the rug, by the fireplace. I have an extra pillow."

"Can we go or do you need to alienate a few more women for me first?"

"No. My work here is done. But let's get one more drink."

Bob lived in an incredibly expensive, modern apartment the size of a London hotel room. Small. Stuff that folded down from the wall. I really did have to sleep on the floor. But I didn't care much. I had to let him use the bathroom first so I went to work a little late. While I waited, I sat on his Persian carpet in my boxers, flipping channels, checking the news, the traffic reports, looking at my watch. Maybe Harrow would be late or would skip today altogether.

But I was wrong. It was 9:30 when I got there, and already Harrow was in his office with the door closed. I started back to my desk, but Esquita called my name. I could tell from her face that she had tried to cover for me but that I was in for it. "He said to send you in as soon as you, um . . . got in." Those were probably not his exact words. I drew a breath and pushed through his door.

Harrow is such a pathetic little man, especially when he is angry. Have you ever been in the room with someone who scares you a little bit, whom you suspect may have a knife in their desk drawer, saved for that really big tantrum? Have you ever sat in front of someone imagining the next day's headlines: "Staff of the Congressman say Abbott had been acting strangely prior to stabbing himself 23 times with Mr. Harrow's letter opener." I finally got out of his office when he took a call from one of his big donors. There was a time when I would figure out things that would make him happy. Get people to call him, bring him funny items from the newspaper that would make him chuckle. I just didn't have the stomach for it anymore.

The press calls about Lixubistan died down and I had time to do more research. CRS, the Congressional Research Service, had a short paper. I tried to get to the web site of the group quoted in the paper but the server was apparently down. In a few minutes though, I had the basics from a quick check of the internet: a little mountainous country positioned near China, Russia, the Middle East. Right in the middle of everything. We say they are an ally. Nasty despot in charge, oppressing his people, but we need to work with him, of course, to try to turn him around. Administration policy. Not just this administration—we had been supporting him for 20 years. So the babe who got to Harrow was hooked up with the Lixubistan Liberation Front, trying to overthrow the government. Just one of several groups, actually.

I called three times before I got through to Sarah. I was smitten, yes. Maybe I was on the rebound. And what did I have to lose? But she wouldn't return my calls so I played dirty: I called the congressional liaison and explained how I was trying to educate myself. She "encouraged" Sarah to have lunch with me. I knew a great little place just a few blocks from the State Department. She could walk. A burger joint, a little better than a student hangout. So it wasn't like I was trying that hard. It was a little windy, but unusually warm for April and I couldn't resist sitting outside. I settled at one of the four cafe tables along the sidewalk, all tables for two and ordered an iced tea.

Smart ass is one thing. But at this point in my life, I'm really not all that turned on by women rejecting me, looking at me with utter disgust. As I waited for her, I had plenty of time to reflect on this and on what I was doing waiting at the restaurant, knowing she was going to try to slam me in my place then get the hell out. If she showed up at all.

By the time she got there, twenty minutes late, I didn't really give a rat's ass what she thought. I had convinced myself I wasn't really interested in her. I still thought about Marguerite, after all, and whether I should try to fix things with her. Then I saw her, unsmiling, cut through the park, cross the street and come down the sidewalk toward me, blonde hair fluttering in the light breeze. I broke out in a sweat. No kidding. I could not remember when a woman last had that effect on me. Like seventh grade or something. I was almost choking. But she couldn't tell. How could she tell when she would barely look at me? She glanced at the three other little tables, all empty, and looked at the doorway, like she was wondering why we were sitting out here.

"This okay?" I offered. "Such a nice day."

She shrugged and sat on the little folding chair opposite me. She ordered bottled water, glanced down at the menu wedged between the metal napkin dispenser and plastic ketchup bottle. It was dog-eared and had a few ketchup stains on the bottom. She didn't touch it but instead, quizzed the waiter on the selection of salads, sending him back to the kitchen for confirmation of the availability of fresh baby spinach. I had a burger I think. I asked her a half-dozen questions about Lixubistan and made no reference to the party. She could barely look at me. Instead her eyes followed whatever went on behind my head. Traffic. Pedestrians. The food came fast. She pushed her fork into the salad like a surgeon probing a diseased gall bladder. "So is the Congressman planning on speaking out again on this issue?"

I strained. I wanted to say, *'How the hell should I know?'* But I knew I could win her over if I could find the right tack, given enough time. She sipped her water. The waiter sloshed more iced tea in my glass and I waited for him to leave the table. "I'm not sure what his plans are at this point."

"Maybe he's planning a trip there?" She almost cracked herself up over this remark, but shut down again, and studied her salad without making eye contact.

I shook my head. "No. Hates to travel. Especially to war zones." I smiled. She tried not to, I think.

She finished chewing a tiny bite. "You know . . ." She lowered her fork and looked at me hard . . . "I get the sense you think this is funny. The State Department takes this very seriously, Jack. I know Lixubistan is a small country, but it is strategically located . . ."

God, the way "Lixubistan" rolled off her tongue. "I realize that. That's why I'm here."

"Really."

"Yes." I dumped some sugar in my iced tea. "Really."

She laid down her fork and dabbed her lips with a napkin. "So, you never told me where you were when the

Congressman made his speech." She looked at her watch and I had a sense that any minute, she was going to pop out of her seat and tell me she had a meeting to go to.

A gust of wind blew her napkin off her lap. I tugged another one out of the dispenser and held it out to her. "I was over on the Eastern Shore." The French fries were cold, but I was hungry. I nudged one with my fork, trying to decide whether to pick it up with my fingers.

"Oh." She closed her eyes for an instant as in, *'Now I get it.'* "You were at the beach. Why didn't I guess that?"

I put down my fork, and for a moment, I didn't care if she ever went to bed with me. "No. I wasn't at the beach. I had a personal matter to attend to." I looked at her smirk and I just could not stop myself. "I promised my father I would spread his ashes on the Chesapeake. I put it off for a year. I dreaded it. But it was the anniversary of his passing and frankly, if the Congressman had fucking declared war, this was more important to me. I told you I had nothing to do with that speech. He trashed the one I wrote. I'm on your side, okay? I'm trying to fix it. Are you going to work with me on this or do I have to go to someone else at State?"

While I talked the smirking face went into mortification. "I'm sorry." She swallowed. "Why didn't you tell me this last night?"

I saw the waiter in the doorway and made the "bring the check" gesture. "Normally I love to bare my soul to strangers, but you may recall, you didn't let me."

"I'm sorry." Now she was looking at me. Trying to make eye contact.

I wasn't sure if I was pitiful to her or whether she was afraid she had pissed me off and I might get her in trouble. She made a half-hearted reach for the check but I snatched it away and handed it, with my credit card, to the waiter without looking at it.

"I really am sorry, Jack." She folded her napkin and placed it neatly under her water glass.

I think it was the first time I actually heard her say my

name.

The waiter brought my card back and while I finished signing the check she rested her elbows on the table and leaned in. "Are you cleared, Jack?"

"No." I shrugged. "With Harrow, I don't need a security clearance. He isn't into national security. Usually."

"It's okay. I have some useful stuff I can give you that isn't classified. And, we can talk. Come on." She stood up. "Do you have a few more minutes? You can walk me back to State and get a cab there."

"I really should get back. The House is in session today."

"Of course." She took a step away on the sidewalk, then came back and grabbed my hand and held it with both of hers, as though she were a politician. "Listen. There's a reception I have to go to after work. Why don't you meet me there and I can give you a packet of stuff?"

I studied her. Why not just put it in the mail? I searched her face, but couldn't read whether this was pity or was she trying to contain me. She didn't need me complaining to the Congressional liaison office again. Or was she a little bit attracted to me? Possibly? Maybe this day was going to be better than I thought. "Okay."

"I'll email you the details." She smiled and released my hand. I watched her walk away for a moment, trying to remember why I was mad at her, what my name was . . .

Three-hour lunches are not the norm on the Hill, at least not when the House is in session. I had taken a taxi to her end of town, waited around for her, and the upshot was, I was gone until almost four o'clock. Back at the office, Martin was waiting for me, literally, standing in the doorway. Before he could say anything, I heard Harrow's voice. "Get him in here."

Being late didn't help, especially when Harrow already thought I was essentially lazy. But what had him furious was the paper, which had only come to his attention in late morning.

There was one little line. "Congressional support for administration policy on Lixubistan seems to be softening, with Greg Harrow condemning US actions over the weekend. However sources say Harrow's level of concern with the policy may have been overstated and that no immediate plans have been made to hold hearings on this issue."

I stepped inside the office and heard Martin softly close the door behind me. Harrow was leaning on one outstretched arm, like he was holding the wall up, peering out the window. At the click of the door, he jerked his head and grabbed the paper, which he whacked on the side of his desk for emphasis. "The whole reason I was fucked is the State Department, and now you're in bed with them. The article looks like I *misspoke*. I meant every goddamn word. Listen, you little prick, the least you can do is get this right. You sure as hell haven't done anything else around here lately. Lixubistan is a problem. The administration is whistling out their ass on this. Maybe I should have a press conference on it, introduce some legislation . . ."

I didn't try to argue. I chose to take the whipping. He wasn't hearing anybody on this, certainly not a lowly flack. I nodded, said "yes, sir" a few times. Maybe he thought I was going to argue. When he paused long enough for me to talk, I pointed out that the press had gotten some of the facts wrong. He really loved that and began to lose steam. Thank God, there was a vote. He left to go to the House floor and never came back to the office. I stayed at my desk until the House went out, about six, then left for the reception.

I thought about walking but changed my mind when I got outside. The sky was black and the wind bent the tree limbs and scattered litter through the street. In a few minutes there might even be thunder and lightning. Everyone had the same idea about outrunning the storm and the streets were jammed, but somehow I was only a few minutes late getting to the Hyatt, which was over on the Senate side of the Hill. She was waiting for me in the lobby, outside the reception, which suited me fine until I started wondering whether she just didn't want to have to introduce me. She had a brown accordion folder under her arm, and an expensive looking purse on her shoulder.

She had taken a cab, so we decided to take my car, which had been parked only a few minutes but long enough to have pale pink Cherry Blossoms stuck all over it and a bright red parking ticket on the windshield. She pretended not to notice. She took in my car, of course. I saw her looking without being obvious. But I couldn't tell what she thought. Some women are reassured by a BMW, no matter how old, no matter what color. Some, not so much. When she got in, her eyes traced the crack in the seat leather and it showed on her face when she looked at me again. It was like she had seen me naked. She suggested Georgetown and pushed the accordion folder onto the back seat. "For you. Not classified, don't worry." She switched on my radio, pressed each of the four presets that worked. Her reaction to my taste in radio stations was inscrutable. Just as we got to M Street, the rain and hail started, and I went for the underground parking down by the waterfront. There were a couple of restaurants there, and we agreed on Mexican. We took the elevator up to the entrance, completely protected from the torrents of rain outside. Cocada Envinada. One of those names you can never remember, after their famous dessert. Very intimate, almost romantic, even with the touristy location. Small rooms with faux adobe walls, flowing curtains separating them, and mellow Mexican guitar music. It had been one of Marguerite's favorites. I have to admit, I relished the idea Marguerite might be hungry, too. We lingered at the door, waiting to be seated. The deluge on the waterfront sidewalk distracted me until the clicks of Sarah's heels on the terra cotta tile floor snapped me to attention. I followed as the maître d' led us to a table.

She still made me nervous. She ordered a mango margarita. They were on special so I got one, too.

We had avoided the rain, but the wind had tousled her hair as we had walked to the car from the Hyatt. I had the urge to smooth it and I think I may have been staring at it.

She pushed the hair out of her eyes with a careless rake of her fingers, leaned toward me, crossed her arms and rested them on the table. "I'm really sorry about your father, Jack." She was almost whispering.

I nodded. "Thanks."

We both lifted our drinks, which took two hands, and sipped.

She rested her drink on the table. "Tell me about him."

I took a long breath. I knew what she was getting at. The Washington question: Was he anybody? Important? Maybe rich? I knew how to bat that one away before I was out of college. "Small businessman." Never failed to shut down the line of questioning. I sucked a long, pensive sip on the little straw in my drink. "When he got cancer, it took about a year. He never had a chance."

"So how did you wind up working for Harrow?"

I had gotten good at this over the years. Relaxed, smiling, smooth and friendly, I went on, "You know John Cook?"

"The Senator?"

"Right. I was his press guy."

"Wasn't he the one . . ." She stopped herself.

"Big scandal, trial, ethics problems, you name it."

"Oh, yeah." She smiled hard, like, *Are you serious?* "So you worked for him?"

"You know, when you do press," I always paused at this part, like doing press was a tad harder than brain surgery, "you actually want to go to the people with the PR problems. Much more challenging. I mean, you can choose, instead, to work for someone boring who just wants to get their name out. But if you really want to make a name, you try to help someone. Someone like John Cook, who is a terrific guy and a pretty good Senator."

She nodded, not answering right away. I couldn't tell if she was about to laugh or whether she was with me.

I leaned in again. "Same thing for Harrow. Then the congressional election came along . . . Then my father found out about the cancer. Harrow turned out to be, well . . ." I gave a knowing shrug. Number one rule in Washington: Never badmouth your boss, no matter what he does. I watched her eyes to see if she was still listening while I gulped some Margarita. "But I think it's time. I'm starting to put out some feelers." I was sure she was going to like that.

She steadied the base of her drink with one hand and touched the salt on the rim of the glass with the slender index finger of the other. "What do you want to do, Jack?"

I really didn't have a ready answer, so the truth leaked out. "I've always wanted to go back to the White House."

She smiled an indulgent, almost pitying smile, like I just said I wanted to join the circus.

I met her eyes, expecting her to ask me for details, and before she could, I changed direction. Instead of saying, *'So how about you? What brought you to the State Department?'* I feigned disinterest in her background. "I'm curious. What's the take inside the State Department on Dexter? Does he look as good on the inside as he does in the press?"

She studied me for a moment, like she was considering whether she could be candid. "Dexter is okay. Some of the people around him . . . well, you know how it is. I don't want to call them hacks exactly, but you know . . . Some of them just don't have the background to get foreign policy."

We ordered some food to share, and I could see she would only have that one huge drink so I got the check and drove her home, just north of Georgetown. The rain had subsided so we decided to take a walk. A few blocks from her place, we started into a small park. The benches were too wet to sit, so we followed the path inside the cast iron fence until we heard a crack of thunder. I grabbed her hand and we ran back toward her place. The rain caught us, pounded us. She would have to invite me in. When we got back to her front door, I had to stand close to her, our dripping suits touching, to get out of the rain, while she fumbled for her keys. Her blonde hair stuck to her forehead and her wet skin glistened under the porch light. As she clicked the lock open, I slipped my arm around her and kissed her.

We didn't exactly hurry inside. She turned on her gas fireplace and got me a towel, a blanket, and a glass of wine. She went upstairs to change then sat next to me on the couch in front of the fire. Not close enough to slip my arm around. Not at first anyway. She poured us another glass of wine and a little later, she yawned. I stood and folded the blanket into a neat square then placed it on my end of the couch. "I need to get home." By the time she was on her feet, I was at the door. I pecked her on the cheek and warned her that I would be calling her for more guidance on Lixubistan.

Of course I wasn't going home. There was no home. I didn't really want to go back to Bob's, but I also knew I didn't want her to have to tell me to leave. I wasn't sure how to play things at this point, so I took the safest approach and implied I would have to call her. Work related, of course. I wasn't sure whether she might have felt a little sorry because of her gaffe about my father or whether I might be winning her over.

The fire had warmed me through and dried my shirt a little, but I was still damp. When I got to my car, I was so tired, I decided to just close my eyes for a few minutes and of course, fell asleep. The only good luck I had was that I didn't get mugged and the police didn't roust me. At six, when it was getting light, I woke up, freezing, with the worst stiff neck. I headed over to Bob's, waited until he was probably gone and went up for a quick shower and shave.

When I got to the office, I really wasn't very late. The thing is, for once it would have been a good day to be late. Esquita didn't look at me but said Harrow wouldn't be in. She said Martin wanted to see me.

Martin wasn't smiling. "Let's go in here," he waved a hand toward Harrow's empty office and shut the door when we were inside.

I sat on the couch. Something bad had happened. I knew that.

He sat opposite me in the leather wing chair, Harrow's usual throne. "Jack," he began. He could look me in the eye, but only for a moment. He went on, "Things have been going badly, as you know. Things have gotten . . . really bad." His eyes dropped to his hands, the rug and our feet. "I've been trying to shore up for you, but he won't hear of it. He wants you out."

"Out? Out where?"

"Out, as in gone. You know." He met my eyes again.

"Oh."

"I'm sorry Jack. I think on one hand, you don't really deserve this. But on the other hand, we both know, it's just a matter of time, right?"

I was still staring at him, letting the words sink in. "A matter of time?"

"Things seem to be getting worse and worse. Think of how long it's been since he's fired anyone." Now he searched my face for a glimmer of acceptance. He swallowed and I sensed how much he wanted this to be over.

"True," I nodded. There was no point fighting, was there? Was there any way to talk him out of it?

"Press people especially usually don't last so long, really."

I tried to focus. I interrupted him. "So what's my deal? Two weeks, a month, until you find somebody?" My mouth went dry. I said that too fast. I was agreeing to leave.

Martin shook his head. "Today. Two weeks severance."

"Today? As in, clean out your desk, take your plant and your ceramic rhino collection and get the hell out?"

"I'm sorry, Jack. I wish I could stop it. If you tell Esquita what files you want from the computer, she can put them on a disk for you. But he was adamant that he didn't want you to touch the computer."

It didn't take long to pack, needless to say. I had a nice little cardboard box full, and a couple of pictures. I carried them to my car and got some cash at the ATM.

As I drove out of the garage, I thought about Sarah . . . "Hi, this is me. Yeah, want to have dinner tonight? Oh, forgot to tell you, I have no place to live right now and I just got fired."

I turned left on Independence. The traffic was thick and I crawled along, catching every light. Which was okay since I didn't know where I was going. I could call Marguerite. Or one of my friends. Bob, or Evan Brett. Then it came to me: I had to get turned around. I had to go back to the Eastern Shore.

Back to the cabin and think.

Chapter Two

About eight a.m. the cold woke me up. Or maybe
something crawled across my hand. The weathered boards at
the end of the dock had made an imprint on my cheek and
forehead. The jolt awake temporarily made me alert and I
lingered on the dock before going in. Through the fog I heard
the squawk of a great blue heron. It slammed into the water
and instantly emerged with a fish.

For a moment, I was the fish.

Eaten alive. Minding my own business and bang, fired by
the worst member of Congress.

I replayed Martin's words again and again. What I
should have done. Should have said. Confronted that SOB
Harrow in person. The spineless piss ant. Whether it was a
mistake. Martin would be calling me. Harrow changed his
mind. But I knew he never did. Maybe someone could
influence him. That never happened. I was an accident
victim, trying to remember what happened and whether it was
my fault.

And what the hell was I doing here? Why didn't I go
back to Bob's place—he would have been okay about that—
but I was embarrassed. Even though everyone thought
Harrow was a joke, letting myself get fired was embarrassing.
Maybe I was hiding but I had to be alone to get myself
together.

I got to my feet and my head was throbbing. I moved
toward the cabin, eyes half closed to keep out the light, but I

could see the birds flee the locust trees. A moment later I heard the barking. It was too late for me to run in the house and lock the door. Our neighbor, Mrs. Lynch, barged through the colonnade of cedar trees and across the yard toward the house. She didn't notice me on the dock at first, as she shifted the paper bag she carried and got ready to bang on the back door. But her dog, a fat beagle, came right out on the dock and sniffed me suspiciously. I was found.

She took a few steps toward me and started talking. "I was surprised to see your car here in the middle of the week. I thought I better come check on you." She was smiling but as she got closer, she stopped and stared, taking me in, head to toe. I was still wearing my suit, without the tie. My shirttail was out, shirt unbuttoned. Her eyes shifted back to mine and she forced another smile. "I brought you some onions and things here. My cold frame is so full, I could feed an army."

I tucked in my shirt and we walked toward the back door. "Thank you." I was suddenly hungry and almost glad to see her. Before I could take the bag from her arms, she flung the door open and went inside. I caught the door and held it for the dog, who sat defiantly on the step. She placed the bag by the sink, gave a pitying glance to me then around the kitchen. "Would you like some coffee?" I asked automatically, trying to remember if the jar of instant in the freezer would yield enough granules to make a passable cup.

She watched me open the freezer and waved me off: "No thanks, I'm fine." She opened the bag, took out the onions like they were Fabergé eggs and placed them it in a line on the window sill. There was a small head of broccoli and a sandwich bag full of tiny lettuce leaves, which she put in the sink. When she was done, she gazed out toward the water.

"I almost expect to see your dad come walking in from your pier . . ." She turned and we exchanged sad smiles. "I saw your car last weekend but I didn't have a chance to come over. Haven't seen you all winter. Thought maybe you finally got married." She smiled slightly at me and wiped her hands on her apron. "Was everything okay when you opened up?"

"Everything was just as I left it. Thanks for keeping an eye on things."

"I still have your key, you know."

"Yes. Thanks."

"Are you still working for the Congress? You must be on vacation." Her eyes darted around the kitchen again, resting on the line of empty beer bottles next to the trash can.

"Uh, not exactly." She waited for me to answer but I didn't know what to say. "How's Joey doing? I haven't seen him in—wow—it must be years."

"Oh! Wonderful. He got a job in Baltimore."

"That's great."

"Yes. It's a great opportunity. Benefits. You name it. So he's sharing a place up there, and he's going to rent out his place down here for the summer."

"The place over on . . ." I waved my arms in the general direction of the next cove.

"That's right. Right nice little place. He has it fixed up with a little pool and a new dock." She smoothed out the bag and folded it into a neat rectangle. "I couldn't believe what he said he could get for a week." She ran her thumbnail over the folded bag to put a nice crease in it. "He just put up an ad in town. He's already had a couple of calls."

I was trying to picture his bungalow. I think I had only seen it from the water and it seemed like a well-kept little place but nothing special. Now I had an urge to go see what the pool looked like. My head was pounding and I was suddenly desperately thirsty. I wondered if I had any aspirin. I took some steps toward the door to try to coax her in that direction.

"Your dad helped him with the pipes. Never would take a swim in it though."

"Mmm. That's great." I kneaded my forehead and backed up just enough to let the dog get a glimpse of me. Maybe the howling dog would get her moving.

"We're still looking for a place for Michael. She took a step toward the door, but her eyes bore through me. "If you think about selling, we're still interested." A tight smile. As though I didn't remember why she was so friendly.

A wave of nausea swept over me, and I thought about dashing to the bathroom. I swallowed a couple of times and my stomach eased up. "I'll remember." I was able to smile and nod. "But I'm not going to sell."

"That's what I thought, but I just wanted to ask again, since a year has passed. I know it's hard for you to get over here." The dog began a mournful howl and it was pointless to say anything further. "Alright, I'm coming, Lady." She squeezed my arm on the way out the door. "You take care of yourself and remember I'm right next door."

I ran to the bathroom but I couldn't throw up. After I drank a gallon of water and a Coke, and let hot water run on my head for 30 minutes or so I felt a little better. In the shower, maybe the blood started getting to my brain and I had the germ of a plan. If Joey could rent his place, why couldn't I rent mine? I might be able to patch things up with Marguerite after all, maybe move back in. Or figure something else out, while I looked for a job. This was the nudge I needed to get out of my dead-end job. Maybe my timing would be perfect— It was an election year after all. Always a good time to make a change.

I made some tea and took my mug out to the end of the dock. I could see the silhouette of the heron across the cove perched improbably in the very top of the pine tree. My plan could work. I was going to be the heron, not the fish. I hadn't finished my tea when my cell went off.

It was Bob. "Jack, where are you? I called your office. They said you didn't work there anymore."

"I was canned."

A pause. "Obviously. What happened?"

I swallowed. "Harrow is a lunatic."

"He's always been a lunatic, Jack. What made him finally fire you?"

"He didn't like the way I handled Lixubistan . . . Thought I was in bed with the State Department."

"Jack, you dog. That's exactly what I thought when you didn't come home. So where are you, actually? Or would you rather not say?"

"Very funny." I put the tea down so I could clamber to my feet. "I'm at the cabin over on the Eastern Shore."

"Damn. So what are you going to do? Be a fisherman?"

"Hm. I hadn't thought of that." I walked slowly to the end of the dock. "Actually, I've been thinking about what we talked about the other night . . ."

"You mean the Dexter campaign."

"Yeah. Or the White House." I took slow steps toward the house.

Bob sighed. "Mmmm. The Dexter campaign has been staffed for months. You know that, right? Unless you want to do Advance or something. I don't think so. Although you would make a great advance man. Well, who knows what could open up? I'll ask around and see what I can find out."

I didn't say anything. I was doing the math on how much money I had.

I could hear Bob puff on a cigarette, I think, before he went on: "Hey, I know. What about Evan. He was looking for someone, wasn't he? You probably don't exactly want to go backwards, but it could keep the wolf from the door. Maybe just fill in for a bit? Until after the election. People in the administration will leave after the election. That's the time to look at the White House."

"Evan was looking months ago. I don't know if he found anyone." I had forgotten all about it, and wasn't sure what to think.

"Well, you might as well check around first. No harm in that. You know, there's always a lot of action on the House side. Especially during an election. Congressional campaign committee. Something like that. You could be the savior, the smart guy. A great interim move—and after the election, who knows?"

I think I mumbled or groaned. I still had my mug so I opened the screen door with my pinky and kicked it wide with my foot.

"Plus, that could cleanse you of the Harrow stain. I could be wrong, but I'm not sure which is worse, that you worked for Harrow or that he fired you."

I stopped walking when he said that. Of course, I knew he was right, but it was a jolt to hear him say it out loud. "Gee, thanks for these rays of sunshine, Bob. Excuse me while I dive off the end of the pier."

"Okay. Can I have your car?"

"Aren't there any flies left in your office to pull the wings off of? How is this cheering me up, Bob?"

"Okay, you're right. So send me your résumé. Oh, wait, I bet you don't have it together yet, do you?"

"Goodbye Bob. I have a large fish on the line." I poured the rest of the tea down the sink. "I'll send you the résumé later today."

"Good."

I ran some water into my mug and stared out the window. My résumé could wait. I realized I could buy time, at least a few months without a job, if I could rent the place. But where was I going to live if I rented the cabin?

Surely I could patch things up with Marguerite. It was true that I couldn't stop thinking about Sarah, but what were my odds? And I hardly knew her. After all, I had been with Marguerite for months.

Like plunging into the cold swimming pool before you can think about it, I sat down and called her. She didn't take the call, of course, so I left her a voice mail. It sounded pathetic, but all basically true. "Hi. It's me. I'd just like to talk to you. I'm afraid I lost my job, so don't call me at Harrow's office or drop anything else off there." Then I sighed, not sure what else to say, and hung up.

A few minutes later she called back. I saw it was her on the caller ID and I braced myself for a whipping. I hoped she had cooled off a little. I was ready to say whatever I had to.

I answered but before I could get past hello, she started, voice soft and almost quivery: "Jack, I'm so sorry."

I swallowed. "Thanks."

"Are you okay?" She sounded so worried. "Where are you?"

"I'm over at the cabin." My mind went completely blank except for answering. "I'm going to work on renting it out, I think." I put a knee on the chair at the end of the kitchen table.

"Oh." A long pause followed.

"Yeah. Apparently there's a pretty good market right now."

She still didn't say anything for a moment and I wondered if we lost our connection. "Marguerite?"

"Yes, Jack. Sorry. I was just trying to understand. So you aren't moving over there. You're selling the cabin?"

"No, I'm not selling it. Renting it right now." My agenda popped back into my head but I couldn't think how to work it in.

She went on, "Oh. But, I mean, have you thought about what you are going to do? "

"A little. Well, not really. I mean, I'm in shock."

"What happened?"

"Did you see the paper with that Lixubistan fiasco?"

I heard her gasp. She didn't really follow the news, but I mean—front page of the *Post.*

"Oh my God, was that . . . you?"

"Of course not. I tried to fix it." I slid into the chair and leaned on the table. "But you know Harrow. A redhead this time. He met a Lixubian redhead, and was convinced I was trying to sabotage him."

"I didn't mean . . . Of course, it wasn't your fault . . . I know that." She was quiet. "Look, Jack. I'm not mad at you any more. You can come back."

"Thanks Marguarite." I swallowed. I couldn't do it.

"I mean it. I want you to come back."

Be careful what you wish for. It was my move. It was so much easier than I thought it would be. "I I I don't know, Marg." I stammered. "I mean, I just don't think it would be right. I think you have put up with my bullshit long enough." I don't know what happened, or why I said it.

"It's okay, Jack." Her voice sounded shaky again. "Take some time to yourself. But I'm just a little worried about you." I could hear her breathe. "I miss you."

"Marg. I don't know how I could have gotten through the past year . . ." My voice cracked.

She interrupted. "I'll keep your stuff until you're ready for it. Just take care. Okay?"

"Sure. Of course. You, too. Take care of yourself."

After we said goodbye I put my phone on the table and stared at it. I thought about calling her back. I was pretty sure I could call her back and maybe say I loved her. Maybe I would have to drive over, see her in person. Bring some flowers. Or I could call her back and ask if I could stay in the spare room. We could just be friends, right? I thought I knew the answer. Hearing her voice, she definitely wasn't mad at me anymore, but I couldn't do it. I needed some time to think. It wouldn't be that hard to find a place to stay while I rented the cabin. Renting the cabin was the greater challenge. That was the thing to focus on.

I pounded out a resume and sent it to Bob so he could read over it for me. Then I decided to get some errands done in town to clear my head and pick up more beer. And I could drop by the boatyard—TJ's—and see if there were any bungalows like mine up for rent. TJ's was the hub for the boat crowd, and since the cabin was waterfront, it was ideal for a boater. Back when I was in high school, a friend got me a job there. When I started, I didn't know anything about sailing. But I learned fast, and by the time I graduated, I was an expert on every boat in the yard, and what kind of car would roll into our parking lot with a likely customer.

I didn't expect TJ's to be crowded in late April and it wasn't. But the Bay was warming up and I could tell business had been good. I walked through the outside lots, one with jet skis and trailers. Closer to the showroom there was a shed with outboard motors. Over by the fiberglass skiffs, fishing boats, trailers or dinghies, little aluminum ones, surprisi probably have to paint mine to sell it and even be lucky to get a few weeks beer money. In the ba showroom, next to the office and the men's room, I fo the stained corkboard just as I remembered it. It reached from waist height up to the low ceiling and stretched down the short hall to the back door. Used equipment of all description. Ads that looked a few years old and which nobody had bothered to take down had newer, cleaner ads layered over them. I scanned the grimy index cards, scraps of paper, and even some neat computer printouts, complete with pictures. Somebody was asking $500 for a trailer. I searched the board for a cabin like mine and almost didn't notice the long tanned legs coming toward me.

"Circe, are you a mirage?" The only thing changed about her was her hair color, which was now a soft brown with blonde streaks. Her shorts and t-shirt were covered with paint splatters that matched the deep red you might see on the bottom of a boat. But it looked good on her.

"Hi, Jack." She slipped her arms around my neck and stood on her tiptoes so we could kiss cheeks.

I really had no idea she was back in town. "How long have you been home?"

"A few weeks. Seems a lot longer though."

"I bet it does. God you look good." Why be stingy with the truth, I thought.

She tipped her head toward the bulletin board. "Looking for a boat?"

"No. I was going to look at your rentals." A quick smile, trying not to look worried. "Just getting some information, because I'm thinking about renting out the cabin. I thought I'd see what the market looked like."

She put her hand on my arm. "Your cabin. Oh my God. Jack. I heard about your Dad. I'm so sorry."

I nodded. "Thanks. It was a year ago." I patted her

...I felt her squeeze my

...Were there a lot of other

...she knew about the whole
...y low key. The cancer was
...wanted to get it over with."
...moment or two and she gave
...wn to business. First of all, you
...line—I mean, if you are serious."
She g... ...pulled me to the other end of the
bulletin boar... ...estate ads are usually on this end."
She jerked her thum... ...ard the upper left side of the board.

"Thanks."

"Let's see. How many bedrooms and baths do you have? Here's one near you." She tapped her finger on the ad and read off the specs: "Hideaway Cabin. Immaculate three bedroom . . ."

"Whoa whoa whoa . . . Immaculate?"

She went on: ". . . three and a half baths, hardwood floors, gourmet kitchen, pool, fifty foot dock with deep water mooring. Wow. They're asking quite a bit."

"Immaculate?"

"I'm glad you aren't selling, anyway. Do you still have that same boat? The one you raced in high school?"

"No. I have a newer one. And I have Dad's boat, the dinghy. Pretty good condition, I think." I waited. "Why? Do you think someone would buy it?"

"No. And you shouldn't sell it, but that's not what I was thinking. "She looked hard at me with a big smile. "Um."

"It hasn't been on the water in a pretty good while."

"Really. Well, that shouldn't be a problem for you, as I recall."

So she wasn't actually talking about the boat. "I'm surprised you remember that long ago."

"Are you kidding? I never would have made it through high school without your 'sailing lessons.'"

A guy with an open shirt and a deep tan stepped sideways past us to the Men's, nodding to Circe. We moved closer, up against the wall.

"Yeah, me too." I said in a low voice. "As I recall, that was my dad's old boat. And it wasn't even a sailboat."

"God that was a long time ago. We're grownups now. How did that happen?" She drew her hand through her hair and I could see the boat paint under her nails, up her arm. "How long has it been since you were in here?"

"I've been in plenty of times, but you haven't been home. Maybe five years ago, or so since we saw each other, don't you think?" I inched toward her and leaned on the bulletin board.

"Right. You were working for some senator. Some guy in deep shit, as I recall." She was about eye level with my shirt pocket and she saw the sunglasses I had stowed there, pulled them out, examined them, looking for the label I guess, then tried them on. They looked better on her.

"Yeah. And you left me—again—to sail around the world or something. What were you thinking?"

"God, that was a long time ago," she said again. She took off my sunglasses, folded them and slid them back in my pocket. "So what do you do for fun now? Do you want to go for a drink later?"

"I would love to. But I have to get this business done. You know?" Plus, there was not much money in my wallet. I couldn't afford bar drinks, that's for sure. I watched her face, trying to think of a way to invite her over that wouldn't sound too obvious, too much of a come on. Frankly, I mainly wanted some company. I knew Marguerite and I were over, and Sarah was probably never going to happen. "Listen, I could use your input on my ad, if you want to come over, we can have a drink out on the dock. Watch the moon light up?"

The tanned guy came out of the bathroom. He squeezed by us again and stood on the other side of Circe, pretending to study the bulletin board. She hooked her arm in mine, pushed me nearer the door, and whispered in my ear.

"Maybe. I'm not sure what I need to do here." She nodded toward the guy. "You remember, the season is starting."

"Okay." I gave a half-shrug. "Maybe some other time." I thought originality was not really necessary.

She released my arm, but held on to my hand and then my fingers as she backed through the screen door. "You should bring your ad in." She was loud and businesslike. The tan guy glanced at me.

"I probably will, I mean, if I decide to rent it."

"Oh. Well, if you do . . ."

"Right. Thanks." I watched her pick up a gum wrapper outside and I must have sighed out loud because the guy gave me a dirty look before he followed her.

I wasn't home long, unloading my beer from the trunk, when I saw a small pickup cut across the front yard. It was Circe.

She would have hit me if I took a step forward. "I brought dinner," she said through the open window, and handed me a bag with two subs and another bag with a magnum of wine in it.

"Wow. I love what you've done with the place," she put her hands to her face in mock excitement.

"I'm glad to see your travels haven't cured your sarcasm." I shifted the bags. "How about getting the door? If you like the outside, you are going to love the interior."

We went through the front door and I put the subs and wine on the kitchen table next to my other groceries. She stood in the kitchen, looked around wide-eyed.

"What do you think?"

She didn't answer, eyes surveying, mouth slightly parted as she glanced at the regiment of empty beer bottles, the cobwebs around the light fixture, the cardboard boxes of old magazines and junk mail.

"A little elbow grease. Good as new, right?" I rummaged in the sink drawer for a corkscrew.

"Jack, you need a dumpster."

I laughed but she wasn't smiling. "No. It's not that bad. A few garbage bags, maybe."

"A dumpster. One of the big ones. I have to work this weekend, but I think I can come back Sunday afternoon and help." She looked around again and hugged the subs. "Let's eat outside. You probably have some chairs out there, right? Or we could sit on the dock, like you said."

"Can you really still smell that cigar smoke? I'll open some windows. I don't smell it anymore." I went to the sink to pry open the window, which had been locked for a year. "Listen, I'd love for you to come over Sunday. Maybe I can cook out. But seriously, you don't need to do anything. I mean, I really appreciate the offer."

I opened the wine, found two jelly glasses and followed her. She carried our subs out to the front yard. I unfolded a pair of decrepit chaise lounges and dragged them to the edge of the afternoon sun. We had a couple of drinks and things looked like they might get interesting when my phone rang.

I debated taking it for a second or two, but it was Bob and I thought he might have news. Plus, with Bob I knew it would be short. As he told me about an opening over at Veterans Affairs, one of the governmental dead letter offices, I saw Circe stand, stuff the sub trash in a bag, and blow me a kiss on the way to her truck. I shook my head no and waved my free arm. I considered dropping the phone and running after her, but she was gone so quickly.

When she left I was sober and unnerved. Veterans Affairs? Was that all I had left? Maybe I would have to go back to the Hill. I switched on my laptop and opened up my résumé again. It had to be perfect. I wasn't going to take a job like that without a fight.

Chapter Three

The next morning, I started cleaning up the place. I opened the door to the shed outside. I could sweep it out, clear the cobwebs, scrape the trim, maybe a fresh coat of paint. Or I could take on the yard: trim the bushes, cut the grass. Immaculate? I would have a ways to go before I could put that on my index card. I would have to work quite a bit to get to "rustic." I worked all day and got up early on Sunday and kept going.

About four o'clock, I was trimming bushes and Circe came over again. "Sorry I ran out on Friday. I had the early shift Saturday morning." She went to the back of her truck. "Brought some crabs." She pulled the bushel basket over to the side. It had a lid on it and she bent the handles slightly to get it off. "What do you think?" She tossed the lid aside. "Why don't you get a pot and we can cook them to eat later."

"Sure." Everyone on the Eastern Shore has a crab pot. We had four, depending on how many crabs you had. I ran inside and grabbed the smallest crab pot, which was blue agate, just like the others, but with less rust on it because it was newer.

"You forgot the tongs, unless you are going to barehand them. Damn Jack. When's the last time you ate crabs? Don't you remember anything?"

I found the tongs but they were rusted stiff. I took off the lid and held it. She whacked the tongs on the ground and they worked a little, not quite closing. She expertly flipped the crabs into the pot. She had eight, capacity for pot number one. When she got them in I clapped on the lid and carried the pot inside.

"Where's the Old Bay?" Before I could answer, she saw that it was next to the stove. She poured a glass of water on the crabs and found a can of beer in the refrigerator and poured that on them, too. Then she pried off the top of the Old Bay and sprinkled the rest of the can over the crabs. She glanced at me. "So, Jack, I talked to Uncle Herman. You remember. Real Estate. He said he could get your place in their rental list if I got him the write-up in the next few days." She switched on the stove. "I brought my camera. You're going to need photos."

The crabs rattled around in the pot as the heat began to build. I always hated that part.

Circe opened the window over the sink. "You have to air this place out, Jack. I'm going to choke in here."

"You know how stubborn Dad was. Still smoked those damn cigars, right to the end."

She tugged at the hallway window. "He told my dad he started smoking them to get past the smell of the honey dipper. Then I guess he got hooked."

"I guess. I think that one is painted shut. I'll get the putty knife."

When I came back in she had opened the door to my father's room. I thought it was locked.

"I haven't really gotten to this room yet, Circe." There was a path through the room between the grocery sacks of papers and other clutter, but it was narrow.

She let out a long, sad breath. "Well. I'm just surprised, that's all. Floored."

"What are you talking about?"

"You know. I thought this room would be empty." She nudged a stack of papers on the floor with her toe. "Especially the way you and your dad . . . got along."

"What do you mean? We got along."

She gave me a sharp look. "Jack. It's me. Not some

Washington airhead who doesn't know you. You did not get along. Frankly, I would have thought you would clean this place out and sell it. Although I'm glad you didn't." Without looking at me she went on: "Do you want me to help you go through this stuff?"

"You were here during one of our rare fights. I was a teenager."

"If you say so." She grabbed some of the clothes out of the closet and tossed them on the bed. "He didn't want you to take the sailing scholarship, did he? Wanted you to stay here and take over the business."

"No. He just wanted me to go someplace closer. He never wanted me to take over the business. He hated the business."

"Okay. Whatever you say. We're going to need some big garbage bags."

I just stared at her, getting mad, not sure why.

"Jack, come on. What are you going to do with this stuff? Can you wear his clothes?"

My father was about four inches shorter than me, as she knew perfectly well.

"You can give them away, Jack. I'm not saying everything is trash."

"Of course. I know. I just haven't had the time. I'm usually only here for a day or two, you know." I couldn't tell her that even after a year, I had so many feelings about my father I could barely touch his stuff. One day I wanted to burn everything, the next day, I couldn't throw away a scrap of paper with his handwriting on it.

She didn't answer. She was folding Dad's clothes into a neat pile. Flannel shirts. Corduroy shirts.

"I'm getting a beer," I said.

She looked up and smiled. "Good idea."

I let her fold the clothes and when she had them all on the bed, I held the garbage bags and she slid them in. Once inside, they probably returned to their happily rumpled state. I lugged the bags to my car and soon we could see the floor of the closet. And we bagged the shoes, the belts.

We went like this until about seven. Circe dumped the crabs on a tray and I got a couple of wooden mallets out of the drawer and some cold beer out of the refrigerator. We took everything out to the end of the dock. One by one, we tore off the shells, ripped off the legs, smashed the claws and picked at the meat with our fingers. I went for the big easy backfin clumps. Circe nimbly gleaned even the smaller slivers. When we finished each piece, we tossed the remains into the water and tried to extinguish the Old Bay with a long gulp of beer.

The sun was low in the sky and the sunset was going to be a good one. When we finished the crabs, I got more beer and a blanket to spread out on the dock. The day had been unusually warm for spring, in the eighties. I got her talking about the places she had traveled while crewing. How the Bay was different than the Caribbean. I didn't expect anything to happen, really. I wasn't sure if she was just helping a friend, felt sorry for me, or what.

The tide was in and we dangled our feet over the side and swished them around in the water. It wasn't very deep, maybe three to four feet at the end of the dock. We were still warm from the day and I tipped my head back to drink the beer. I could see her out of the corner of my eye, pulling her shirt over her head. She didn't have a bra on, a fact I was already well aware of. There was nobody on the water in our little cove. Nobody on the other docks. Probably a few ducks further up, maybe a heron. I was frozen, like when you walk through the woods and discover a wild animal you don't want to scare. I had already pretty much worked out what her breasts looked like, partly from memory, but they were even better without the shirt. She stood up and unbuttoned her shorts, eased them over her ass and let them fall to the dock. Her panties were black bikini. I would have guessed a thong, but no. Bikini. She whisked them off with a smooth motion, sat on the dock, then slid into the water.

"Come on, Jack."

This was a no-brainer, right? I got my clothes off in record time and slipped in after her.

The thing is, swimming at the cabin is not like the beach. The bottom is muck. Several inches. I jumped in and my feet slid into the cold mud, maybe three or four inches down. She was already swimming out to the end of the dock, so I went after her, kicking my feet hard to get the mud off.

Damn she's a good swimmer. Finally she let me catch her out by the boat. The stern was tied to a stake out from the end of the dock so the water out there was a little deeper. The bottom was still gooey but I didn't let it slow me down. I planted my feet and held her slippery body close to mine and we kissed a long time. She swam away, climbed up the dock and grabbed her clothes. I went after her and followed her into the house.

When we came back out, it was dark and cool. A thunderstorm was coming up. We grabbed my beer bottles from the dock and went back in.

We made love again and fell asleep for a little while. When I woke up, she was getting dressed. "Where are you going? Stay with me."

"I have to work tomorrow. And to be honest, I don't want to get hurt again."

"What are you talking about? You dumped me. You started seeing some guy and left to crew with him."

"Because you were going to move to Washington. What the hell did you expect me to do?" She pulled on her shirt. I grabbed her arm and eased her back into bed. She rolled on her side, close to me, laid her hand on my face. "I thought we could just have fun, you know? Old friends. But you are a damn tar baby. I'm not going to get stuck again."

It took me off guard. I wasn't going to lie and tell her that I wasn't going back to Washington. "Whoa whoa whoa. You broke my heart. You fucking left the continent."

She laughed. "Broke your heart? You couldn't wait to get away from here, Jack. I remember. You wanted to get away."

"So did you, as I recall."

"Yeah, but not like you. Honestly, I really am surprised you haven't sold the place already, now that your father is gone."

"Never." I brushed the hair out of her eyes. "I might leave but I always come back."

"But maybe you should sell, Jack. Cut the roots. You can reinvent yourself with no baggage. No embarrassing dad. No ramshackle cabin to worry about."

"What do you mean ramshackle?"

"Come on. By Washington standards."

"I don't think it's ramshackle. Quaint maybe. Charmingly rustic."

"So what do you tell your Washington friends? Do you say he was mayor?"

"Funny." I rolled to my back. "I'm not going to apologize for putting myself in a positive light. I never lie."

"Okay, poor Jack. You never lie but you know, what we just did, you know how to do that to the truth. It's a gift." She patted my cheek. "I don't get the big deal, anyway. Everyone loved your dad. And hey, somebody has to take care of the septic tanks, Jack. It's pretty important around here."

"Right. Your dad owned the boatyard."

"If you love it here so much, you know. Roots and everything . . . my uncle could put you on selling real estate. They make really good money, even by big city standards."

"No kidding?" I feigned interest.

"You know, Uncle Herman remembers you. The illustrious Jack Abbott, sailing sensation, went away to Newport on that big scholarship . . . sailed in the America's Cup. You were famous around here. How could you put that behind you?"

"I haven't put it behind me."

"When was the last time you went sailing?"

Time to go on the offense. "Don't you get tired of crewing on other peoples boats?"

"No, not really. It's just fun. If I get a crew I don't like, or an owner who is too grabby, I just come home."

"Yeah. Well that wasn't exactly an option for me. Or not an option I wanted."

"So you think you are going to get rich and buy your own boat in Washington? How do you do that in Washington, exactly? And stay out of jail, I mean."

"Ha ha. Funny."

"So you should see Uncle Herman's boat. Sweet. Think about it: You sell some real estate and make some serious money. Buy a boat, run for Congress or whatever. Then you have Washington, and a boat."

"And you." I pulled her closer, and kissed her.

"If you say so." She wriggled out of my grasp. "You can dream." She slid out of bed and turned to me as she slipped her shorts on, "I'll get you a meeting with him."

I watched her. I knew what would happen if I said no thanks. She wouldn't be back. So I nodded thoughtfully.

Over the next day or so, I somehow talked myself into it. I thought, what the hell? I can talk to the guy—and if I can make some money, stay alive until after the election . . . why not give the idea a chance?

Circe set it up for Tuesday morning. I woke early and I was nervous. I shaved and went through my clothes. The cleanest shirt I found had French cuffs but I couldn't find my cufflinks. I went to Dad's room and rummaged around in the dresser, in one of those personal junk drawers I hadn't cleaned out yet. In the back, I recognized a box with puffy tissues folded neatly inside, like a tiny pillow for a set of Presidential cuff links and a tie clip. I had given them to Dad for Christmas several years back, when I worked at the White House. I remember his face, stunned and solemn, for once. No joke about my job, trying to knock me down a peg or two. I never had the heart to tell him they were inexpensive and not all that hard for me to get.

I had no choice. I put them on and went to the real estate office on High Street. My meeting was at ten. I sat across the street in my car. I watched the door, studied the parking lot. My hands got sweaty. Circe's uncle's Lincoln Towne Car was in the parking lot, clean and shiny. One of those dried flower wreaths hung on the front door of the office. It looked very respectable, very solid. Probably pathologically cheery inside. There wasn't a thing wrong with the look of it, really. A small round woman with too-dark, kinky curly hair around her moon face carried a white bag inside, probably filled with doughnuts.

I watched the door and imagined myself talking to my Washington friends. What are you doing now, Jack? *Selling real estate.* Oh. In other words, you are dead to us as far as Washington goes. You are no longer one of us. You have officially changed careers.

They wouldn't say that, of course. We would lose touch and soon, I would be telling people around town about how I used to work in Washington.

And what about Sarah? Circe had blocked Sarah out of my mind, like an eclipse of the sun. But Circe was already showing signs of impatience with me. If I didn't sign up with Uncle Herman, there was a good chance I would be sleeping alone. Either way, she would probably leave in a few weeks, as soon as someone called with a crewing job for her. I imagined calling Sarah. Could I tell her I was selling real estate? No. I would just never see her again. What were the chances she would see me anyway? Right now, I needed money. Maybe I would have to put my pride aside so I could pay my bills.

It was almost ten. I thought about going in, sitting down and having a sugary doughnut and pretending to drink a cup of coffee. Which I hate. I don't actually drink coffee. I could see myself, sitting right there, and mid-fantasy, I saw someone in the window. The figure at the window moved toward the door. He would come out the door and wave me in. For a moment I stopped breathing, I'm not sure, maybe my heart even stopped. I didn't wait to see if it was going to be Circe's uncle. Without looking over at the office again, I swung the car out of the space and turned the corner, never looked back. I felt I was going to choke when I got to the stop sign at the corner. I turned and kept going until I was in Washington, around the corner from Bob Carson's office.

Chapter Four

I called Bob from the car. "Bob, remember that job at Veterans Affairs?"

"Uh. Yeah."

"Have you heard anything else about it?"

"Well, kind of. Just a second." He clicked me off the speaker phone and picked up.

"What I heard is . . . they want a woman."

"Shit."

"I don't know for sure." He paused like he was thinking. "But you know how rumors like that go. Usually some truth."

"Would I have to wear high heels?"

"We talked about this. You don't really want Veterans, do you? Jack?"

"I could do it."

"I didn't say you couldn't do it. You could clean toilets, too, right?" I could hear him sigh. He went on, "If you want a real job, get your ass over here. Sleep at my house a couple of days, get some interviews. I can call a couple of congressional offices. You can set something up with them. Find out what's going on."

"As it happens, I am here." I waited, trying not to sound desperate. "Should I come by?"

"Sure. Come up to my office. I'll make some calls, we can walk around the Hill a little, then you can buy me lunch."

I looked at my watch. "How about a half hour?" You can't be too needy, even with your friends. One loop around the mall would easily kill thirty minutes so I drove around, crossed over to Constitution Avenue and past the White House then back to Bob's. I nudged into a spot by a fire hydrant where I could see the top of the Capitol dome and I killed another ten minutes.

Bob's parking lot was full, as usual and it took another ten to find a space near his office. Near being a relative word. He was in an ancient townhouse, just this side of shabby, which no doubt gave the members of his trade group a lot of satisfaction that they weren't wasting money on overhead. Bob put me in a conference room with the *Washington Post.* "Make yourself at home, Jack. We've got a lunch on the Hill with Tim Baumol, staff director of the Policy Caucus."

"I've met him a couple of times."

"You didn't smart off, right?"

"Um. I don't think so. I was my usual quiet self."

"Right. Well, it's a start. He usually knows everybody on the House side who is looking for somebody."

The lunch went even better than I expected. Baumol had a couple of ideas, and even offered to look into putting me on his payroll temporarily, to do some special projects. We set a meeting for the next morning, and I went back to the cabin feeling a lot better about everything. I called Circe's uncle and apologized then called her but she cut me off. I went by the boatyard just in time to see her sliding into the some guy's sports car. I guess that would have to do for closure for now.

When Wednesday came, before I got to the Beltway, Bob called. "Baumol has to reschedule. But come on in anyway."

Bob was waiting for me in his office. He closed the door and sat down across from me. He held his coffee with two hands. "Jack, I didn't tell you everything about Veterans, I'm afraid."

"What do you mean?" I tried to stay controlled.

"I'm not completely sure, but when I called to check on the job, Annie, one of the gal's in the Secretary's office, mentioned Harrow."

I couldn't believe he said "gals" and I blinked, wondering if my old friend still had his edge or if he was trying to be funny. But he wasn't smiling.

Bob watched me, then went on, staring deep into his coffee. "Like, was he the one who had a problem with his references? Then she thought better of it and wouldn't tell me anything else."

"Shit."

"I knew you would say that. But listen. This doesn't have to be fatal. That crazy SOB can't stop you from getting a job."

"Well, no offense Bob, but I wasn't that excited about going to Veterans anyway."

He nodded. "Of course. The thing is, it turns out Baumol is a wimp. A fool. I had him all wrong. He's an idiot to let one Member stop him from doing something—one Member most people think should be in stir or possibly in a home someplace."

"Oh, God. Baumol too? What did he say?" The adrenalin washed through me, felt like it was going to squirt out my fingers. I may have changed color.

Bob stared at me. "Are you okay?"

"No." I swallowed. "What happened? What did he say?"

"Some bullshit about how he'd have to have a consensus to go forward and he just hadn't realized you were so . . . um . . . so controversial." Bob blinked his eyes like I might punch him. "Said he would keep his ear to the ground."

"What happened, Bob? I was straight with him. I told him Harrow was mad at me. He seemed to hate Harrow as much as everyone."

"Harrow called him and reamed him out. Said if he hired you he'd get him fired. And, that he should pass along to other members that he didn't want to see your face around here."

"But they all hate him . . ."

"True, but they don't want him to scream at them. You

know what a bastard he can be. You know. Why make him mad over a press secretary?" Bob went to his desk, opened the top drawer, found a pack of cigarettes and got one out. "Don't·worry. I'm not going to smoke it, it just helps me think."

"Shit, Bob. I don't even want another House job, you know. I mean, I think this is good. It forces me to focus on what I want. You know, I haven't even called Evan. I should have called him already. Just tell him what happened. I want to go to the White House . . . Get my name in there. You know?"

"Sure. Maybe Evan can get John to give you a couple of months. And maybe, if nothing comes up now, you will be in position for after the election."

I was aware that I had stretched Bob's positive attitude muscles as far as they could go. "I'll call him and see if he can have lunch today."

"Sure, do lunch if he can." Bob walked over to the window, fingertips holding the cigarette. But he just sat on the sill, and switched hands again. "I think I can get some tickets to the Orioles game Friday night. For all three of us."

I called Evan. He couldn't have lunch so I asked him about the Orioles game. "Bob has Orioles tickets. What do you think?"

"Orioles? What about the Nats? Why drive all the way over to Baltimore, for God's sake?"

I relayed this to Bob and the two resumed their argument, with me as the go-between.

Bob gave me a disgusted shrug: "Because they are bland and without a soul, just like this city."

"Okay, Evan, here's the thing. I don't know if you heard, but my incarceration with Harrow has ended. I'd really like to debate the Nats versus the Os but I am preoccupied by this job thing. If you can't make the game, could I stop by later on today or tomorrow?"

"Shit, Jack. When did it happen? Did you quit? You didn't just quit did you?"

"No. Of course not. He's on this Lixubistan obsession at the moment. I just neglected to fetch and carry to his satisfaction."

"Oh, yeah. Saw the front page of the *Post*, whenever that was."

"That wasn't me. I'll fill you in when we get together, if you want the whole download."

"Um. That's okay. I'm just glad he fired you and we aren't reading about your body being found floating in the sea grass along the banks of the Potomac. The crazy SOB."

"Yeah. Me too."

"Damn, you know we were looking for a flack for months. We just hired a guy."

"I remember you were looking. I figured you long-since found somebody. Listen, I would really like to go somewhere in the administration. Maybe the White House, if I could find a spot."

"Sure. Good idea. I'll do some checking."

"Great. Thanks." I was so relieved he wasn't going to harass me about wanting the White House I almost forgot the excuse for the call: "What about the game? Are you in?"

"Hell, yeah. I can't let you two go all by yourselves."

We made plans to meet at the game. Bob and Evan would drive out from DC and I would come up from the cabin. When Friday night came, they were waiting for me at the 'Will Call' windows. Evan looked good. I started to tease him, asked if maybe the Rogaine is working. He had lost a few pounds, and he looked relaxed, like he was enjoying life. We went inside toward our seats. Bob and Evan argued about whether Camden Yards was better than the old stadium, which threw me back into some memories of drinking beer there with my dad. But it's hard not to like Camden Yards, even for Bob, for all his complaining that it felt like he was at the mall, not a ballpark. Carpeted floors. Clean bathrooms.

We went to our seats and watched them call out the players. Bob got a bag of peanuts. I didn't remember seeing him eat before.

In the middle of the first inning, Bob leaned toward me. "So Jack. I heard about something at OMB." The Office of Management and Budget. I had been there before, but it was a start. The only place better was the actual White House Press Office.

"Really?" I was bracing for a jab—maybe a joke.

"Yeah. A friend of a friend, you know, called. Left me a message. He was gone when I called back. Some kind of press gig, apparently. He said it was White House, second only to the Press Office. That has to be OMB, don't you think?"

Evan listened. "Want me to nose around at my end?"

Bob nodded.

"Yeah.' Evan paused, thinking. "We need to get you an interview with the White House Personnel Office . . ."

I was elated, trying not to show too much.

Bob shook his head. "Evan, if we can find somebody who wants him, they can grease it with Personnel. I know you like to dot your I's and all, but it is just a waste of time unless somebody wants him."

Evan ignored him and we went back to watching the game. The Oriole pitching was better than usual and the game flew by with Bob throwing his peanut shells on our shoes. Bob insisted on waiting to get our beer until the National Premium vendor came by, which didn't slow us down much. The row in front of us had a neatly dressed man with his son and a bearish looking fellow with a couple of teenagers. Every time the Orioles scored he climbed up on his seat, arms stretched over his head and screamed. By the time he sat down again, a half inning had elapsed. Bob's face got redder and I was afraid he was going to say something, but the guy left during the seventh inning stretch and never came back. The Orioles won 7-4.

After the game, we shuffled out of the stadium with the crowd, toward the Hyatt to get our cars. "Let's go over to J. Paul's and get a drink." Evan offered.

"What about Little Italy?" I suggested, thinking it might

be cheaper and not quite so touristy.

"Sure." Evan liked the idea. Bob didn't seem to be listening. We left Evan's car at the Hyatt and I drove, headed for Little Italy. Evan was hungry. But before we got there, Bob, who had been dozing in the back seat sat up and growled, "Turn here." About ten minutes later, after following his grunted directions, we pulled up to a bar: "The Baltimore Blues Club" in huge gold script, with enormous *B*s but a few other letters missing, such as the T and I in Baltimore. Evan and I exchanged dubious looks. I had my hand on the door latch when I spotted several motorcycles near the entrance. "Bob, is this a biker bar?"

Bob had dozed off again. "Are we there?" He didn't seem to hear what I said.

Evan looked amused but worried. "Bob! Bikers! Hello, hello? Is this a biker bar? Have you been in there?"

Bob looked around like a groundhog sniffing the air. "No. I don't think so. Look, those are just biker wannabe bikes. You know. Accountants on Harleys."

"So you've been here before?" Evan said.

"Oh, sure." Bob started to get out of the car. "Barbecue. Come on."

Now Evan and I traded worried looks. "Do you feel lucky?" he whispered.

As soon as we got out of the car, you could hear the music. We followed Bob inside. There was a small blues group. The lead singer, 400 pounds of sincerity, dripping with sweat, eyes closed, sang with soul-piercing purity. The crowd was mixed and Bob surprised us again by sliding his chair over to a table of black women, and dancing with each of them. We kept the beer coming, and didn't leave until the music stopped, which coincidentally was when they started putting the chairs up on the table.

I drove a few blocks and saw that Bob looked like he was asleep again.

Without opening his eyes, and maybe his lips, he said, "So where exactly is this cabin of yours, Jack?"

"About 90 minutes from here."

"Sounds good. Let's go. I need a vacation."

Evan reclined his seat. "Me too."

I knew their eyes were closed but I froze a smile on my face. "Wow. I've always wanted you guys to come over. Thing is, I'm not really set up for guests." I wasn't worried about my lousy housekeeping. I was thinking about how unsuitable the place was by Washington standards. Not rustic with antique beams and brass doorknobs, but rustic, as in one bathroom, linoleum on the floor and a Formica kitchen table. And, I was wondering what they would think about the pictures on the wall.

Bob opened one eye. "Is there any beer there?"

"Of course."

"Then shut the fuck up and drive."

"Yeah, Jack. We're tired. We aren't on vacation like you."

"Ha. Nice. You have to know what you are getting into. You know, it isn't the beach. Not Ocean City. Not Rehoboth. In fact the beach is at least an hour away. It's the Chesapeake Bay. Peaceful but boring. Very rustic. It is not a large country house."

"Are there beds? I don't have to sleep with Bob do I? That's where I draw the line."

"Yes. I have beds. And beer."

"Then, shut the fuck up and drive."

"Are we there yet?"

They were both asleep before I crossed the bay bridge. I rolled down the window and turned up the music to keep awake. I thought about the OMB job. Was it in the NEOB? The newer building crammed with OMB analysts and functionaries? Or OEOB. With the Director. It could even be over in the East Wing of the White House, with the congressional relations staffers. We got to the cabin and I led them to their respective bunks.

The sun was warm and bright at about nine and made a direct hit on Evan's face. I was already up, rearranging the pictures on the wall.

"Jack. This place is great." Evan rummaged around the kitchen, found some instant coffee in the freezer and put some water on to boil. He stopped in front of the kitchen window. "Is that your boat?"

I nodded, mouth full of tea. Bob appeared in the doorway, looking disheveled. Eyes bloodshot, unshaven. Even worse than Evan. I wondered how I looked.

"I'll make some eggs." Bob yawned, tugging the refrigerator door open. "Oh," he said when he realized there were no eggs and very little else to eat. Evan was still looking at the boat.

"Want to go out for a little ride before you go back?" I wasn't really thinking straight. The boat wasn't ready to go into the water.

"Sure."

"Where's the coffee?" Bob was over by the sink, looking around. It seemed to be a struggle for him to get each word out. He picked up one of the onions on the counter and looked it over, like he was considering biting it.

Evan got him a cup and filled it for him.

"Sugar." Bob said.

"I'm not your type," Evan said back.

I got the sugar bowl out of the cupboard and put it in front of Bob. He scraped and stabbed at the hardened sugar with the spoon.

"Sorry. The dampness here—it does that." I rummaged through the cupboard for the sugar bag, which had only a cup or so left. I folded it down and stomped on it, then poured the lumps into the sugar bowl. Bob picked up a large chunk with his fingers and dropped it in the coffee, then stirred with the sugar spoon. He walked around the kitchen, studying the pictures on the wall. "Hey Evan, it looks like Jackie boy here used to be a big time sailor. How about that? Did I know that?

"You knew."

He stopped at one of Dad with a fishing pole in his

hand, not the one in front of the Honeydipper Septic Service Truck, which I had slid under the counter. "What did your Dad do, Jack?"

"Small businessman. A little of whatever was going well, you know?"

"Just like you." Bob slurped some coffee. "I had you pegged as a rich kid. This is much cooler."

Evan picked up a pen from the jar in the middle of the table, read it out loud: "Honeydippers," and put it in his shirt pocket. "What's a honeydipper, Jack?"

Bob had his coffee mug tipped up, draining it and stopped mid-sip, spilling a few drops on his shirt. "Shit."

I froze, not sure what was going to come out of Bob's mouth next. His eyes cut toward me but he went on fussing with his shirt. I picked up my tea and jerked my head toward the door. "Let's go out to the dock."

Bob refilled his coffee mug and they followed me outside. The dock was bathed in morning sun and the warmth had medicinal qualities. There was a spring high tide and the river was way up. At the end I stepped out of my shoes, sat down on the side and plunged my feet into the cool water. Bob and Evan exchanged uneasy glances, but followed my example.

I sipped my tea. "Evan, I don't think there's enough wind for the sailboat . . ."

He nodded. There was barely a ripple in our cove.

"We can take the dinghy out if you want . . ."

He shook his head. "No. That's okay. I guess we have to get back, you know." He sighed. "God, this is sublime, Jack. How do you leave here? Seriously, have you ever thought about living here?" Evan pulled his feet out of the water. His pants were wet at the end. He leaned on a piling and stretched his legs out on the dock, one straight, one bent.

"Sure. All the time. But the commute is a bitch."

"Jack, don't listen to Evan." Bob hacked out a laugh. "You could never leave Washington. It's in your blood."

"No it isn't, Bob." Evan shot back. "It's in *your* blood.

Along with a river of gin or whatever."

We all chuckled and opposite Evan, Bob stretched out on the dock, his hands under his head, eyes closed, smile tranquil. "Seriously, this is beautiful, Jack. We really have to get you out of here." Bob opened one eye. "Evan, don't you know somebody who needs a hired gun?"

"Wait a second, I'm not a hired gun. I have standards." I wanted to say, '*Hey, what about the OMB job?*' Was that a fiction Bob made up to make me feel better?

"Oh, that's right." Bob said. "That's why you went to work for Harrow."

Evan picked a sliver of wood from the end of the dock and flicked it at Bob. "There must be something to do here to make money . . ."

"How about you, Evan? You could move over here. I'll rent you a room. I won't have much time to come over when I'm at OMB, after all." My tea was almost gone. I eyed Bob as I tipped the cup to get the last drop. ". . . Unless you're going to work for John for the rest of your life?"

"Maybe."

I could work the conversation around to OMB, but it might be the long way. "I guess he's running again?"

"Of course." Evan shifted on the dock and I was hoping he didn't pick up a splinter in his ass. "We've got plans, too, you know."

Bob scratched his neck. "What's that supposed to mean? Are you getting married?"

Bob and I exchanged looks. "Is he looking for an administration job? Maybe an ambassador? They can always use a rich guy over at the Court of St. James, you know."

Evan stared at Bob for a moment, perhaps trying to figure out if he was making fun of John. "Come on. You know John better than that. He'd go crazy." He sighed. "No. You know. Same old thing. I've been talking to him about making a run."

Bob eyed Evan back. "That's a long way off, isn't it?

"Sure. On the other hand, he's still a young guy. While

we're on the subject, what about you, Bob. How long are you going to work for those crooks in your association?"

"As long as they keep paying my exorbitant salary, I guess." Bob yawned.

"Don't you miss being on the inside? Making policy?" Evan asked.

"Smoke filled rooms?" I added and laughed at my own joke.

"Not in the least. Anyway, who says I don't make policy?" he closed his eyes. "Evan, you could do with a touch of humor, you know. And subtlety."

Evan sat up. "What if John does run in four years? You would support him, right?" He shifted on the dock. "Are you saying you wouldn't want to go to the White House?"

"Sure. I'm pretty sure I would support him. Nothing personal, but it might depend on who else is running." He closed his eyes again. "I don't do the Don Quixote thing, you know. It would depend on his chances."

I wasn't sure if Bob was tweaking Evan, or if Evan was going to get mad.

Bob went on, "Of course that's a long way off. Jack here, on the other hand, is your man. If we can get Jack on the inside, get him into the big game. OMB maybe. It's a start. A solid guy like Jack, with some White House experience under his belt. Think how that could help John. Maybe this job I heard about . . ."

Chapter Five

On Monday, I couldn't wait for the elevator in Bob's dingy building so I took the stairs two at a time, and wondered if I could do three.

"Okay, here it is." He perched on the edge of his desk and fixed his eyes on me. "It isn't OMB. That was wrong. It's Cunningham's office. They're looking for a press guy."

I caught his tone, which was roughly like he just told me I was terminal, but ignored it. After all, it was a job in the White House. "Are you sure?"

"When are we ever sure, Jack? All I can say is, I can't get any verification on the OMB job. But a couple of people mentioned Cunningham."

"Great!" This was it. Perfect timing. My luck had finally changed. As soon as I had expressed my longing to go back to the White House, this opportunity presented itself. I was only a little wary that he might have a punch line.

Bob shook his head slowly. He squeezed by me to get to the window, pulled it open and lit a cigarette. He perched on the window ledge, hand stuck out the window and looked at me without saying a word.

"Okay. I know what you're going to say."

"Jack. You don't want to do that. Come on, Jack. James Cunningham? You can't work for that guy. I don't care if it is the White House."

"Sure I can. I already told you, I could work for Satan."

"You don't mean that." He flicked an ash and sucked on

the cigarette. "But that isn't what I mean. I also heard that Dexter is going to dump him."

"Wait a sec. I thought you said Dexter was thinking about dropping out."

"That was just a rumor. You know. Some cold feet, but they're going ahead. Dexter will pull himself together. He's not going to just walk away from being president for god's sake."

"So much the better for Cunningham."

"That's what you say. But that isn't what I hear. They barely speak, you know."

"Yeah. I've heard that. But you have to look at it from my point of view: That much more reason he needs a flack. A real flack."

"So if they don't dump him, the next question will be, how long before he fires you." Bob flicked the cigarette. "They go through flacks like shit through a goose. You don't want to be goose shit, do you? And once Cunningham fires you, you won't be hireable by the White House, you know."

I could imagine a completely different outcome, but there was no point wasting it on Bob. "Bob, what are my options? Do I get to be picky here? Do you know about any other leads?"

"In due time. We just have to find a quiet cove for you until the right thing opens up. Evan could open up a temporary spot for you. Like we talked about last week."

"No. I told you. They got somebody."

"Just temporary. You know. Speechwriter or something for a couple of months."

"Who could I talk to about this Cunningham spot?" I wasn't going to let the Vice President's office slip through my fingers.

Bob watched me while he took another drag. "First of all, Jack, even if you wanted this, which I can't believe, I can't really see Cunningham wanting to hire one of John Cook's people . . ."

"But everyone says what great terms John is on with the

White House."

"The *White House*, not Cunningham. You know that. But, you think you can get in there for an interview and they will love you, because of your charm and your silver tongue." He shook his head again. "I'm not even sure we could get you in the door. Come on. Cunningham?"

"What about Evan? Do you think Evan might know anyone who can get to Cunningham? A former staffer? Somebody from his state?"

Bob drew in the last drag of his cigarette and put it out on the window sill. "Go ask him. I have no idea." Bob was getting pissed. "If you get in there, it will be a career killer."

"How could it be worse than working for Harrow?" I couldn't afford to alienate Bob, but this was my life, after all. "It is the White House. I could have exposure to the White House press office or OMB . . . Something better . . ."

Bob picked up the remote and flicked on the tiny TV in the corner of his office. It was already on CSPAN. The House was deserted, about to start the proceedings for the day. "No. Jack. You aren't getting it. Cunningham is locked out. They don't even let him go to funerals. They think he is a complete disaster. When Dexter had to scramble to pick a new Vice President, they thought they were getting "the affable Senator James Cunningham." Remember? They didn't really know him. They wanted someone super-low-key, after the John Cook fiasco. He was a quiet guy, everybody assumed he was serious, hardworking, would fit in—you know."

"Come on, Bob. He can't be that stupid. How did he get elected to the Senate?"

"He's not stupid. I never said he was stupid. He's a lightweight. He lacks judgment. Nobody could have known that. He was untested." Bob opened his desk drawer and got out a fresh pack of cigarettes.

"Exactly. That's exactly what makes it an opportunity . . . to introduce some judgment . . . some press savvy."

"Plus, it turns out he isn't all that affable." Bob stood up with his coffee cup. "At least not to staff. Haven't you had enough of staff abuse?"

"How's his aim?"

Bob shook his head. "I give up. Go ahead and call Evan. See what he thinks."

I wasted no time. Evan took the call and talked fast, like he just had a second. "Jack, I'm glad you called. I've been thinking. Our press guy is okay, but we still have some room"

"I talked to Bob and he says the White House job is actually Cunningham's office."

"Shit."

"Yeah, yeah. I know. And he gave me a ration of it already. Said there was no way to get in there, and that I shouldn't want to."

"Jack, you aren't serious. They would never do us a favor. They probably see John Cook as their chief rival, after Dexter's term."

"Isn't there someone they listen to that could help us? Someone we could get to?"

"Jack, this is all wrong. You don't want to go there. Come over and we'll talk about it."

It took me about forty five minutes to get to the office, since I walked. There is even less parking on the Senate side. I had to wait for him to get out of a meeting, but not too long. "Evan, I thought about what you said at the cabin. About gearing up for John's run. I want to be in on that, you know. And the best way I can make a contribution is to get some more experience. Boots on the ground. Inside the White House is a completely different game. If I could get some national exposure, maybe get into the campaign . . ."

Evan unfolded his arms and inhaled. "God. That would be great."

"Yeah. I know. So if Cunningham is the only way in, we have to make that work."

Evan squinted at me, like he was thinking hard. I was about to say, *get me in the door* and leave the rest to me. I was about to remind him that I knew how to make myself indispensable, after all. But before I could go on, John came into the office, back from a vote.

John grinned and grabbed my hand, then gave me a bear hug. "It's good to see you, Jack. Evan's been telling me we might be able to convince you to help us out for a while. Get the old band back together . . ."

I shot Evan a look and John realized he had missed something.

Evan gave him the latest: "Bob had a line on something in the White House. It was going to be great. But it turned out to be Cunningham."

"Is that want you want, Jack? The White House?"

"Hell, yeah." Evan interrupted before I could say anything. "I'd love to get him on the inside, especially during the campaign."

I nodded.

"White House press is a little different than the Senate, isn't it. Evan, have you checked around over there? Is there anything?"

"No. There isn't anything. The campaign is set. The press office is not hiring. I checked. Nothing. I called our legislative guy. Willie Lavas. He nosed around for me and couldn't find anything."

"Except for Cunningham."

"And that is a non-starter." Evan crossed his arms.

John nodded to follow him into his office. "I have to call the Chief of Staff on something else—this budget mess. I'll just ask him. I don't know the press secretary. What's his name? Crane?"

I didn't answer. I have to admit I was doing the math on whether being John Cook's guy was going to help or hurt. John was still a Senator, of course, and had more power than ever in the Senate, but wasn't there still a tiny bit of bad blood with the White House? Having to drop him as the candidate for Vice President four years ago? Having to scramble to get away from his scandal? Tyler was Dexter's key guy back then and he had been especially angry.

John and Evan were looking at me. What could I say but, "Sure. That would be great! Fantastic."

"Never hurts to ask. Isn't that what you taught me?" John leaned forward and spoke toward the open door, his words aimed at Helen, his ancient assistant who was just within earshot. "Helen, get me Phil Tyler over at the White House, please."

Evan and I waited until Helen confirmed that she had left a message with his office. We started toward the door. I figured it might take a day or two to get a call back so I was surprised, to put it mildly, when Helen pushed us out of the way and barked, "Line one, Senator. Phil Tyler returning your call."

We eavesdropped from the doorway. John's voice was low, but I heard the words "first rate" and "loyal" and the hairs on the back of my neck stood up. He put the phone down and gave me the thumbs up.

He scribbled a name on a notepad and gave it to me. "He suggested a detail. In the Press Office. Help out in the run-up to the election. Call this guy in Personnel. He'll set it up."

Evan frowned at me. "A detail. That could work." He punched my arm. "You are such a lucky bastard."

I grinned big and thanked John. On the way out of his office, I let the words, "Detail from where, I wonder?" slip out. I knew what a detail was, of course. The White House borrows an employee from an agency for a few months.

"Who cares? You can get your foot in the door and get a permanent job."

I called Tyler's guy in the personnel office. He asked me to come down on Friday, put me on with an assistant to give them my blood type and shoe size so I could be cleared in with the Secret Service. I spent the rest of the week looking for an apartment. For the time being, I moved over to Evan's condo, a Spartan townhouse in northern Virginia. I knew I needed to keep after other job leads, and I did, but just nominally. I thought about calling Sarah, but what would I say? '*I might have a job at the White House? Sorry I haven't called in weeks?*' No. It would be better if I waited a few more days. Feeling sorry for me wasn't going to win her over.

Friday, I took a cab, of course, to the visitor's entrance of the Old Executive Office Building on Pennsylvania Avenue, just like they told me. The OEOB is next to the White House. Most of the staff of the White House actually works there, so I was fine with that. I went through the iron gates to the little outdoor security post. I waited my turn. There were several in front of me. Uniformed Secret Service, very pleasant, looked me up, motioned me through the metal detector, handed me a visitor's pass on a chain. The stone steps in front of the dove-gray double-pillared façade were steep but I could have taken them two at a time. I went through the massive double doors, which were propped open, and inside, on the right, another Uniformed Secret Service agent, seated at a formidable desk, stopped me before I could orient myself. "Can I help you?" I told him I was looking for Personnel and he motioned me to the office just across from the entrance. Since I hoped I would be working there soon, I didn't want to embarrass myself. This was no big deal, right? So I did not notice the 22-foot ceilings or gawk up and down the halls, looking for a familiar face.

I crossed the dark gray and white checkerboard marble floor to the Personnel Office. The door was not open so I twisted the knob and pushed—it was quite large and heavy. I assumed my interview would start in Personnel, go through the preliminaries, maybe fill out some papers. Possibly get my security clearance started, although this was supposed to simply be an interview. Then they would take me over to the White House to meet with David Crane in his office.

Instead, I was back outside the gate in less than a half hour. I never talked to David Crane, the Press Secretary, just some pimply-faced guy in Personnel who was more nervous than I was. A courtesy interview. Like I needed a courtesy interview. I knew there was a problem when I noticed his pass, tucked in his shirt pocket with just enough of the top peaking out. He didn't even have a White House pass. How was he going to take me over to the White House without a White House Pass?

I walked back down the gray stone steps as inconspicuously as possible and dropped off my visitors pass. The Secret Service buzzed open the gate without my asking and I left without giving them my usual friendly nod. I felt like a complete fool. I walked briskly to the corner of 17th and Pennsylvania, like I had someplace to go, and waited for the light.

I figured I had three choices: I could forget the whole thing. No way. I could run back to John and get him to make another call. Maybe. After all, this isn't what he was promised. But wait—it was Friday. Was he still in town? Probably not. I could wait until Monday, try to get him to call again. Or, I could try to call Tyler myself. Today. Right now. Take matters into my own hands.

I fondled my cell phone, the light changed and I crossed 17th. What was my best shot? Because now was the time to take it. I stepped near the edge of the curb to get out of the foot traffic, punched in the area code of the White House and the next three numbers, 2-0-2-4-5-6 . . . A bus roared by, honked its horn at a minivan that had strayed into its lane. *Take your best shot* . . . I spun and went back to the intersection. If I went a couple of blocks up 17th, I could get the red line of the Metro to Union Station, just a short walk from the Senate side of the Hill. Much cheaper than a cab. I could use the phone in John's office. Not take a chance on sounding like a lunatic, ranting on my cell on the corner, with street noise in the background. Better to have the caller ID say "Senator John Cook" or whatever. And call from a quiet office. Nobody but tourists stand still in front of the White House. I kept walking.

Still, it was a pain to go back to the Hill. And just like I thought, it was Friday afternoon, so Evan and John were gone. None of the old-timers, people who knew me, were left in the office. I had to do some sweet talking —had to get Evan on the phone—and I finally got into Evan's office. With the door closed, I sat at his desk, called the main White House number and asked for Phil Tyler. He wasn't going to take my call, of course, but I might be able to get a message through. I waited only a moment, until someone named Susan asked if she could help. I told her about my interview. I asked if she could find out if John had misunderstood what Tyler had said. I left John's office number for callback.

About 15 minutes later, she called me back. "I have a message from Mr. Tyler. He asked if you are available to meet with him on Monday at 9:30 a.m." A meeting with the Chief of Staff? Probably just a courtesy to keep John happy, but a no-brainer. I knew this meant something good. Like a job.

I wasn't going to blow this by getting stuck on the Bay Bridge on Monday. I spent the weekend at the cabin, but came back to Evan's place Sunday night. Monday morning I went directly to the White House visitor's gate, as instructed. There was no line. The Secret Service buzzed me through the gate. At the security outpost, I stepped through the metal detector and got my "visitors" pass. Before I could take a step toward the White House, the agent said "Wait here, sir." I swallowed and sat at the end of the row of fancy folding chairs. From my seat, I studied the part of the lawn where the TV reporters set up to do their stand-ups, so the White House would be in the background. But there must be no news because dark green covers shrouded the lights, tripods, and microphone stands. In the distance, the doors of the West Wing lobby swung open and a slight young man in shirt sleeves with the coveted White House pass dangling from a chain around his neck came down the driveway toward me. "Brian *something* with the Chief of Staff's office. Mr. Tyler asked me to meet you, sir. This way please." And he motioned with one hand. We went in through the Lobby, passed more Secret Service, then left. I hadn't been in the

White House for years, and that was actually a tour from a friend, but I knew the Press Office and Press Briefing Room were to the left. Maybe we were going to stop there first? Meet Crane? But no, we kept going and passed the Cabinet Room, door propped open for show, I guess, then the staff office that led to the back door to the Oval, where his appointment secretary and a few others sat. Our footsteps on the carpet did not make a sound. Nobody in the halls. No voices. It was like church. We kept going, past the closed door to the Oval. Secret Service sat in the hallway, nodded at my escort. We continued on past the closed doors to the President's private dining room and some other small offices on the left and the Roosevelt Room, on the right, which had its door closed. I could hear a faint murmur. Muffled voices, calm and orderly, but a sign of life. We stopped just before the corner and went through the open door on the left. When the receptionist greeted me, I almost expected her to whisper. She spoke quietly and I recognized her soft voice from my phone call on Friday. The phones rang, but they were set to a low pitch. I sat on the dainty furniture and waited briefly, noting the pictures and sculptures displayed tastefully around the room. Controlled harmony. And power.

I realized that coming in the long way, must be part of my young friend's training, make sure when you visit the chief you know where you are. If you come in the other way, you might not notice how close his office is. The closest, in fact, to the Oval.

I didn't have time to get comfortable. Tyler came right through the door, shook my hand. "Let's go in here and talk." He led me into his inner office, which was probably the second largest in the White House. Larger even than the Vice President's, but perhaps not that big by corporate standards. He motioned me to the conference table.

Tyler was a small handsome man, perfectly proportioned, athletic, immaculate dark suit, full head of white hair, although I don't think he was that old. Younger than Dexter. Like a bird of prey, he eyed me from the small round conference table, where he had been working. Stacks of papers were aligned on one side. He waved me to a chair on the other side, where the table was clear. He sat in front of the piles. I glanced at his desk, which was picture perfect. No stray papers, almost bare but for brass, or silver, leather and wood. I crossed my hands in front of me while we talked and at one point I noticed his eyes on my sleeve. I remembered my cufflinks and cringed. I never thought they would be noticed. They were mostly gold, after all, and at a glance were pretty nondescript. But Tyler noticed everything. It was like he saw me naked. He stopped the smile from spreading on his lips, but he couldn't stop his eyes. He had my number.

He wanted to know all about John, my history with Harrow, what I had to do with the Lixubistan fiasco. John had even mentioned my father and his cancer. Tyler told me how sorry he was. I suspected he was trying to find out if I was still a basket-case, or I could handle a high-stress environment. It was the most intense five minutes I ever spent with my clothes on. Then he had a woman, a slinky, dark-eyed brunette, walk me over to the Press Secretary's office. He said her name but I didn't catch it. I didn't want to ask again and run the risk of sending the wrong signal.

I waited at least a half hour, but I finally got to meet the famous David Crane, the President's Press Secretary. He was shorter than I thought, receding hairline, back past his ears, and thin, like he hadn't had a good meal in a year or two. I think Crane may have been mainlining Freon. I'm not sure. Maybe liquid nitrogen. He was not very friendly.

I knew it was going to be temporary. Crane didn't say much but I knew he wasn't happy. "We have a couple of projects we need some help on, Phil tells me." This was his very nice way of saying, *this isn't my idea. Hiring you is a payoff and we aren't about to be stuck with a loser like you indefinitely.* What he actually said was, "I wouldn't be surprised if you find some opportunities in the agencies after you are here a few weeks."

A few weeks? Translation: '*We're going to shove you*

down the throat of some agency the first chance we get so don't get comfortable.'

I really wanted to ask when I was going to get my first paycheck, but I decided against it. I know he was trying to put me in my place, insult me a little so I would have no expectations and would stay out of his way. But I didn't care. Really. I was inside the White House, breathing the air and knowing what you can only know because you are on the inside. The only thoughts going through my mind were, *if you think you're going to get rid of me that easy, buddy, you're going to learn something.*

The brunette walked me back to Tyler's office. I tried to see her name on her pass but knew I shouldn't stare at her chest. She told me Tyler said I could start the next week. Then she added, "Personnel will handle the details."

Uh oh.

Chapter Six

The following Monday, I went back to the northwest gate, where they clear you in if you are an employee. They told me to go to the visitors' entrance, in front of OEOB. I figured, okay, whatever. It's my first day. I waited in line behind a half dozen agency staffers, or lobbyists, or whatever. Each guy in front of me—they were all men this morning—slipped them a drivers license or agency ID, said he was here to see so and so, waited, tapped his fingers, and after a few minutes got a tag on a chain to wear around the neck.

My turn finally came. No record of Jack Abbott. Nothing. I suggested they call the Press Office—They had never heard of me. Okay, please try the Personnel Office, I asked real nice. They started looking a little nervous, like this was right out of the lunatic gunman scenario. Any second I was going to pull out my Uzi. The Personnel Office, at least the person they spoke to, knew nothing, of course. Wasn't this in one of Kafka's stories? Or maybe in one of my many anxiety dreams? But I wasn't going to just go away. I stepped away from the desk and pulled out my cell phone—slowly. I called the Chief of Staff's office. I got Susan again, and I asked her to give Tyler a message. "This is Jack Abbott. Mr. Tyler offered me a job last week. You told me to report today. I am down here at the northwest gate right now, and nobody seems to know anything about it. I'm going to wait about ten more minutes here, and then I'm going back to Senator John Cook's office. Do you have all that? Thank you." I stood near the door, avoiding eye contact with the guys behind the barrier. A few minutes passed, I heard the phone ring, then they called me over and handed me a pass. "Report to the Personnel Office. First Floor. Room 145."

I knew where it was. I went up the stairs, past the Secret Service agents inside, and crossed the hall with a certain satisfaction. Clearly Tyler's office had alerted them. They showed me into a small conference room and the morning dwindled away while I filled out security forms. At the end of the day, I still didn't have an office. I still hadn't been to the Press Office. When I asked to see the personnel director, I found out she had to leave early. I left, reluctantly, when they closed the office. If I didn't know better, I might have thought that something was wrong. That perhaps I didn't really have a job. But I had been here before. I knew all about the glacial bureaucracy that can miraculously start to move. However, you do have to be persistent.

The next day it still took 45 minutes to get a pass. I still had to report to Personnel, but instead, cheeky devil that I am, I went by way of the Press Office, the one in OEOB, where all the grunt work took place. Only Crane and his secretary were over in the West Wing. I figured, after all, I was supposed to be in press, right? I walked up to the receptionist and introduced myself: "I'm new. I'm not sure where I'm supposed to go . . ."

The receptionist looked like she was still in college—and was very cute. She eyed me suspiciously and buzzed someone on the intercom. "There's a Jack Abbott out here. He says he's new." She put the phone down "She'll be right out."

She? Who was *she*? I stepped back from her desk just as a tall, wan man, thin and blonde in an unhealthy sort of way, breezed in and waved at the receptionist. I recognized him from somewhere, surely not TV—as Deputy Press Secretary Scott Goodington.

"Hi Scott," she called out.

Scott looked at me over his shoulder, and answered her with a curt nod.

I passed about ten more minutes, hands clasped behind me, but no "she" came out. I edged close to the receptionist's desk again, leaned in, affable but confidential, and whispered, "I met David Crane last week. Is he here? Maybe he can tell me where he wants me to go."

"No." She shook her head with certainty. "He's over in the White House." Of course I knew that Crane's office was in the West Wing but I thought he might be over in OEOB sometimes to meet with staff.

After she shared this with me, she had that "*Uh oh. Shouldn't have said that . . .*" look.

"Of course," I nodded and retreated a couple of steps and eyed the chairs. Should I sit down or head back to the Personnel office, where I was supposed to be?

"Here . . . have you read the clips?" She handed me a thick pile of papers stapled together. I remembered this from my old days: The White House news summary.

I had a smile pasted on my face, but it was getting harder and harder to hold it. The obvious thing to do was throw around the name of the Chief of Staff. But I had the idea that would be a mistake. This guy Crane didn't want me, and if I was going to ingratiate myself with my usual charm and overwhelming competence, it wouldn't do to start out by invoking the weight of the big boss. I was going to be an asset, a team player.

So I read the clips twice and memorized all the photos on the wall. Dexter and Crane, Crane and Dexter, Crane and Dexter with the Queen, Crane and Dexter going over some papers on Air Force One. Just Crane, briefing the press corps. I began to realize there was something really wrong. It was almost lunch time. A medium-height, fortyish brunette rushed out of her office. "Marilyn Bezzmatier," she parsed, hand outstretched, unsmiling. "It looks like we have some kind of mix-up here."

"Oh?" I tried not to look worried. I was sweating.

"Some kind of misunderstanding . . ."

"Uh, huuh," I said, inflecting my voice in a matter-of-fact-way. It flashed through my mind that this might be the part of the dream where I find I am on my way to math class in my underwear.

She wasn't smiling. She stared at me, waiting for me to explain myself.

"I was told to start yesterday." I watched her. Nothing registered. "Mr. Crane met with me about a week ago . . ."

"He's in briefings all morning. I'm not calling him on this."

What else could I do? "Perhaps you should call the Chief of Staff's office. I think they know all about me." I kept watching for a sign, a glimmer of recollection, but nothing, so I went on. "I met with Phil Tyler . . ."

This got the *ahaaa* reaction. The smug smile.

"I'll call over there." She said the words like she wasn't really talking to me, turned and went back to her office. I really didn't like the way she said it. Like I had somehow given her some advantage. What was I, an intern? Was there a civil war going on, or what?

So I eased back in the chair and waited. The receptionist, who was still chilly despite my friendly comments, tried to get me to go eat some lunch. Was I paranoid to think that if I left I might never get in again? Finally, they had another junior looking aide, perhaps secretary, named Elaine, escort me to the far side of the building, the side along 17th street. I remembered the building was like a square doughnut. The inside row of offices had windows to the courtyard, if they had windows at all. We took an elevator to the fourth floor and she managed to answer all my questions with yes, no or a skeptical smile. We crossed to a small flight of stairs and climbed it. The fifth floor. Actually, the attic. We passed several uniformed men and many doors with complicated-looking locks. We came to a door on the inner side of the building and she unlocked it. There were two desks piled high with boxes and a number of file cabinets with combination locks on them. Safes. They store sensitive or classified documents. It looked like a storage room. The desk had a phone, but after Elaine left, I realized it wasn't connected. At least she gave me a key so I could let myself in. She couldn't look me in the eye. Clearly, she had to know that I was a power guy.

I sat down at the desk even though I would get dust all over my pants. For a few moments, I have to admit I was upset. I considered calling Tyler's office to complain. But first, I'd have to have a phone that worked, unless I wanted to use my cell again. And, I had played the card once. If I did it again, there would be no hope of working with these people. Anyway, I did have a private office. Not bad for day one.

I spent the rest of the week going back and forth from the downstairs press operation back to my cubbyhole, armed with the White House news summary, which I read cover to cover, since I had nothing else to read. Or do. On Friday someone showed up to install my phone. Getting a phone wasn't a sign that I was finally in. I got the phone through my own initiative. I struck up a friendship with some of the fellows who shared my hallway. Dapper military types from something pronounced as WAAkah. Later I found out this was the White House Communications Agency.

It was Thursday before I got up the nerve to call Sarah. Harrow had made the White House news clips for three days in a row. I thought about how I could offer to help, give some insights on how to castrate the little bastard. Once my phone was in, I stared at it for a minute or two, sucked in a breath and called her. She picked up her own line.

"Hi, it's me, Jack."

"What?"

"Jack Abbott. Listen, I've had some major setbacks that have prevented me from calling you, but I'm back in town now. I'd really like to see you." I had rehearsed this line so I wouldn't say anything even more stupid.

There was a long silence. "I really don't think so, Jack."

"I'd like to see you. Harrow . . ." She cut me off.

"Yes, thanks, I've been fine. And what exactly caused

your amnesia, preventing you from making a phone call until now?"

God, what an idiot I was. Why hadn't I left her a message? I was trying to think of a response to that gut punch but before I could get anything out she went on: "Your boss is keeping me busy, as if you didn't know. I have another call." Click.

She was entitled to that. It was up to me to call her a half dozen more times, beg for forgiveness, and maybe I'd have a chance. Send some flowers once I got paid. I wasn't going to give up.

Friday morning I stopped in the press office, as had become my little routine, tea in hand, *Washington Post* tucked discretely in my briefcase. In the past days, I learned the receptionist's name, Donna Wiggins, and had ingratiated myself to the point of knowing I could elicit a shy smile from her. So when I opened the door and saw her avert her eyes, I knew there was a problem. And there he was, in the corner, ostensibly scanning a memo or something, but almost certainly waiting for me. It was the skinny blonde guy, Goodington. I walked to him eagerly offering my hand. "Jack Abbott," I said, with my most disarming, sincere smile.

He looked at my hand like I had leprosy.

"I just started this week." As if he didn't know. I didn't know much about him really. Just what I'd heard from Bob Carson. Very low profile. Like a snake. Strongly suspected of being incompetent. I went to the pile of news summaries and picked one up.

"You have to be on the list to get a summary." He said, still not looking me in the eye. "We've been short all week. I guess you are the reason."

"Oh, sorry. How do I get on the list?"

He acted like he didn't hear me. Then he glanced at me and said, "David has to put you on it."

"Oh. Okay. I'll ask David."

This idea seemed to make him even madder. He took a couple of steps toward me and said with a big, phony smile,

"You know what? You need to go back to your office and stay there until somebody calls you down. You don't get to talk to the Press Secretary unless he sends for you."

I wasn't sure how to answer this one. It was still in the back of my mind that I was trying to be nice, trying to ease my way in to some kind of role. When in doubt, grovel. And I was working on something obsequious to say, too, but he turned and left, the door closing in my face. I watched him give a wink to Donna, who was pretending hard that she was very busy and not listening.

So there was no point in trying to play nice. These people were out to gun me down. It would be wrong to let that happen. Unless I did something, they would have me shoved out the door before I could say "White House Mess."

Chapter Seven

During the week I never saw Evan. He was a great roommate. He had an extra bedroom so I didn't worry about being in the way. Plus, he wasn't a neat freak. And he didn't smoke. He spent a lot of his free time with his long suffering girlfriend, or at work. Friday night I picked up some beer and a sandwich on the way home, went to bed early and got up early on Saturday.

Evan came downstairs after ten, unshaven, in faded running shorts with no shirt on. I was sitting in the living room, reading the papers on my laptop. I was trying to think of an excuse to go to the office, but I knew I would get hassled at the gate. The sight of Evan startled me. I hadn't seen him all week. But it was an election year, so the Senate took the weekend off. "Hey, Jack." Evan yawned and scratched his stomach.

"Evan. You're alive!"

"I think so."

"There are some doughnuts in the kitchen."

"Mmm. Thanks."

He waddled into the little galley kitchen and put on a pot of coffee. He came back into the living room with a sugar doughnut. "So how's life at the other end of Pennsylvania Avenue?" He stuffed half the doughnut into his mouth.

"Not too bad."

He nodded, chewing.

"I have my own office." I said cheerfully.

He swallowed. "Wow. That's great? Not in the West Wing. Where?"

"OEOB. Fifth Floor, over by 17th Street."

"Fifth Floor? I didn't know there was a fifth floor." He thought a moment. "Isn't that a storage area? Who else is in there?"

"Sort of. Just me." Then I had this pang of defensiveness, like he was going to think I screwed up or something.

"That's kind of weird, don't you think? What are you working on?"

"Nothing. I think . . . That's just it. Nothing. It's like I don't exist." I didn't like the way that sounded. "On the other hand, I'm just getting settled in. I mean, one week."

"Sure. You can't expect to run things the first week you're there." Evan went back to the kitchen, opened the doughnut box and frowned at the contents. Without looking at me he said, "Jack. No offense, but are you sure you didn't do anything? You know, flirt with the wrong person or something."

I wasn't sure if he was kidding. "No. No way. It has been like this from the moment I showed up. I haven't figured out what's going on."

"You want John to call?"

"Maybe. I'd say that was the nuclear option. Plus, I'm not sure it would do any good."

He shrugged. "I guess you knew it was temporary. After all, that's how we sold it."

"Right. I knew it was supposed to be temporary. They just don't understand what invaluable qualities I have. Yet. I'm going along with it because if I make a flap, I might get sent somewhere even worse. So I'm sitting tight, watching for my opportunity. Maybe I can worm my way in to Crane's good graces."

"Yeah. Maybe. What are you going to do all day though?" Evan drank the rest of his coffee and picked up a puffy glazed doughnut.

"I'm going to solve the biggest problem they don't know they have. I was hoping to get rid of it, but Harrow has been stirring up this Lixubistan mess. Who better than me to contain Harrow. I think I could enjoy this."

Evan looked up. "What do you know about Lixubistan?"

"Don't you remember? That's what got me fired from Harrow's office. He became obsessed with Lixubistan and when I tried to smooth it over he freaked out and fired me."

"It could work."

"I think so. It's perfect exactly because no one else wants it."

Monday morning I heard Evan call my name as soon as I was out of the shower. I went to the kitchen wrapped in a towel and he handed me the *Post*, folded open to page seven. "You lucky bastard. You are the luckiest son of a bitch I have ever known . . ." The headline was "Harrow Plans Lixubistan Mission." He had announced on Sunday he was going to Lixubistan. He didn't have permission from the State Department, but he was going, by God. He was hoping to lead a congressional delegation, which he was planning to recruit in the next few weeks.

As soon as I got to the office, I called the White House legislative liaison office and asked for Evan's friend, Willie Lavas. It was glorious. "This is Jack Abbott in the Press Office." Willie didn't know who was handling the Harrow problem. When he called me back, he had won the prize of the crisis du jour. I suggested we meet and before I could tell him I would be in his vicinity in the next few minutes so he wouldn't see my office, he said he'd be right over to meet. Ten minutes later there was a timid knock on my door. Willie pushed the door open and peered in at me. His eyes were open like I had just goosed him. He looked around my office like he was on Mars.

"Never been up here, eh?"

"Uh, no." He looked at me really hard, like he was trying to decide if I was for real, if this was a joke, or if I must have pissed somebody off so, so big. "So how do you know Evan?"

"We worked together a few years back."

Willie gave a quick nod. " Okay, so you were saying, you worked for Congressman Harrow?" He forced a quick, nervous smile and sat down in the chair I had already dusted and placed by my desk.

"Right." I started to ramble on about it not being my proudest moment of course, but he held up his hand to interrupt:

"So you saw the paper. I don't really know Harrow. He's supposed to be on the House floor this morning. Do you have a TV?" Again he looked around, like he could have missed something as big as a TV.

"No." I was grateful to have a desk. "It doesn't matter. I can probably tell you word for word what he will say." I shook my head slowly, to underscore my disgust. "I know I'm in the press office, but I thought my background might be useful to you and I'd like to lend a hand." Nobody wants to share turf, even when it is stinks to high heaven. I knew I would have to sell him on the idea and went on, "I didn't exactly part on good terms. Lixubistan was one of the problems."

Willie studied me some more and unable to stop his eyes from moving around the office, still trying to decide whether I was some crazy must-hire they had stashed in the attic. "Whatever. Sure. We can always use some insight on these guys. There's a meeting over at State later today."

"Oh. Good. I don't have a clearance yet. But I was pretty well briefed a couple of months back." I wasn't even sure the press office was trying to get me a security clearance, except I knew I had to have one to work in the building.

"You don't have a clearance yet? Shit." He sighed. "I'm not sure you'd better go to the meeting."

"I can step out if you need to get into classified issues, Willie. I have insight on Harrow I know would be useful." I thought a moment. "You can check me out with Tyler's office." I knew he wouldn't of course.

His eyes snapped back to me and he nodded. "I brought

you some material, but you aren't cleared. So let me . . ." He thumbed through a two inch thick pile of papers. I could see several classified documents. Then he handed me a folder with articles in it. "You can look at these press clips. They're pretty good, really."

"Sure. What time is the meeting?"

"Two o'clock. I'll meet you at the Southwest gate, okay? We can walk."

I read the clips and met Willie downstairs at the gate at 1:45. I had to turn in my pass on the way out, as usual, which always made me nervous. I still didn't have a permanent pass, let alone a White House Pass.

We crossed 17th Street, passed the side entrance to the Corcoran and went another block up to the park that separated eastbound and westbound E Street. I hadn't expected it to be so hot, even though it was June. Of course, I was usually inside during the day. I wondered whether Willie liked to walk, or if perhaps he didn't have enough pull to rate a car.

The long strip of park, with tall sycamores along the street gave us some shade, but when we got to the State Department, my shirt was more than damp, and my hair was matted with sweat. Thank God Willie was with me because I really didn't have any credentials, other than my driver's license. Even with Willie and his White House Pass it took me 20 minutes to get cleared in to State. The meeting had already started. Willie took a seat along the side of the conference table. I took a spot by the wall, just behind Willie, and scanned the room for Sarah. I was numb with anticipation of seeing her. Extremely nervous. The room filled up and I recognized Defense, Commerce, and several from State. An officious staffer introduced himself to us as Ralph Prixell, seated himself at the head of the table and proceeded with the meeting. He passed around a draft statement in opposition to Harrow's trip, explaining why we weren't going to allow it. For a moment or two I went deaf.

She came in through a side door and there she was. I hadn't seen her in weeks. She didn't look at me. Gave no hint of recognition. For an instant, I wondered if she could have completely forgotten me. I decided to ask a question, mainly so she would notice me. And, I swear to God, my voice completely failed me. I wasn't tongue tied. My mouth opened but no words came out. My face got red and I was afraid someone was going do the Heimlich maneuver on me, if they noticed. I smiled and coughed. I focused on the draft statement. When I found my voice, I leaned over to Willie and whispered. "You can't let them put that statement out. Harrow will have a field day."

Willie looked at me. "Really?"

"Yes. Listen to me on this. If you can't talk them out of it, stall. What Harrow wants more than anything is to get into the news. If you put this out, you have created a problem: 'Harrow takes on the White House.' He'll be on cloud nine. And he'll be on cable news 24/7. Front page of every paper. Not page three. You won't be able to put the genie back into the bottle."

Willie studied me for a moment, nodding slightly, then turned back to the meeting. He listened patiently to the background and when the speaker stopped, there was a brief lull. He held up one finger, pointed at the ceiling. The table fell quiet. Willie looked at Prixell hard and spoke carefully, clearly and quietly, without smiling, "I need a day or two on this. I want to run it by my boss. Don't put it out until you hear from me."

He slid back his chair and left. I followed, not nodding or stealing one more look at Sarah, who had refused to make eye contact with me the entire meeting. But I know how to play hard to get.

Outside in the hall, we hurried toward the elevator. Willie said in a low voice, "I hope you're right, Jack." We got to the elevator and he swatted the down button with his open palm.

The arrow light went on: "I know I am." I said without

even thinking. Because I at least knew that. "I'm not sure what we should do, but that release is a disaster."

The elevator doors opened so I stopped talking while a man in a motorized wheel chair surged past us, followed by a young man sporting an overlarge bow-tie and a few non-descript bureaucrats. We got on the empty elevator just as the doors were starting to close and I pressed L for lobby. As soon as the doors closed, Willie glanced over at me, then looked up at the numbers. "I do think what you said made sense. Let's stop by Linda's office and tell her where we are. Then you can go back and tell Crane, in case it comes up in the briefing."

Tell Crane? Right. I'd be lucky to get to tell the receptionist. "Okay. Willie, can I ask you something? You know I'm new . . ."

He nodded.

"Who is Linda?" The elevator stopped and the doors opened.

Willie grinned. "Linda Saracen. She works for the Chief. You know, Phil Tyler."

"Very funny." We rushed off the elevator and dropped off our State Department passes. I thought a moment. "Is she that good-looking dark-eyed woman? I think I met her."

"Yep." Willie gave me a sly, knowing look. "Deputy Chief of Staff."

Willie held the door and I hurried through it and started down the sidewalk, hoping I was going in the right direction. "Okay." I stopped and faced him. "Here's the deal. I'm new. I'm temporary, you know?" I waited for a flicker of camaraderie, of understanding of my plight. "I'd like to brief them with you, but you saw my pass." I waited. Willie could just walk over on his own and cut me out of my golden opportunity to shine.

Willie shrugged. "Jack, there is so much going on, they are not going to want to have more than a sentence on this. I doubt they will want to meet with either one of us. But if you want to, you can walk over with me . . ." He touched his

White House pass, slipped it in his shirt pocket. ". . . and we can drop off this release of theirs—and see what happens. Come on, I'm already late for another meeting."

I didn't worry so much about the heat or the sun on the way back to the White House. I was so preoccupied with whether they would let me in the Southwest gate, like Willie, or make me go around to the front. And could Willie get me in to the West Wing? With my lowly pass? I couldn't remember what it took to get inside.

They cleared me through the gate, returned my temporary pass to me—and Willie waited for me. We walked down "West Exec," the street between OEOB and the White House, where the senior staff, the big Kahunas parked. The street was enclosed at both ends by large iron gates and every possible security precaution—tucked discretely out of sight of course. We got to the canopy covered side entrance to the West Wing and pulled open the white double doors. More uniformed Secret Service agents scrutinized Willie's pass and then mine. I was ready to turn on my heel, laugh it off and retreat to my garret, if they stopped me. But they didn't and I followed Willie, past the elevators and the entrance to the Mess and the Situation Room, up the stairs, past the Press Briefing Room and down the hall. Before we got to the Oval, the dark eyed woman I now knew as Linda, stepped into the hall, followed by Tyler, who was moving in slow motion, still talking to the assistant inside, the one who sat outside the President's office. Linda's eyes jumped to me, then Willie then me again. "Willie, Jack. What's up?"Willie stood at attention. "Just a brush fire over at State. Jack is helping us corral the errant Congressman."

Tyler let go of the doorway and started toward his office in a hurry. He slowed when he saw Willie and when he saw me, he looked puzzled and almost stopped. "What does that have to do with press?"

"Lixubistan." I said quickly "It's about stopping State before they make Congressman Harrow a household name." I swallowed when he wasn't looking. I hadn't been sure he would remember my name, let alone that I was in the press office.

Tyler looked at Linda. "Christ. You need to get involved in this. State never understands how to deal with Congress. Keep me informed."

She tipped her head toward the open door down the hall. "Stop by my office for a moment."

Willie said, "Linda, I have another meeting. Can Jack bring you up to date?"

"Sure. She took a couple more steps with Tyler, then turned. "Jack is there anybody else from your office you need to bring over to brief me?"

"My office?" I swallowed again. "Uh. I don't think so."

Tyler and Linda both stopped walking and turned to face me. "Who are you reporting to there?"

This was not the way I had hoped the conversation would go. "I don't seem to . . ."

Tyler interrupted. "They haven't given you anything to do, right?"

I offered a weak smile. "I have a lot of knowledge and expertise on Lixubistan and Harrow. I just thought I would lend a hand."

Tyler and Linda exchanged looks. I thought it was disgust. I was pretty sure it wasn't directed at me.

Tyler resumed walking, even faster now. Linda went after him and called back to me, "Go ahead back to your office, Jack. We can meet later."

I waited until about 7:30 p.m. and was almost convinced she had forgotten me when my phone rang. Linda told me to come over right away.

She met me at the West Wing entrance, walked me into Tyler's office and shut the door on her way out. Tyler was behind his desk writing. He nodded toward a chair. "Linda got a briefing from Willie. Good job at State." He straightened the papers on his desk and folded his hands. "We are going to move you out of Crane's office and make you a Special Assistant to the President reporting to me. The first thing you can handle is Lixubistan. As I understand it, you're an expert. Your clearance won't come in for a while, but as you pointed out, your friend Mr. Harrow is stirring things up. We need someone right away who understands the subject, knows the press *and* the Congress. We may have to send somebody up to testify. But whatever we have to do we need to coordinate this, you know. For public consumption."

Sarah was going to love this.

"Where are you now?"

"Fifth floor OEOB."

He shook his head. "You are moving. Not sure where, but we'll find something."

"Okay."

Tyler bent his head and he was quiet, almost like he was praying for an instant. He went on, somber and steady: "I hope you know, Jack, we didn't bring you up here as a favor. It may have looked like it, but the President values John Cook's opinion, and he says you are the best, and that you can be trusted." His eyes were candid and imploring. "We may be in for a bumpy ride. We obviously have some internal staff problems that we're trying to work through . . ."

It began to sink in that he used the future tense, as in, I might really be able to pull this off.

I heard the door open behind us. Linda held it and nodded at me, without smiling.

She followed me outside the office where a small woman with a very bored expression sat by one of the secretary's desks. "Do you know Leslie, Jack?" Linda asked.

I stuck my hand out.

"Leslie is going to take you to your new office and find out if there's anything else you need." Then she turned to Leslie. "Give him what he wants. He's going to need nice furniture. You may have to paint, new drapes . . . I'm not sure where you're putting him."

"Yes, ma'am. Already taken care of." Leslie beamed at her and shot me a skeptical glance. "Whenever you're ready, Mr. Abbott."

"Wait." Linda reached in her desk. "Lorraine is on vacation so you can park in her spot until we get you something more permanent. I can't do anything about your pass until your FBI clearance comes back. Probably a few more days. "

I followed Leslie back across the street to the OEOB where I was startled to see my name etched in a sign outside a first floor room. The Vice President's OEOB office was the closest to the West Wing, ground floor, directly across from the White House. But I was close too, just across the main corridor, down one of the side halls. The meager contents of my desk upstairs were in a box on top of my new desk, a beautiful antique looking thing.

My inbox had clippings in it and the President and Vice President's schedules for the day, which would have been confidential if they were not past-tense. I was pouring over them when I heard Linda's voice at my door. It was almost nine o'clock.

"Do you have a secretary or assistant or someone you'd like to bring here?"

I shook my head.

"We'll see who's available." She looked around the office, not with that vacant, isn't this nice air, but more like, '*Okay, what's wrong with this.*' "What do you think? Space is at such a premium around here. Of course, you come from the Hill . . ."

"Right. This is great. My last office was a cigar box compared to this."

She smiled for the first time, like a dam breaking, like she could breathe. Her face looked completely different. I actually stared for a moment. She was quite lovely, in an understated way, almost like she was trying to hide it a bit.

"I'm settled in. Let's get a drink somewhere. We need to get out of here."

"Sure. Love to. But not tonight." She flashed another smile and held the door. "Keep me posted on your crisis, okay?"

I stood up and some of the papers I was looking at fell to the floor. I shuffled them together. I figured she was probably just shoring up that I wasn't going to run to John Cook complaining. And I really didn't care. A friendly face, even if it was phony, was better than nothing.

Chapter Eight

Getting cleared in the next day was surprisingly easy. I was early, and was feeling much better in my new office. Tyler gave me a job to do and I was going to astonish them with my ability. I figured Sarah still wouldn't take my call. Instead, I got her boss on the line and explained that I had to be brought up to speed on Lixubistan. I had been out of the picture for weeks and I needed to be briefed, even if I couldn't be told anything classified. I could have gone over to State, but you know. My new office . . . Nobody had seen it yet.

By some standards, it wasn't much. The desk, on closer inspection, had a few nicks and scratches and the upholstery could have used a good cleaning. But by OEOB standards, it wasn't bad.

Sarah made no sign of noticing my furniture or superb office. She was furious. She didn't scowl or yell at me. That would have been better. If she were any colder, she would have been dead. She brought three other people, junior staffers she didn't need, but obviously she didn't want to be alone with me. I was businesslike, icy right back at her. She had her assistant, a skinny guy with bad skin, give me the high school civics lesson on Lixubistan.

I let him go on for a moment, then interrupted: "Is there anything to the nuclear rumors?"

They squirmed. Shot glances back and forth.

"I know you're about to tell me that information is

classified. But listen. I read it in the fucking newspaper. How can it be classified?"

Sarah rolled her eyes.

"I'm serious. Talk to me about the rebels. The LLF allegations. The average rainfall, interesting though it may be, can wait."

Her two minions looked at her for guidance. She started softly, like she was talking to a kindergarten class. "The Lixubistan Liberation Front is not a reliable source, Jack. There is no information that the government is trying to develop a nuclear weapons program."

"What about biological, chemical?"

She glared at me.

"Okay, you aren't going to answer. Tell me about human rights? Political prisoners, slamming people in jail for inappropriate clothing, stuff like that. Is it true?"

"Yes and no. It's a different culture, Jack. You can't evaluate their society against our values."

"Gotcha. They're pretty much guilty of everything the LLF says, only we think it's okay if they do it to people in some other country because they're allies."

"Once again, Jack . . ."

I looked at my watch, interrupted and cut the meeting short. Thanked her. My clearance could come through any day, I told her and I'd expect to be briefed if there were any developments.

She couldn't have had time to get back to her office when Willie called. "Harrow just put out a press release. He's making another statement on the floor right now." I held the phone and switched on the little TV that had materialized in my office overnight. Willie went on. "Linda said you are handling this now."

Great. Before I could get on top of the issue, there is Harrow on national TV s going on about how he will lead a delegation to Lixubistan. He had a little press coverage and he wasn't letting up.

Willie sounded so tired. "What do we do with this guy?

Is there a way to turn this off?"

I knew of course there was no way to contain Harrow. He's a flake, a loose cannon, and everybody knew it. Nobody more than me. But that's what I had to do. "Is there any interest? Are any other Members interested in this?" I asked. "I haven't seen anything in the major press . . ."

"As far as I can tell, not outside of Lixubistan. We haven't gotten any calls yet. And there seems to be zero interest on the Hill."

"Good. Listen, the likelihood is, he's going to self-destruct on it. We're going to need a statement. I'll draft something."

"Okay. There's a meeting at State in an hour. You can fill me in on the way over."

If I couldn't take care of this, I knew I would never be heard from again. I'd be flacking for the Bureau of Lost Change. Department of Dental Floss. The State Department was having convulsions over the idea of Harrow in Lixubistan. If they did let him go, it would have to be tightly controlled, which would look terrible and give Harrow exactly what he wanted. So we had to turn it off. Sarah's boss had set up the meeting with their congressional guy and Ralph Prixell, whom I had already met. Prixell, it turned out, was Assistant Secretary for that part of the world.

Willie and I walked over. "Take a look at this." I handed a short draft to him.

He skimmed it and stopped in the middle of the sidewalk. "Jack, this is crazy."

"Hear me out." I explained.

"Oh, Christ. I don't need this." He looked at his watch. "We're late. Start talking."

I thought I had him pretty well convinced when we got there, but at the guard's desk, he got a call on his cell. "I have to go back to the office. Just go up and listen. You float this thing, they're going to think you're crazy. Seriously."

At State, they were agitated and waiting for me, sort of.

"Where's Willie? We need to get started." Sarah's boss asked.

"He had to go back. We should start. I don't think he's coming."

"Okay. Here's the draft press release." He passed around the same statement we had seen two days ago. "I'd like to put it out immediately, so we can get our response in Harrow's story."

Prixell studied the group over his bifocals. Everyone turned slightly and looked at me.

"Well, you all are the policy experts, of course. But I've given this some thought, and I really think we need a different approach with this Member . . ." I passed out my release.

Sarah came into the meeting and sat at the far end of the table. She wouldn't look at me.

Her boss passed her my paper.

"It's just a draft. Change the wording if you want."

Prixell dropped his copy on the table and it slid toward the middle. "We can't say this." I could tell from his tone he meant, '*Are you nuts?*'

But they had to hear me because I was from the White House. "Listen, I used to work for this guy. He's mentally ill, I think. If you try to talk him out of his position or try to kill the trip, he's going to have a field day. Now, you don't really want a lot of publicity on this issue anyway, right? If we say sure, go ahead and go, he's going to get zilch play on it. Nobody will notice or care. It isn't a story. It's only a story if we fight it." I scanned the faces around the table.

They blinked at me, thinking, brains laboring over this obvious fact to find the flaw. I went on. "Do you *know* this guy? If you know him at all, you know there's no reasoning with him. The only other thing is to blast him. That's what he expects, of course. What he wants, actually. Then, you get all kinds of press and so does he."

Sarah spoke up in a defiant voice: "Why can't we just quietly brief the press that he's crazy? That he has to be protected from himself . . ."

"Put out a press release that a Member of Congress is wacko? Sure." I smiled amiably. "I'll volunteer to write it."

"I'm not talking about a press release, Jack." Her pique was obvious. "I mean off the record."

"Okay . . ." I nodded. I was trying not to be a smart-ass. "You know somebody who will buy that he's crazy just because we say so? You have his medical records? I don't."

Prixell stared defiantly at me but was still silent.

I went on: "If you issue my release, the story is, "Congressman Plans Trip to Lixubistan." What page do you think that will be on? On the other hand, if you tell him he can't go, the headline is, "Congressman Fights Dexter State Department." It might even make the evening news."

Sarah exhaled an annoyed sigh.

I went on: "Listen, our position on Lixubistan is that we are optimistic they will work out their problems. How can we object to a Congressman going over to encourage them? We can't."

"But . . ." Sarah began.

I held up a hand, fingers spread. "We aren't going to let him go. Of course not. Although it is tempting, considering the terrorists there would love to send him home in little pieces in a body bag. But no. It would be wrong." None of them got my joke, of course, or maybe they chose not to laugh. "He has the attention span of a fly. If the redhead in charge of the Lixubistan Liberation Front Washington operation loses interest, he'll drop this thing faster than you can say, 'Get a life.' Or any number of other things could turn him off. Listen, isn't there some other great congressional recess junket going on? The Paris Air Show? The Holy Land, perhaps? It doesn't matter. I have a few other ideas to get him off this thing."

Prixell finally spoke. "So you're saying he won't really go."

"Of course not. You guys start scheduling shots for him. Malaria. Cholera. What's that thing they have in Africa? Ebola. Is there a shot or something for that? That would scare the hell out of him."

Sarah smiled at this. I saw out of the corner of my eye.

"Listen, we might want to get the Secretary to call him up and say he'd like to take a delegation. We can think about that one. Then, if he doesn't fold as soon as we think, the Secretary can always reschedule the trip. He will be totally screwed. Put it off long enough, it will go away."

"The Secretary's schedule is way too busy for that, Jack."

"But he wouldn't actually go, see?"

They wagged heads NO in unison.

"Okay. Maybe someone else."

One of them, Prixell I think, offered, "The Vice President? He could do this."

"Sure. That would work. Listen, I've been on hiatus for a while, so I'm not up to date on the nuances of our policy with Lixubistan. But can't you use this on the Lixubians? I mean, if they think a delegation is coming over, won't they clean up their act? Especially somebody openly hostile like Harrow, who has called them a bunch of butchers? The Lixi government will have to behave, and they will see the level of resolve in the Congress, encouraging them to soften their line and even reform."

Of course they didn't react to this, because, God forbid, a lowly flack would suggest policy.

Prixell cleared his throat. "Jack, I think it's too risky, but if you are ordering us to put this out . . ."

What a little weasel. "No. If you think it is better to have a page one story, get called up for hearings, maybe get some other members interested in it, you should go ahead with your release. I'm merely here in an effort to help, with the sole intention of trying to support you and our policy." I smiled an obsequious smile and blinked sincerely at them. They knew I was right.

When I got back to the White House, I had three messages from congressional relations and the press office. Standing in the hall was Scott Goodington. Like he was just running into me.

"Abbott . . . What's going on with the Harrow trip?"

I hate it when people call you by your last name. So unfriendly. I didn't try to conceal my dislike for him, but I was civil. "Has anyone called you?" I asked him.

"Yeah. The Asian bureau of the *Wall Street Journal.*"

"Okay. We can handle that."

"No Jack. *I* can handle that. Not *we*. Crane asked me to handle this. We can't have any more freelancing on this, okay?"

I took a step closer to my door and put my hand on the knob. "What are you talking about, freelancing? Tyler asked me to deal with it."

"After your clearance comes through," he said, like he was warning me I was going to burn my fingers.

"I have a temporary clearance." I twisted the knob and put my shoulder to the door.

His anger got more frantic. "Jack, there's no such thing. You have a temporary pass. This is the kind of fast and loose we just don't play here." He took a step toward me like he was going to follow me in my office. "What happened at State?"

"I know enough to talk to the *Wall Street Journal.* Unless you want to wait until they get a clearance, too? But I don't have to call and neither do you. The State Department will be issuing a statement. Refer them over there."

I didn't say goodbye or attempt any pleasantries. I went inside my office and shut the door in his face. He had left two messages and must have thought I was refusing to return his calls so he made a personal appearance.

Before the door clicked shut, it opened again and I braced myself for another round, but it was Linda. She came over to my desk and leaned on the arm of the sofa. No hello. Strictly business. "What's the latest, Jack? What did Goodington want?"

"He wanted to welcome me and ask if he could help in any way."

She cracked a slight smile. "Oh, right. I don't see any bullet holes. Are you okay?"

I patted my jacket and shook my head. "I guess his gun wasn't loaded, it turns out."

"So, what's up with Harrow?"

"I talked State into saying they'd love for him to go."

She stopped smiling and leaned toward me. "You're kidding, right?"

"No. I told them to send over some people to give him shots, get him ready to go."

She stood up and gave me a frightening look. What a rush.

"Listen, I know this guy. If they told him not to go, he'd be on a plane tomorrow. If they help plan it, they can control it, control the timing. If he doesn't back off in a couple of days, they're going to get someone to say they want to go with him."

She didn't react, sat again, thinking for a moment. "Not bad. A bit risky . . ."

I went on ". . . The Secretary or the Vice President." I folded my arms, because you know, it was pretty brilliant.

Her dark eyes sharpened and drilled into me. "The Vice President? Is that wise?"

"He won't really have to go."

She gave me a long, worried look, then got up and walked to my window, "Jack, you have to be careful about the Vice President." She was choosing her words very carefully. "He is extremely able, of course."

"Really? That isn't what I've heard. But what?"

She sighed, faced me, leaning on the window sill. "When he gets involved in something, he stays involved. As I said, he is extremely capable and he's always looking for more to do."

"Oh. Shit. But he knows our policy there, right? So he would stay with our policy. Not try to free-lance?" I swallowed, discretely I think.

"Sure. Probably. But you know how these guys are. They think anything they lay their hands on will be fixed. So he could start thinking about what a positive force for change he could be. And how presidential he would look. And how it might help him in the polls, which wouldn't necessarily be bad. But it would be better all around if he stays out of it."

"Oh. Gotcha." I put my hand on the phone. "It can't have gotten too far. I'll just call State and make sure they hold off on that."

I wasn't really that attracted to her but I liked her and the way she handled herself. And she was on the inside. I hoped she would invite me for a drink or something and was a little surprised when she didn't. Maybe more disappointed than surprised.

She moved toward the door. "Keep me posted, okay?"

"Definitely." I jumped out of my chair. "In fact, I wonder if you could have dinner? I still need a lot of gaps filled in around here."

"I can't, sorry. I have to go back over." And she slipped through the door without saying goodbye.

I got Prixell at State on the phone and told him to go slow on the Cunningham connection.

"It's okay, Jack. I know some of his people. They're on it."

"Oh. Do they understand we need to low key this? That we don't really want him to go."

"Sure. Of course. They're top people, Jack. Very smart."

"Maybe it wouldn't hurt to talk to them again. Make sure they understand." I was caressing my forehead to keep it from exploding.

"Oh, I don't think that's necessary, Jack. Really."

The State Department had to play out the charade, of course. Harrow agreed to a meeting with them, and naturally, I briefed them and went over with them, carefully staying away from the inside of the office.

I waited in the hallway of the Rayburn House Office building, right around the corner from Harrow's office. After they went inside to meet with him, I slipped in and gave

Esquita a little hug, then went back out to the hall to wait. At the other end of the long corridor, down by the elevators that would take Harrow to the Capitol, I could see a redhead, presumably Harrow's Lixubian friend. This was going to be harder than I thought.

Maybe thirty minutes into the meeting, while I was trying to get a good look at the redhead, the bells went off. There was a vote on the House floor. I heard Harrow's door open behind me and ducked into the men's room to avoid him. A few moments later, Sarah led the State department suits out of Harrow's office and down the hall. I took a stairwell and met them on the street.

At first, Sarah wouldn't look at me. We waited for our cars, which weren't there because they had assumed the meeting would be longer. The sidewalk was deserted so I asked one of the staffers what happened. He looked at Sarah nervously but she didn't stop him.

Harrow had greeted them with his usual wary, confused look. Sarah explained how relieved they were he was taking on this important but dangerous diplomatic mission. As I had suggested, they began with a list of the shots he would need and the various epidemics he would be exposed to, and the dismal nature of the medical facilities in case he got sick before he got out of the country. Then they went over proposed itinerary for him: A fascinating tour of farms and factories. He would need warm clothes, probably long underwear and lots of sweaters because there is almost no central heating. I was pretty sure that Sarah would be more than he could take, considering how stunning she is. But as far as I knew, he didn't seem to take the bait. They were about to talk about the possible terrorist hazards, such as having his hotel bombed, when Harrow ended the meeting and left for the vote. Overall, it went pretty much as planned. A little short, but they planted the seeds.

Our cars pulled up. Sarah got in the first one, I got in behind her and turned to the other four. "I need to get back for a meeting. Sarah said she would fill me in on the rest, drop me off and see the rest of you back at State for a recap. Great work guys." I closed the door in their surprised faces and slid into my seat. Sarah glared at me.

We pulled out from the curb and I had to grab the armrest to stop from sliding into her. "I hope you don't mind dropping me first. I hated to take everyone out of the way."

Sarah was quiet for a moment, like she might explode. She looked out the window and ignored me for a block or two. Then still with her back to me, "It didn't work, Jack."

"What do you mean, it didn't work?"

She looked at me with such annoyance. "No reaction. He's still going."

"You have to be patient. You didn't think he was going to change his mind on the spot, did you?" I said. "I mean, you did send him running from the room."

She went on, voice going up a little, getting madder: "Not funny. So what are we supposed to tell our people in Lixubistan? That this is all a ruse? That Harrow is just an oversexed stooge?"

We stopped at every light. The car crawled along, dodging double parked tourists and taxies, probably making her even more anxious.

I stretched out my legs by putting them on her side of the car. "Do you mind? I'm cramped over here." She didn't answer so I went on. "I don't know, Sarah. You're the diplomat. Can't you just use innuendo with our own people? You do know you can't put anything in a cable, Sarah. You know not to put anything in writing on this, right?"

"Of course. That's the point. How do we let them know he isn't really coming?"

"Oh, come on. You say something like: 'The Congressman's precise schedule and availability is still uncertain and may have to be altered or even indefinitely postponed if his Washington duties require.' Bla bla bla. Something like that. He'll postpone it in a few days. In the meantime, can't you get your people to use his possible visit to leverage some changes?"

She gave me a strange look, and I thought for a moment she was warming up a bit. But then she exhaled one of those sighs of disgust. "That's such a simplistic approach, Jack."

"I know it is. I'm a simple guy. I know you don't think about things the way I do. I mean, if I were you, I would be milking this for my career. I would be making contacts, showing off how smart I am. Instead of wanting it to go to the back burner and go back to handling a forgotten backwater country, never invited into the big meetings. I mean, I guess you could spend your whole life handling Lixubistan and their problems. Well done. My hat is off to you."

Before she could answer, we stopped at a light at 17th, near the White House on the State Department side. "I'll get out here," I said to the driver. I opened the door without waiting for him to pull over to the curb and climbed out.

Chapter Nine

The only way to stop Harrow from going on the trip was to get him stirred up about something he wanted even more. But was there anything he wanted more than redheads?

Maybe. For two years, I had written every speech, every statement for the House floor. I knew every bill he had introduced or cosponsored for the last two years. Most of them he did out of obligation, or to protect himself politically. To kill the trip, I needed something he really wanted. Something he had to have.

I remember Harrow asking me "Hey, Abbott, how do you get a road named after you, anyway?" He was ebullient that day. Over the next few weeks, I had the bill drafted, and we debated whether he could introduce it himself or whether he would need to get another member to do it. After that, he got interested in post offices. He had an uncle who was killed in a postal facility in the line of duty. For the most part, of course, these bills have languished in their respective committees.

Bob and Evan helped with a few well-placed calls from friendly staffers, suggesting the possibility of hearings on some of these pet initiatives over the summer. Soon, I was doing double steps up the stairway in the West Wing with a press release in my hand. Harrow had postponed his trip. He was going to have hearings on Lixubistan instead.

Linda was hurrying down the hall outside her office when I got there. She didn't say hello: "Does this mean what I think it does?"

"He's not going? Probably."

"Of course, hearings are not optimal, Jack." She stepped into the doorway of her outer office and I followed, past her secretary. She paused, dropped a handful of classified files in front of the secretary without a word, and held the door of her tiny inner office for me.

"You didn't think he was going to drop it completely, did you? Not right away."

She pawed through her inbox. "I guess not," she said without looking at me. "How do you get the hearings turned off?"

Before I could answer, I was distracted by unmistakably loud, angry voices. Linda's door was open a crack. I listened for a moment. Crane and Tyler were having words. I looked at Linda. She had a blank expression like she didn't hear it. Maybe not a blank expression, more determined. Like she was commanding me to ignore the noise.

Which I did. "Turning off the hearings will be a little tougher. I have to admit, I never thought Harrow would stay interested in this one for this long. He may have to have the hearings, Linda, but with a little help, I think we can be sure they will be his usual fiasco. Zero press coverage and his peers think he's a lunatic."

"Not going to cut it, Jack. You know that. We need to turn it off."

"I'm not a hit man, babe."

She actually cracked a smile on that one. And the argument outside her office had abated. She stood up, the universal sign of 'Time for you to go.' "Jack, this may come up at State's press briefing today. You need to go over there."

"I do? And do what? Watch?"

"Yes. Watch. Give them guidance. You know."

"Okay." I didn't move.

"Did you need something else?"

"Yes. I need something else. A scorecard, a map of the land mines? I was wondering if you could grab a bite with me and fill me in on some of the eccentricities of this place. As you know, I am in the deep freeze in the press office, and I need some friendly advice."

She didn't answer right away.

"I mean, I'm staying with John Cook's guy, you know, and I know the Hill and all, but I could just use a little guidance here." I saw her blink when I mentioned John Cook, like she had forgotten the connection and perhaps wouldn't want me to go crying to them.

When I got to State, Sarah met me at the elevator. She leaned her head close to my ear and whispered, "Jack, I need to talk to you . . ." She nudged in more and I felt her breath on my face. I was turned on, of course, except that she was obviously upset. "The Vice President wants to go to Lixubistan. With or without Harrow."

I didn't want to believe her. Maybe she misunderstood, or had bad information. "I don't think so. Prixell told me . . ."

"No." She put her hand on my arm. "Now, we are rethinking the policy. Now we are considering, you know, maybe the Vice President could exert some pressure . . ."

"Shit." I looked around. "All I did was mention his name, for Christ sake."

"Prixell used to work for him. On his staff. Didn't you know that?"

I didn't answer. I didn't say what I was thinking: *Sure. I've memorized the résumé of every flunky at the State Department.*

"Ralph says, of course, this could be challenging for our work there. But the Vice President is convinced he can make a contribution. Move things forward." She smiled a cheery, fake smile.

"Normally I'd have to make a joke. But listen: I need a phone. Not your cell."

"Sure. Follow me."

I got through to Linda right away, a near miracle. I told her what was up. "I don't think he should go and I'm going to put the Kibosh on it if I can," I whispered. "Unless you want him to go."

She caught my drift right away. "Do you understand, up here it's going to look like you are responsible for this, right? You pulled him in, after all. If I were you, I'd do what I had to do. But, um. I'd rather not have any blood on my skirt."

Nice girl. I knew I liked her.

The press briefing was just starting when we got there and I stood just off to the side. The State Department spokesman glanced over, and seemed to recognize me from the recent meetings. As usual, there was no shortage of problems to talk about. Normally, it would have been hard to come up with many of less interest than Lixubistan. Still, after about thirty minutes, a reporter asked whether we pressured Harrow into canceling the trip. The spokesperson denied it, said we welcomed congressional interest, even in this very sensitive area.

Another reporter said she heard the Vice President was going anyway. Leading a delegation of business people, going to encourage investment and free markets in Lixubistan.

The press spokesman looked at me. I nodded back like it was all planned. I walked to the podium and introduced myself: "Jack Abbott from the White House. The Vice President asked me to come over today and tell you there is no truth whatsoever to those rumors. As always, Vice President Cunningham works very closely with the State Department on sensitive matters such as this one. It is true that he was considering such a trip in conjunction with Congressman Harrow's trip. However, he told me, quite emphatically I might add, the schedule does not permit a visit in the near future. He is far too involved in his other activities. He continues to be deeply concerned about the people of Lixubistan and will continue to be involved with our policy making on this issue."

There were no follow up questions, not from the press anyway. Prixell glared at me until the briefing was over then followed me out of the room. "When did you talk to him?"

"What?" I said.

"The Vice President? I talked to him last night and he was very excited. He phoned some friends in business . . . So when did this happen?"

I gave him a puzzled look. "You must be mixing up some other issue. Remember, we said this was just a possibility to involve the VP? Not part of the plan. You know the status of that country better than I do. It's sure as hell no place for Vice Presidents."

I left him standing there. He started to follow me out of the room, but one of his staff diverted him.

I wasn't going to leave without talking to Sarah, now that she was speaking to me. I caught her eye and she waited for me. "We need to talk about the hearings," I said in a low, conspiratorial voice. "But I really need to get back. Could we have a drink tonight and talk about this then?" The words shot out of my mouth before I remembered I had made plans with Linda.

"I'm having dinner with Carl and his parents tonight."

"Carl?" I held my face in a friendly smile, hoping to conceal my pang. I glanced at her hand. No ring. "Your fiancé?"

"No. I'm just meeting his parents."

"Sounds serious." I gave her a theatrical sigh and pressed my hands on my heart. She gave me a half-smile, head-tilted. I went on: "Listen, if you hear that Harrow has actually scheduled the hearings, get the White House to find me. I'll handle it. Frankly I think he's cooled to the whole issue. At least for now. He has some other hearings coming up."

Sarah let out a breath. "Good. We could use a break." Her eyes dipped around the conference room like she was trying to decide whether to go on. "Listen, what you said about our policy there . . . I want you to understand . . ."

I waved her off. "I understand, Sarah. It's just that I'm dealing with the press."

"We have to have allies."

"Of course."

"We think we can work with them to moderate their policies. It isn't just a line. If we prance around denouncing them . . . we won't even have a dialog."

"I understand that. I get it." I got up to leave. Please spare me the fucking lecture. Don't spin a spin doctor.

I was both disappointed and relieved Sarah couldn't go for a drink. She was seeing somebody, but at least we were finally on a friendly basis. I was also thankful I didn't have to make excuses to Linda, in case I could get her to go. If Sarah had said yes, I don't think I could resist.

I worked in my office until 8:30 p.m. then called Linda. I told her I needed to fill her in on what happened at State. After a pause, she suggested we meet at Dolan's, a small, quiet restaurant in Old Town. She said it would be nice to get away from the office.

I was about to go into the restaurant when I saw her get out of her car. How she had lucked into such a close space, I don't know. Her car was one of those sensible BMWs. Not the cheap little one, or the sporty one. One like an investment banker or a patent attorney would drive. We were late enough I had to step out of the doorway as customers filtered out, and I grabbed the swinging door and held it open for her.

"Hey, you're pretty good at that," She winked as she went through the door.

"Thanks. You never know if you might need another line of work, you know?"

The dinner rush had passed so they were able to seat us right away. We ordered some drinks and they came quickly. I hoped they weren't going to rush us. I poured my beer in the glass and waited for the foam to fizzle down.

"So what happened at State? Everything under control?" She took a sip of wine. Red wine.

"I think so."

"Well, tell me what happened."

I related my deft deflation of the Vice President's plans and it seemed like she was amused. Like she was trying not to grin. Finally, she couldn't stand it anymore and she laughed out loud. "Jack. Tell me you are making this up."

"Okay, but I think they may have filmed it. They tape those press briefings."

"Good. Seriously, that is the greatest, funniest thing I have ever heard."

"I hope the Vice President thinks so," I said, mouthing the words Vice President, so no one would overhear. "I don't know what is going on there. I think he must have some horrendous staff around him, people who don't know how to redirect his energy."

"Maybe." She sipped her wine again.

"So, what was the fracas outside your office all about?"

She held her hand on the base of the wine glass, rested on the table, and seemed to be looking into it for the answer. "Oil and water, basically."

"Oh. So you aren't going to tell me."

She opened the menu. "Aren't you hungry?" I didn't answer. She sighed and rested the menu on the table. "They're always arguing about something. Tyler has known Dexter for years and he's never gotten used to Crane. He's really good, of course, but a Prima Donna. Wants everything his way. You have to be a team player sometimes, you know."

She stopped when they took our order and brought the warm bread. She had told me next to nothing of course, but if I could get her primed, maybe she would go on. "So is Crane going to stay after the election?"

Linda lifted the linen napkin covering the bread and studied the contents. "Sure. Of course. He loves being in the White House." She picked out a dark roll, tore it in half, placed it on her plate, dipped some butter with her knife, iced the roll and bit in. She was as hungry as I was.

"No lunch, eh?" I picked out a muffin and buttered it. "What about his staff? You know, I hang around over there. I got to see them up close and personal."

"So?" She shrugged, mouth full. She swallowed and went on, "What are they up to?"

I stared back at her, my eyebrows raised. "They don't

seem that bad, really. Except for the disloyalty thing. I mean, Tyler is the Chief, right?"

"Yeah, yeah. Whatever. Crane has some um . . . problems in his office. But we know how to handle them."

The beer tasted good and I gulped it a bit. "Almost like they think Crane is the boss, maybe the boss of the President sometimes?"

She smiled and chewed at the same time. Then she finished and got a big smile. "You'd like to see yourself in his chair, wouldn't you, Jack."

"Maybe." I think I tried not to squirm. "Someday." I gave her my best boyish smile. "I never apologize for wanting to advance." Then I leaned a little closer to her. "Let's face it, none of us get this far without having colossal ambitions, do we? Do I want to go down to the mailroom and help out? Do I want to ride along on the plane, just to have a seat? Am I that kind of guy? What do you think?"

She held her wine without drinking and seemed very amused. "I think I better tell the Secret Service about you. Make sure you walk through the metal detector every morning." She took a sip. "Seriously, I'm going to tell Tyler how you handled everything."

I smiled back at her, which wasn't hard. "I hope you will put the proper spin on it."

"Of course. He will be pleased. And relieved. It has been a while since I've heard his laugh."

Our food came, we ate, and had a couple more drinks. It was the weirdest thing. The whole night I sat there, talking to her, almost like I might talk to Bob or Evan and she was fun, kidding around the whole time. I had planned to ask, if I got the chance, if she thought I might get to go to the Convention. Or was I going to be put out with the trash as soon as Harrow got off the Lixubistan kick? But it never seemed like the right time. We kept each other at arm's length, cat and mouse.

I noticed her eyes. Dark brown. After looking in them all evening, I decided they were the smokiest, sexiest I had ever seen.

I walked her to her car. The night had cooled, the tree-lined brick sidewalks were empty. She was relaxed, almost lighthearted. I didn't really think about it, I just pulled her close to me, half closing my eyes in case she hit me. I figured it was worth the risk but before I could kiss her she touched my face, slid her hand over my cheek and held it a moment. A friendly move, but no kiss. After a moment I felt her push away from me and I let go.

"Want to go for a nightcap or something?" I whispered. What a stupid thing to say but she knew what I was getting at.

"Yeah." She took a step away. "But we can't Jack. It's late. Call me tomorrow." Before I could answer she slipped into the car and I watched her until she drove away.

Chapter Ten

First thing the next morning, as usual, I went for my news summary.

Scott Goodington lingered in the reception area, studying his summary. Was he waiting for me?

"Abbott. Got your things packed yet?"

I was almost out the door with my mail, but I stopped.

"I heard you were moving over to Veterans . . ." He was trying not to laugh.

I shrugged, working my face to register boredom.

"Yeah. I heard they needed somebody really creative." He turned and scurried back toward his office.

I kept my bored look and left the office but clearly something was up. I was in trouble. Deep trouble. It must be Cunningham. I deduced this because next I saw Cunningham's deputy chief of staff in the hall. He smiled at me, not a friendly smile, but like I had toilet paper stuck to my shoe.

So the question was, could Cunningham get me fired?

I had to call Linda. "I think I have a problem."

"You could say that. Stay there. I'm coming over."

Before I could react to being kept on my OEOB leash, my door opened and two neatly suited men stood tentatively in the doorway.

"Mr. Abbott? Agent Hewlett and Agent Groff. FBI. We just have a couple of questions regarding your clearance. We were nearby and took a chance you might be in, but if this isn't a good time, we can come back."

Holy shit. What was I going to say? "No, not at all. Come right in. I do have a meeting in a few minutes."

"This shouldn't take long."

They peppered me with a few questions and were letting themselves out when Linda arrived.

"What was that all about? Dope smoking in college?" She laughed.

"I'm not going to tell you my dirty little secrets," I said, pretending the FBI didn't have me flustered. They just asked a few questions, mostly about Dad. Was I going to have a problem with my security clearance? They didn't act like it, but then, would they? I went around my desk and perched on the edge of it. An appropriate distance between us. "Not unless you tell me yours first."

She stood right inside the door, like she was only going to stay a minute. "I have none. No time. Yours I will probably have to know about whether I want to or not."

I started talking, almost automatically: "My father had colon cancer. He died a little over a year ago. It was a tough time . . ."

Linda held out her hands to stop me. "I was only kidding Jack. You don't have to tell me anything. Not unless you think there really is a problem with your clearance."

"No. Not that I know of."

"Good." She moved toward the couch and sat on the edge. "Guess who came to see Tyler this morning? Cunningham came over first thing to personally yell at Tyler."

"Oh, shit." I stood up.

"I think Tyler would have thought it was funny, but Cunningham was so angry . . ."

"Goodington . . ." My throat tightened up. ". . . had great fun congratulating me on my move to Veterans."

She didn't meet my eyes. Always a bad sign. "He's such a prick, isn't he?"

"So what happens now? Am I toast?"

"Not yet.

I looked at her, waiting for her to go on. "What should I do? Should I apologize to Cunningham?"

"No. I don't think so. I will tell you that Tyler told the Veep very calmly that he was absolutely right, of course, about how inappropriate your handling was, but that it was totally ludicrous for him to think about going to Lixubistan, especially without airing it with the President."

She stood up and backed toward the door. "Can you stay out of trouble for a few days . . . maybe even out of sight?"

"Done." I swallowed.

She left and I deduced the best way of staying low was to get out of the building. I thought I might even eat lunch. Payday had come and gone, and perhaps I could treat Evan and Bob. They had called several times to get me to come to the Hill but I didn't think I should go. Now, however, I needed moral support. I wasn't sure I wanted to tell them about the trick I had played on Cunningham, because they might kill me. All the trouble they went through to help me get the job. Only a few weeks had passed since I had started as a temporary hack, lucky to get a paycheck. Now I had a title and an office with a nameplate. Couldn't I just keep myself out of trouble until the election?

Both sides of the Capitol were in session so Evan couldn't leave the Hill. We agreed to meet in the tiny restaurant on the Senate side of the Capitol, open only to staff and Senators and their guests. I was only about five minutes late but Evan and Bob were already there, waiting for me like a couple of vultures. They had a round of iced tea and the waiter came as soon as I sat. We ordered without checking the menus. I didn't care that Senate Bean Soup was for rubes and tourists. I always had to have some, even in the summer.

As soon as the waiter left, Bob glanced around the restaurant, checking to see who was nearby, who might be listening. Then he leaned toward me and whispered, "So what's this we hear about Dexter?" He paused, studying me. "Having AIDS?"

"What?" I really thought for a minute I had

misunderstood.

"Dexter. You know . . . the President . . . AIDS?"

I looked over at Evan and he was staring at me, too. They weren't smiling.

"You're joking, right?"

Bob shrugged. "Listen, we've both heard it from separate sources. Sounds like there's something to it."

"Bullshit." I glanced back and forth at them, still uncertain whether they might be messing with me. "Bullshit. There's no way they could keep that quiet."

"Um, Jack. They haven't," Evan whispered. "That's the point."

I waved it off. I tried to laugh but I couldn't manage it. All I could think of was that Linda must know if there is any truth to these absurd rumors. I tried to rerun the tape in my head of everything she had said, to see if she had given me any hints. But I got nothing. I wanted to leave, go back and check with her. I certainly couldn't use the phone on this one. But I managed to finish lunch.

Stay low, she had told me. Did I dare go to her office? If Tyler saw me, would it be over? I didn't care. This could not wait. They had to know about this. Christ, this could make the stock market tank if it got any further. They had to put something out to shut it down. I went straight to see Linda.

She was standing in the hall outside her office, so I didn't have to go through her assistant or wait for her.

"I just heard the damnedest thing and I really hope it makes you laugh out loud. Because it's going around the Hill, both sides, like wildfire."

"Jack. This isn't what I told you to do." She waited.

"Listen to this . . . Dexter has AIDS."

She rolled her eyes. Then she shook her head. "Come on, Jack." She whispered, motioning to her office and I followed her.

"You aren't laughing."

"Sorry." She closed the door. "Long day already. No, Jack, he doesn't have AIDS."

"Walk me through this then, will you? This is coming from somewhere. They come up with some wacky stuff up there, but it usually has some kernel of reality."

"Calm down, okay?" She was murmuring, or kind of hissing at me. "The President does not have AIDS, Jack, and if you go around asking this, you will just look like an ass."

I lowered my voice. "A thousand dollars says there'll be something in the *Washington Post* by the end of the week on his health. Now what is it? What's going on?"

She didn't answer. Face unmoved, unimpressed. "There's no AIDS, Jack. No AIDS. I have a meeting." She opened her door and glared at me until I left.

I went back to my office. I wanted to call Evan and Bob and reassure them. Tell them they were so full of shit. But something in my gut said there was a problem. Or maybe it was the edge in Linda's voice. After a couple of hours passed, I began to entertain the idea that my gut was wrong. There really wasn't anything to it. Linda expressly told me to disappear. If I didn't cool it, I would be on my way out.

About six o'clock, the call came. Linda's assistant told me to come over right away. I feared the worst. My meeting with Martin was still rather fresh in my mind. I broke a sweat on the way.

I forced a carefree grin for the Secret Service on the way in to the West Wing and they eyed my pass and nodded. As I climbed the back stairs, I tried to take in everything, just in case I wasn't coming back.

Linda was in with Tyler and when she saw me, she waved me in, then left, closing the door behind her. Obviously I had blown it, but I wasn't going to go down without making a pitch at least, for one more chance.

Tyler nodded me into a chair. He came over and sat next to me. I was going to get the full treatment. He looked so concerned, so caring. I was ready to throw up.

His voice was low and steady. "Jack, we are really glad you're with us, because John Cook says you are a loyal person." He paused, watching me. "If you're going to leave, do it now. Because things could get rough around here. So decide. "

I tried not to look confused. What was the part about *going to leave?*

Tyler didn't wait for me to commit. He went on in a slow, even voice. "President Dexter has had a brief, recent brush with cancer. Colon cancer."

Tyler must have seen me wince and his jaw flexed but he went on. "He's already been treated. He's doing fine. The doctors believe he's going to make a full recovery."

I heard the words and began to realize the meeting was not about firing me. As I listened to Tyler explain the President's condition, all I could think about was my own father, of course. I never expected this. Obviously, this was where the AIDS rumor came from. I wanted to know how long they had been sitting on this, but I couldn't come out with that. "When does this become public?" I asked.

"We were going to let the President enjoy the Fourth of July holiday, get a little extra rest, then announce that he had it . . . it's over . . . he's better." Tyler chopped the air gently with his right hand for emphasis.

"And you want him looking his best when we say that." I thought of Crane. Is this what they were fighting about? Nobody was asking my opinion but I had to say something. "The thing is, I think, I mean, it looks like something's already out there. This has to be where the AIDS thing is coming from."

Tyler nodded slightly.

"So what's Plan B?"

"We don't bring it up, but if we're asked about it, we have to tell the truth because, obviously, it will all come out eventually."

"Always does."

Tyler gave me a sad nod.

"So if a reporter asks me, what can I tell them?" I pictured the transaction and before he could answer I shook my head. "I don't think you can wait. It will break over your heads and be the only news for a month. I wouldn't be surprised if they try to have some kind of investigation on it."

"Exactly. We need to put out a statement. Do a press conference, whatever."

"I think, Crane . . . I don't know who would handle that . . . should get that statement ready."

Tyler never took his eyes off me or missed a beat. "I want you to handle it." He paused, and looked hard at me. Dramatic effect, I guess. Then he went on, "Draft it tonight—this weekend and have it on my desk as soon as possible. I want you to give me your plan, Jack. How you see this playing out. Linda has the medical reports—you can make calls to the docs if you need further clarification."

I just stared at him. Speechless is the word. I had a million questions. I was working all the math, all the angles and I knew better but I couldn't help but say it. "I'm sorry, I don't get it. This is a major announcement. Why me instead of Crane?"

Tyler sighed but still smiled. "Jack, the press likes you." His eyes met mine unflinching, no bullshit, no niceties. "If someone besides Crane handles this, particularly, someone a bit more, well, junior, it underscores that we aren't worried about it. We don't want to make a big deal about it because it's over and we want to move on."

He could see my skepticism.

"And, you have some credibility on this because of your father. I remember when we met, we talked about your father . . . that he passed away a while back . . . that he had cancer." He paused. "Again, I'm sorry."

"A little over a year." I nodded. "And yes, he did have colon cancer."

He nodded sympathetically, looked at the carpet, solemn faced. "Of course, if you feel this situation with the President is too close to home, too uncomfortable," he shrugged, "too difficult . . ."

I needed air and sucked in a big breath. I think I closed my eyes for a second. "It is pretty close to home, but then again, I know the lingo. I've been through it. My dad couldn't make it but a lot of people do. You should know— I'm all too aware of that." I swallowed. I knew exactly what to say. "There's nobody in town that can do a better job on this than me. My dad would be proud, and we all know, one great thing about the President going public is that more people will get checked."

"Absolutely." Tyler narrowed his eyes. "The President believes that is the most important part of the story. But you know, of course there will be people in the party, in the press, who will say the President needs to step down or at least not run for reelection. As I said, this could be a long grueling ordeal all the way through the election." His eyes x-rayed me. "You have a reputation for loyalty . . ."

I nodded slowly. "I appreciate your saying that. Loyalty means a lot to me." In my head I was replaying the fight I overheard in his office the day before. Were they fighting about who would handle this, or how it would be handled? This was my chance to find out. But part of me didn't want to know. Maybe Crane didn't want me to handle this. Didn't see the logic. I was half listening when my good sense returned with a jolt: This was my chance and if I wanted to stand around questioning it, I might just blow it.

"Loyalty works both ways of course. I have to be honest with you, Jack. If the announcement goes as we hope it will, I think we will be in a good position to give you more responsibility. You can be running your own show, getting critical management experience."

I nodded, not sure where this was going.

"You know the campaign staff is already set, and our press operation is fully staffed. If you move to run a press office until after the election, we'll be in a position to bring you back after the election."

"Run a press office?"

"Yes. I think you are ready. Linda has briefed me on how you've handled the Lixubistan matter so far. This is the kind of superb effort we need."

"Thanks." I said quietly.

Tyler chuckled. ". . . Cunningham, what a stunt . . ."

He went to the door and opened it before I could formulate a question. He patted me on the shoulder as I stood next to him in the doorway. "Linda will fill you in on the details." He turned to go back to his desk but I didn't move.

"Sir, just a second." I closed the door. "So you're saying that if I handle the announcement well, I will have to leave?"

"Just temporarily. To an agency. To head a press office."

"I appreciate that, but I would rather stay here. In a non-managerial role. I mean, won't there be follow up? Won't it look bad if you move me out?"

He sighed, seemed to strain at explaining this to me again. "Jack, this is clearly an extremely delicate matter. But it is our thought that it needs to be in proper perspective, which is that it is not really material to the election. We don't want to overplay it. We don't want a recurring theme. If you handle it, every time the press sees you, they will remember the story and want updates. That takes the focus off our narrative, which is key to reelection." He stopped and just studied me for a moment. "But you know, who can say? I'm not in stone on that. Let's wait and see, after the announcement. Maybe there will be a way to keep you around." Then he smiled.

Chapter Eleven

Before I got back to my office, I realized I hadn't asked him the most obvious, difficult questions. First, when the President goes under the knife, and anesthetic is used, he is supposed to pass power to the Vice President. Obviously, they didn't do this. I would have read about it. Holy shit. Second, why had they waited to disclose this? I mean, a good why. Not some bullshit about privacy. I was going to need a real reason. The President went for a physical and somebody, Crane, I assume, said everything was fine. That's called lying.

Except in this case. I called Linda and went over the medical records with her. First of all, incredibly, the colonoscopy was done "without sedation." I must have said, "Really?" to her about five times, but apparently, it wasn't uncommon. The timing issue was a little more complicated. We pulled the statement the press office put out after the procedure and luckily, if you want to call it that, it was worded very carefully. "The President's physician believes that due to the President's age and medical history, a colonoscopy should be performed at some point, but is not urgently needed." Linda pointed out that an MRI had revealed the probable cancer during the exam, and the colonoscopy took place almost immediately. Really, all we had done was delay reporting the results. She had a good reason for this, too. We were trying to schedule talks with the Chinese. Everybody knew it. Having a sick President would have interfered with the sensitive negotiations. As for the President's wan appearance, he was undergoing chemotherapy, just to make sure the cancer didn't spread. He was a little nauseous. Had lost weight, wasn't his usual energetic self, but was mentally sharp as ever. And, he was already at the end of the third week of a five-week treatment.

And what about Cunningham? What would he say about all this? Would he be supportive? Where would he be when I made the announcement? I wondered who knew on his staff and how I could coordinate with them.

I stayed at work until after midnight trying to figure out how the hell to detonate a nuclear device and convince everyone it was just a firecracker. My plan was to parse the information out over two days. I would start, make the announcement, give the details of his treatment, surgery, and finally, let the reporters at the doctors themselves. The second day would be hell: follow-up. After the reporters spent the night on the internet scraping up information, we would give the doctors another session. Tyler was to call a few key congressional leaders and a couple of columnists he leaked to and give them a heads up.

We would have to control the flow, get everything out there. After the news conference and the first 72 hours or so, we would show the President being president, making other news. And, we would have to answer the big questions before they were asked: Could the President go on? Could he run for reelection? Was he up to it? Everything else will fall into place—with a little luck, and some other news—if we could shut down the idea that Dexter had one foot in the grave.

I'm not saying we would have to start a war or anything like that. But it would be helpful if some celebrities would decide to get divorced, shoot each other, et cetera. We couldn't count on such things, so I would call my friend Willie in Legislative Affairs, and we could cook up some issues. Nothing too strenuous. A bill signing, a visit to a school. We could put together two weeks of Dexter agenda items, a new message every day.

Cable news would beat the story to death around the clock for the rest of the week. By Sunday, we would have a good read on it. There might be lingering doubts about the President's health, in which case I would be unemployed again, or they might be ranting at us about disclosure. Also not good for me.

The Sunday interview shows would have to spend five minutes on the President's health, at the very least. With a lot of luck, the pundits and pollsters would conclude the people believed us and it wasn't important. With a lot of luck, it would go off the radar screen. And maybe, I would be saved.

Of course, I knew, worst case, the disclosure issue could play worse than the cancer itself. There could be a call for a Special Prosecutor—Justice Department investigations and a general furor. A full blown scandal was a possibility. President plummets in the polls. The press smells blood. It was a little bit like trying to feed a shark bare-handed. There was a good chance it was going to gobble me up. At some point it dawned on me that this was how they got Crane to go along with letting me handle it rather than Scott Goodington: If it didn't go well, I was disposable. What I didn't know was what to do about Cunningham. Tyler was going to have to fill in the blanks on that one.

Cunningham was the lynchpin. If he was appropriately supportive—as the heir apparent—and enthusiastic about Dexter running for reelection next year, it would reinforce us. If he didn't, he was going to look like an ass, but more important, it would encourage others in the party to take on Dexter. Was the Vice President going to think this was his big chance? Really, he had no choice but to go along with the plan, whether he agreed or not. If he gave a hint of disloyalty, it would be over for him. Maybe not right away, but he would be toast. Would he realize this?

I worked most of the weekend to finish the press release. I took it over to Linda's office Sunday afternoon. I went back to my office and while I waited, I got a call from a reporter I knew from my John Cook days. I categorically denied the

AIDS rumor both on and off the record and told him off the record not to run anything or he'd be very embarrassed. I alerted Linda. The story was about to break. She told me to come over, that Tyler was going over the release.

Tyler's door was closed and his secretary wasn't at her desk so I just leaned in the doorway, shifting my feet, wondering if there was something wrong with the ventilation or was it me. Tyler came out of his office with the release rolled up in one hand, like he was going to bop me on the head with it. I shuffled a step or two toward him, unsure what to do, where to go. He cruised past me to the door. "Come on. Let's go over this with the President."

My mouth went dry, but I managed to follow him without tripping. He strode into the secretary's office, just off the Oval, and I followed him like a baby duck. He paused briefly and exchanged nods with Doreen, the little gray woman at the desk.

We had to walk through the Oval to get to Dexter's study, on the opposite side. I tried not to gawk, I tried not to think about where I was but the air got thinner and my heart pounded. The National Security Advisor and a uniformed staffer filed past me, nodding at Tyler. Dexter was relaxing in the study. From the back I could see the familiar silhouette, large head and powerful shoulders. My nervousness gave way to shock as I could see he had a blanket tucked around him like an invalid. His well-known face was tan as usual but looked deflated. Before he noticed me, I saw his eyes, sad and tired.

"Mr. President. This is Jack Abbott. He's the one John Cook sent us."

"Yes, of course." The President came to life and flashed that gorgeous, radiant smile. "Forgive me Jack, if I don't get up."

"Of course, sir." I smiled back agreeably.

"Jack has developed a plan for release of the medical information, sir."

The President just looked at me and nodded.

Tyler motioned me into a side chair, I think so the President wouldn't have to lift his head up as much to look at me. Tyler sat next to me and tipped his head in an unmistakable sign I should start talking.

I began and the President sat there, blanket snug around him, head bowed, his fingers kneading his temple.

This was one of the most important events in his political career so I knew he wouldn't want just the highlights. I was on about the third paragraph when I suspected he was asleep. I stopped talking and looked over at Tyler.

"Go on. Finish, Jack." Tyler said impatiently.

So I went on, and as I was finishing, the President lifted his head and looked at me. At first I thought he was about to say, *'Who the hell are you,'* but he just nodded. "Sounds fine, Jack." He reached his hand out and when I jumped to a half crouch and took it, he clapped his other hand over it. "Good finally meeting you. Thanks for coming aboard."

That was it. I was whisked out of the office before I could say another word. Tyler walked me around the corner, back to his office. Of course I was elated. After all, I just met with the President. But I hadn't been prepared to see him like that. I could still feel his hands, bony and cool, on mine.

Tyler looked at me warmly, with his whole face in a casual smile. "So are we ready?" You almost didn't notice those piercing eyes.

"Okay." I nodded firmly. "I'll put it together." Proud I wasn't wetting my pants—yet. "But one question, one thing I didn't cover . . . What about Cunningham?" He wasn't press, after all.

"What about him?"

"Is he going to be cooperative?" I caught myself, not wanting to sound disrespectful. "I mean, given how he's handled some of the Lixubistan issue, I know he can be unpredictable."

Tyler hesitated. "He doesn't know yet."

I think I may have blinked. "Shouldn't we tell him first?"

Tyler sighed and stared at me a long, uncomfortable

moment. His face was inscrutable. "Well, if we tell him, Jack, he'll leak it."

"Really?" I blurted it out and immediately wished I hadn't.

"Yes, really."

The magnitude of the Vice President's presumed disloyalty reverberated in my mind. "Well, what will happen if he finds out on CNN?"

Tyler didn't answer.

"We have to tell him, don't we? Just before we go public?"

"I guess so. Yes, of course."

"Do you want to call him?"

"No." Tyler shook his head. "No, Jack. I don't have time to listen to his temper tantrums. He'll use the opportunity to tell me the President should step down." He shook his head. "Listen, you need to talk to his press guy. Make sure he gets it. That's the way to handle it. Tell his staff." He waved his hand like he was shooing a fly.

I tried to follow. ". . . how disloyal he will look, how he will be unelectable if he screws us on this?"

"Exactly," he nodded.

"Okay." Last week, Cunningham had tried to get me fired. Maybe, if I was extremely lucky, I could handle this at the staff level. Even that was going to be a nightmare.

Monday morning, the President and Crane left for Camp David, ostensibly for a meeting with his economic team. Most of the White House beat reporters headed up to Camp David, hanging around in case some news happened. So I was going to have to deal with the extra hungry sharks— the ones who wanted their jobs. I got the doctors and spent two hours going over questions with them.

Then, I went to see the Vice President's Press Secretary, Ted Valbrun. I had never met the guy, who had been hired about the same time I was. He must have filled the opening Bob heard about in the VP's office. I didn't take more than five minutes to tell him. He took it in, nodded thoughtfully and said he agreed, didn't see any problem. But about ten minutes before the press conference was supposed to start, he called me. His voice was thin and tight. "Jack, I have some concerns, on reflection, about this . . ."

My guess was, he went back to tell Cunningham, and the VP went ballistic. The problem was, I was the only one left to yell at. The President and Chief of Staff were en route and it was clear they weren't going to take his calls—at least for a while. When he found out they were gone, he demanded to see me.

Cunningham sat in his office on the first floor of OEOB, behind the large desk, his chair turned away from the door. The windows behind him looked out to the West Wing. He had an office in the West Wing, but it was mostly ceremonial. When I went in, past the Secret Service and past his receptionist, he didn't turn to me. Didn't look at me. Didn't say hello. He directed his words to Ted: "Thanks, Ted. I want to talk to Jack for a minute."

Ted backed out of the office and closed the door.

He pressed his hands together, just in front of his face, almost like he was praying. He was thinking, blinking. Finally he looked up at me. "How long have you known?"

He didn't ask me to sit, but I did, in one of the nice little antique chairs in front of his desk. "Not long."

One eye was half closed, like he was aiming a gun. "When did he find out?"

I nodded at the question, like it was logical to wonder how long the President had withheld this information, but not wonder about the President's prognosis, how he was holding up, etc. "I think Ted probably told you it was discovered during a routine physical. The President considers it a private matter. It isn't *necessarily* life threatening, you know, at least at this point."

"So you won't tell me when?" He pushed his chair back like he was getting ready to stand up. "I should have been told."

I didn't answer. I was inclined to agree.

"On a good public policy level, I can't believe a matter so critical to our country as the continuity of leadership would be handled in this underhanded way." Then he leaned back and looked at the ornate ceiling. "It's personal. I know that. But what I don't know is, why? Why does he treat me like this? Like I'm the enemy or something. He goes out of his way to embarrass me . . ."

"Sir, the Chinese . . ."

"Bullshit!" He leaned forward again and shouted at me. "Save the bullshit for the press, Jack . . . If he decides to pull out of the election, he's not going to give me five minutes notice. He'll treat me like any other candidate. After serving with him . . ."

"Sir," I interrupted softly, "he's still planning to run, sir."

"Sure he is. That's what he says now." Cunningham narrowed his eyes again, suspicious, and angry. "But I've seen him, you know. I know the drawn look, loss of color. No, he's going to pull out and leave me hanging."

I just shook my head 'no' and hoped my eyes weren't giving away my own doubts.

"I suppose they want me out there, sweetness and light, telling everyone, lying to everyone that I'm completely on board . . ."

I watched him for a minute while he waited for me to say something. I drew in my most sincere, tired breath. "Wow. It's been a long time since I saw someone take their career down over an issue of principal like this."

He straightened and for a moment didn't say anything. "What do you mean?" he growled.

"You know. If you go out there, shaking your head, angry at the President over this, you must know that your political career is over. DOA. Of course you would bring down the President, too. But I don't have to tell *you* how the press works." I gave him my best admiring smile, no note of sarcasm in my voice. "If anyone gets wind that you are not on board with this, they would just tag you with disloyalty;

probably suggest you're trying to push him out so you can take over. Yet you have some legitimate concerns you say can't wait, and after all, you are one heartbeat away from the President." I couldn't hold this pose much longer so I stood and took a step toward the door.

Cunningham squinted at me. "My career is over if I stand by Dexter, and this thing blows up in his face."

"But it isn't going to do that." I said it without a hint of jocularity.

"How do you know that?" he growled.

"Because I'm handling it." I let that arrogant remark hang there for a minute, then went on, "You know, you can always see if I can bring it off. You can always criticize me or the President, or whomever later, if it blows up. You can go on *Meet the Press* and pound the table that you begged us to follow your advice. On the other hand, if you come out criticizing us now, I really don't know how angry that might make the President. Or Tyler. You might keep in mind that the President is facing a potentially life threatening illness here . . . The press will probably be looking for you know, good wishes, common decency . . ."

"Very funny."

He thought I was kidding.

His eyes shifted at the floor, left and right. Then a glance at me. "I just can't believe the disregard for the American people . . ."

I took another step sideways toward the door. "Sir, I'm already late for the press conference. Is there anything else?"

He pushed a button on his phone and asked Ted to come back in. "Ted, Let's get to work on a statement." Then he turned to me, "That's all, Jack."

No good wishes, no best of luck, no hint of what would be in the statement. As in, fuck you, I went out the door without saying the usual, mindless, *'Thank you, Mr. Vice President.'*

Chapter Twelve

We let the press know only that an announcement was coming at 3:00 p.m. This would be on the evening news, and the closer we were to air time, the more we controlled the story. If we looked too controlling, of course, it could backfire. At 4:00 p.m. we would have Dexter's doctor answer questions, beginning with a lengthy explanation of colon cancer. We had debated how many doctors to march in. I thought three was good, but Tyler said it would look like we were trying to spin the thing. So we settled on two. I would set up the story, answer the basic questions but defer all the medical questions until the 4:00 briefing. The next day, we would follow up with a second panel of the President's doctors, who would again walk through the disease, treatment and prognosis, then take questions.

I started the press conference about a half hour late, to make sure I had their attention. First my statement would go on the wires and instantly on Cable news. The doctor's would lead the network news. Tyler told me to go ahead and take as many questions as I felt I could. I guess they wanted to know what they were up against and let's face it, if I bungled it, they could just quietly execute me.

I walked in and went to the podium. Reporters gave me a bored glance, like maybe I was adjusting the microphone. I just stood there and quiet swept over them as they realized Crane wasn't coming. I read the statement:

"Ladies and Gentlemen, one month ago, the President

underwent a routine physical. As part of that physical, he had a routine colonoscopy. During the colonoscopy, three malignant polyps were discovered and removed. Since that time, the President has undergone routine chemotherapy as a precautionary measure. There is presently no indication of continued cancer in the colon or elsewhere. The President says he feels fine . . ."

The press who had been milling around, ignoring me, rushed to their seats, forgetting to wait until I was finished, shot their hands into the air and shouted questions at me. I thought a couple of them might require medical attention.

I went on. "As to the timing of this announcement, it was the President's wish to delay the announcement of this health matter during this period because he had a number of duties he wanted to complete without his health becoming a factor.

"I can refer any of your technical questions to the President's doctors who are here with us today: Dr. Wayne Wilson, the President's personal physician, and Dr. Bart Roberts, gastroenterologist at Walter Reed.

"Again, the President is deeply grateful to his doctors for their skillful handling of this matter and reports that he feels very well indeed. I'm going to open up to questions now, but let me say that I know some of you are going to want us to be available on this for several days and we will be ready to do that."

Very cool, very sincere. Definitely not flippant or witty. I answered some of the questions, but turned to the doctors for the more detail.

It was clear right away which reporters knew what they were talking about. Which ones had encountered the Big C before. And which ones had not. They wanted to know if we were going to make his x-rays available or tell the specifics of the treatment. Was he going to have one of those little ostomy bags, and if so, would it inhibit his diplomatic duties? I was expecting the next question to be whether or not he could still have sex, but it never came. There were a lot of very basic questions, too. After about a half hour, I cut it off.

Once we established the rosy prognosis, the quicksand would be the "What did you know and when did you know it," questions. It was in the statement but of course they asked me again and again—I told them, off the record, the same thing, which was the truth: We had held back on the announcement because the President wanted the crucial, long-planned meeting with the Chinese to take place without his health issues being a factor. The public had a right to know, of course, but not instantly, not if it jeopardized national interests. And we could hardly go around trumpeting that the President had kept quiet about his health issues so the Chinese wouldn't try to take advantage of him. As I smacked every question out of the park, I realized, much to my well-contained jubilation, that there was nothing I had failed to anticipate.

You may think you can picture the press conference, but I doubt you could feel it like I did: Like I had my fingers in the light bulb socket. An almost out of body experience. But it wasn't a dream. The entire world had seen me and would see me over and over for the next week at least.

I went to Linda's office when it was over, a bit damp around my shirt collar with sweat. Okay, I was soaked. If I kept my coat on, it wasn't that noticeable. Her assistant was gone but her door was open and Linda was sitting at her desk, on the phone with Tyler, and she waved me in. Tyler and the President had watched the whole thing at Camp David on CSpan. I took Linda's remote and flipped. The cable channels had a trailers of the news conference "President Dexter treated for colon cancer. Full recovery expected." Above was a loop of the President playing tennis. File tape, of course. The networks had the President taking a brisk walk and waving at the camera. Déjà vu. The initial diagnosis, the hope, following through on the treatments. The networks went back to regular programming and I switched back to cable, waiting for Linda to get off the phone and give me my real review. Her face began to relax and when she put down the phone, she was smiling. "Tyler said the President is pleased, Jack."

I nodded. "Good." I shut the door and sat in one of the dainty chairs across from her desk without asking.

"I don't think it could have gone any better."

"Thanks."

"What next?"

"They're all running to the experts, to the internet now, trying to find somebody to dispute what we said. Tomorrow will be more detailed. But we know this stuff."

She shook her head impatiently, like, *'You don't get it.'* "Right. What I guess I'm asking is, when does it end?" I realized that for once she wasn't flipping through a memo or looking at her computer screen while she talked to me.

"Oh. Well, if we're lucky, the Sunday interview shows should be the end. They will want updates through the election, of course."

"So Sunday, you think. You can shut it down by Sunday?"

"Wait a minute. I said, if we're lucky. Look, I don't know what else will happen this week. I don't have a crystal ball, you know. But if I'm downtown planning the Sunday interview shows, I have to do a segment on this. We should think about who to send out on this." My blood raced at the idea of going on *Meet the Press.* "Unless some bigger news comes out. I mean it is only Monday. A lot can happen in a week."

Linda's cat-like, almost purring support turned fierce. "Jack, no. We really don't want them to do a whole show on it. There must be something you can do to derail it."

"That's not the way it works. This is news. We can't squelch it. We can't look like we're squelching it."

"Oh bullshit, Jack. The news? Is it really news that the President is going to be fine?"

I got up to leave, but remembered the other detail I needed to tell her. "I almost forgot. Cunningham is pissed. He made me come over and meet with him before I went out there. Damned inconsiderate . . ."

"So—what is he mad about?"

"Guess. He wasn't told, first of all, but here's the big bug up his ass: He thinks the President is going to pull out of the election, and if he supports him on this, he's going to be blamed as part of the so-called cover up."

"What did you tell him?"

"I said the President is running, period. If he looks like he doesn't support him, he's going to appear very disloyal and his career will be over."

"Is that all? It seems unusually sensible for you, Jack." She crossed her arms and allowed a smile.

"Why, thank you, Miss Linda. I did tell him to go ahead. I guess you could say I egged him on a bit." My hand twisted the doorknob, but I didn't open the door.

"What's he going to do?"

"I don't know. He went out of his way to not tell me. I don't think he likes me."

"Duh."

I walked toward her and stood at the edge of her desk. "I'm new around here but is it normal for the Chief of Staff and the President to refuse to take the Vice President's calls?"

"They never, never, refuse to take his calls, Jack. I'm surprised at you." She stood up and straightened the papers on her desk. "They aren't instantly available for everyone. You know? I'm sure they'll be very eager to talk to him and hear his views."

I rolled my eyes. "Well, I don't know if you heard, but I already answered the question about when the Vice President was told. I said, 'I don't have the exact day and time for you, but I can tell you he was informed at the earliest possible time, as was appropriate given the nature of this matter.'"

Linda's hand was on the phone. "Not bad. I'm calling Tyler back to give him a heads up."

"Fine, you should do that. But I really don't think Cunningham is going to do anything. His eyes, you know. That look. Fear, I think it's called. He's not going to self-destruct. He can't go after the President on this without going down himself."

"Is that what I'm supposed to tell Tyler?" she smirked. "That you read his eyes?"

I blushed on that one, but I dropped the friendly smile. "Funny. Look, I'm just saying I think he gets the self interest on this. His good government façade does have limits, you know?" She looked down at the phone so I stepped toward the door again. But there was one more thing I had to know: "Would you mind telling me where the hell Crane is through all this?"

"Yes. He's with the President. Strategy. Reelection."

"Right. One of the most important announcements of the Presidency . . ."

"Depends how you look at it, Jack. It isn't important unless you screw it up. That's how I see it." She smiled brightly and put the phone to her face.

I left. Still damp, still feeling good, but not as good as when I went in. There was a lot at stake. I just didn't know what it was.

For the next two days the country was immersed in the President's colon. I briefed again the next day, after everyone had a chance to do some research and call their favorite doctor to give me some hard questions. We went over the same facts again and again, like they wanted to see if I had my story straight. After the second day, all we needed was some big news. Almost anything, an earthquake, a coup on some other continent. Shameful, I know. But I had to divert the Sunday interview shows—let them ask the questions about the President and his health as an afterthought.

The President came back to the White House to meet with his economic team. We had a photo-op. The President posed with his genial smile, and gave a wink and a thumbs up to the "How're you feeling?" questions blurted out by the media.

By Thursday night there was still no news in the Middle East, no new presidential hopeful. No coup, no earthquake.

No other news. I had to tell Linda all three networks were planning to do the President's health on Sunday.

I always like to give bad news in person.

She glared at me from behind her desk. "Are you sure?'

"No. Of course not." I leaned in the doorway. "They could change their minds six more times before Sunday. You know that."

"Oh well, we can always hope." She said, but her voice didn't' sound very hopeful. She gave me a dismissive look, like, *'Oh well . . . you tried.'*

"It isn't over yet, Linda," I tried to stall, "And let me remind you, the Sunday shows, well, if they have to cover it, that would be the end of it. The consensus being, the President's fine, life goes on."

She looked at me like she was trying to decide whether I would leave on my own or would she have to tell me to go.

"By the way, what has happened with Crane?"

"What do you mean?"

"Is he back? I mean, is he coming back?"

"Yes. Of course. Why wouldn't he?"

I got the uncomfortable feeling that maybe I was going to be the one leaving.

"What about Cunningham? Has Tyler talked to him?"

"Of course. The Vice President leaves tomorrow for Michigan."

"Huh?"

"Sure. Tyler suggested he could do some campaign stops up there."

"Campaign stops? Is that wise?"

"Probably not, but it gets him out of town."

"God, Linda, I hope you know what you're doing. Some eager beaver type will track him down and if he breathes a word of misgivings over the President, it will be . . ."

"Relax. We're sending our advance people. We'll whisk him in and out. It will be totally scripted. Completely controlled."

By late Friday, I was beginning to consider committing

some terrorist acts myself. Then—and I had nothing to do with it whatsoever—there was a coup in Ecuador. Now they wanted the Secretary of State, the head of the Drug Enforcement Administration, various congressional leaders. They would probably mention the President's health at the end, but no fireworks. All except one network. Roger Castleton didn't want to do a me-too story. They wanted to keep the story on the President. They somehow got the idea to talk to a panel of cancer survivors, big name people, an actor, a former Senator, a CEO and, they always love this, one of their own, a TV correspondent. Castleton wanted, of all things, Cunningham, to put his imprimatur on the story. In other words, what does the heir apparent think of the President's health? I was screwed. I was sandbagged. I smelled disobedience from the Veep's staff. They peddled this, sure as God made cheerleaders. All it would take was a moment's hesitation from the Vice President, camera tight on his face, and I was dead meat.

I had to do something. I waited until Saturday morning for that feeling of spontaneity, and I called the show's producer. There was nobody I could trust to do it for me. It took about twenty minutes, but I managed to let them talk me into going on the show, to talk about my own father's cancer. For insurance.

Saturday night, the comedy shows had a field day with the story. On one, they had the networks making a huge model of the President's colon, with the anchor doing the news from the inside . . . The inside story. It was a good sign that the country was relaxed enough about the President's health to laugh.

The next morning, I went to the studio and waited with the others. If I couldn't stop him from going on, I could try to explain what he said. They were going to do the satellite link to the Vice President first, with us as a follow up. What was he going to say? The odds were that he'd utter the same boring, supportive, predictable baloney. But there was too much at stake and I'd already begun to suspect the Vice

President's judgment couldn't be trusted.

Cunningham looked tired and slightly rumpled. He clearly knew nothing about cancer. They tried to nail him on the question of whether we should have revealed the cancer as soon as it was discovered. Cunningham meekly parroted all his lines. He looked sympathetic, caring. Probably nudged his approval ratings up.

It was too late for me to get off the hook. I grinned stoically, told my story. My voice got gravelly with emotion. My eyes filled at just the right time. Given my up-close experience, I was able to be quite emphatic that the President's case was nothing like my father's.

After the show, I went to the office and worked the phones the rest of the day. Sunday night around eleven, I went home. I kept waiting for a call from Linda, or Tyler, or even the President, thanking me. Telling me a job well done. I drifted off to sleep with my phone in my hand, wondering, Had something gone wrong I didn't know about? Where was Crane?

Chapter Thirteen

I certainly succeeded in getting the story off the Vice President. Cozy features dribbled out for days about my tear jerking revelations on Sunday. Inside the White House, it was now clear to everyone why I was hired and why I was given that particular job to do.

By this time, I knew I would have a paycheck, whether I was in the White House or whether I got the boot to an agency. So when Bob called to tell me a neighbor had a small apartment to sublet, I took it. Small place, similar to his, semi-furnished. Good location, but a lot cheaper. One reason was the view. Bob's apartment looked out on a park. My view was a brick wall about ten feet from my window. So I had no direct sun in my apartment. That wasn't a problem because if the sun was out, I definitely wasn't home.

On the weekend, I drove to the cabin. The worst heat of the summer was still a month away, but it was warm enough that I slept on the screened porch. On Sunday, I loaded the car. I got most of my clothes, the work clothes, at least. There were a few boxes of stuff I had from before I moved in with Marguerite. Books. A couple of ugly lamps I got at a yard sale. A pair of spindly rockers and a small folding table I used for dining, working, you name it. I took the books. If they wouldn't fit on the shelves in the apartment, I could put them in the coat closet. The car was getting pretty full, but I knew I might not be back for a while, if things went well.

I went into Dad's room. We had emptied his closet.

There were a couple of file boxes stuffed with papers. The bureau was empty now; the clothes were all gone, too, thanks to Circe. I grabbed some of the pictures on the wall, most of them fuzzy snapshots I took of Dad in the boat, various waterfowl.

In the bottom of the closet I had stashed his fishing box. It was probably forty or fifty years old, made of some pretty wood, mahogany, I think. A stitched leather handle on top. Not very useful. Not very practical. I don't know where he got it, but it was solid. I remember kidding him, asking how much it would bring on Ebay. Not much, he had told me. I put it in the car. Eventually I might be able to bring myself to look through it, think of fishing with him, straighten up the old lures, ancient hooks, dried up bottles of pork rind that used to be bait. I had to move an armload of clothes and wedged it on the floor. I couldn't see out the rear window on the way back and had to stay in the slow lane most of the time.

While I waited by the elevator to take some of my stuff up to my new apartment, Bob appeared with two shopping bags full of wrapped presents. I eyed the bags. "Wow. I didn't get *you* anything."

"No shit? I'll have to take these back, I guess."

But he had my curiosity piqued. I thought I knew all there was to know about him. "Bob, I don't want to get too personal, but are you in love or what?" The packages were covered in birthday paper—kiddie wrap. Cars, balloons, cartoon characters.

"You might not believe it, but I have a brother in Gaithersburg. He has a family. I have twin nephews. They turn seven next week. On the Fourth. Uncle Bob visits. Brings presents."

"Uncle Bob? That's scary."

"Want to come?" Bob's squinty, small eyes watched me, wondering I suppose if I was some lonely basket case with no place to go.

When the elevator came I got on and held the door for him. I pushed nine and fourteen.

"Uh, let me check my calendar." I looked up at the elevator ceiling. "Let's see, I'm busy that day."

"Going to your cabin? All alone . . . how sad."

"You're jealous."

"Sure. I can picture it. Booze. Broads in camouflage gear with fishing accessories." The elevator door opened and I started to get off on my floor.

Bob stuck out his foot and stopped the door from closing. "Listen, I was going to call you later anyway. I've been hearing some strange rumblings about Crane. Word is, he's toast."

"No kidding?"

"Yeah. Dexter is pissed at him."

"Oh." I pushed my box against the wall to give me a break from the weight. "So what does that mean for me? Have you heard anything?"

"I don't know. All I know is, Crane is supposed to be out. He's been tagging along with Dexter trying to save his ass. To no avail, the word is. No word on you."

"Frankly, I wish I could believe you." I remembered how Bob's friends didn't know about the job at the White House in the first place. "Sounds like wishful thinking, don't you think?"

"Maybe. But we think it's true. We think, therefore, we pass it on."

The elevator closed and I went to my apartment. What was going on? Bob's rumors were usually wrong, but not completely. Of course, I loved the idea that Crane was out. But they weren't going to give me the Press Secretary job. Not this soon. What if it really meant a new press secretary who would come in and clean the place out. Even the interns would be lucky to stay. My stomach churned.

The next morning, Tyler's office called. I was summoned. Not that I didn't expect the call, but I had hoped my affability, as reported by the press, combined with my handling of the cancer announcement would have gotten me a reprieve. Now I could hope for timing, and for a good spot to land.

I waited outside Tyler's office for over an hour. I heard his secretary say he was going up to Camp David to meet with the President in the afternoon. Linda passed in the hall, gave me a friendly wave and even said "Hi Jack." Usually no one will make eye contact when you are about to get the bad news. Before I could ponder the meaning too deeply, Tyler burst from his office, without slowing down, grabbed a briefcase waiting on his secretary's desk, and said, "Come on, Jack. You can walk me to the car."

Getting fired on the way to the parking lot. That was a new one. I ran after him. Down the stairs and out the door. There were staff every few feet it seemed and he didn't say a word to me. When we got to the car, he looked at his watch and sighed. "Get in. You can ride up with me."

I scrambled in the other side. Tyler's car was one of the dark sedans from the motor pool, of course, complete with a military driver.

I waited. I sat on the edge of the seat, cocker spaniel eyes, wagging my tail, waiting for him to hit me with the rolled up newspaper. But he ignored me. Reached into one of the briefcases, pulled out a stack of notebooks and papers, switched on the overhead light and started reading.

I flipped open my portfolio and pretended to make some notes.

We rode for a half an hour, crossed the beltway, cruising north toward the Catoctin Mountains. I stole glances at Tyler, who went through paper after paper, signing, initialing, scribbling. "Damn!" he barked. He threw his pen. "Jack, do you have a pen?" He rifled his briefcase. I slid down and handed him a ball point.

Didn't say thanks. Went back to writing. Finally, we were about to get off I-270. Couldn't have been much more than ten minutes to Camp David. He looked up. "Jack, we need to go over a couple of things before we see the President."

Did he say, "We?"

Did he say, "See the President?"

Tyler actually looked at me. "As you know, we need to get things organized for the campaign. Crane is going over to the headquarters to get the campaign press office up and running and act as a liaison to us at the White House. I want you to take over the White House press operation."

I worked at keeping a poker face, but I couldn't help a huge, involuntary swallow.

"Jack, we've talked to you a lot about loyalty. I'm going to say to you again, that you need to think this through and decide if you're in or out." His voice softened. "I know when things got tough for John Cook, you moved on. I understand that. But things are going to move fast between now and the election and we need a team that will execute the plays we call, not second guess every decision. Not freelance."

I figured he must have been talking about Crane. I tried to count to ten, pretend I was thinking about it. "I'm in." My voice came out strong and I nodded my head in a supportive, definite way. But there was a big question and my mind wrestled with tactful ways to say it: Why me? I knew I couldn't ask that. And what was he saying that I would be Press Secretary? Holy shit. "Um. I'm not clear on what exactly you want me to do. Press Secretary? Acting? Or what?" Nobody ever said I didn't have nerve.

He smiled. "No, not Press Secretary." I think, for a moment, he was trying not to grin.

I felt like an eager puppy that just peed on the rug.

"Listen, I don't know about titles. I haven't worked that out yet. But you'll be in the Press Office. Detailed from my office. You keep your office for now, but you are in there, the daily press brief, the whole show. I want you to be my eyes and ears there, you know?"

"Is Goodington going with Crane?" Please please please, I thought.

"No. He's staying." He thought a minute, then leaned in close. "You have to make it work. I saw what you did at State. That's what I mean. We need you in there."

Tyler's phone rang again and he took the call. "Tyler," he growled, like he might bite the phone. He listened. "We're just pulling in. What's he doing right now?" Pause. "What did the doctor say?" Another pause, this one longer. Tyler looked down, no clues for me to pick up from his face. "Oh. Okay then. Get my call sheet ready."

I was watching Tyler and barely noticed the car go through a set of gates. We were coming up to a guard post and another set of gates. The car came to a stop. Our driver took our White House IDs and handed them to the guard. He looked at us and nodded, while another guard walked a dog around the car. The huge gate opened slowly. We drove through and stopped at the main building.

"You start next Monday." I smiled casually while trying to believe I had heard him right. He went on, "The President is resting now. We'll get you in to see him when he gets back." He tipped his head toward the driver. "Steve will take you back to town." Tyler put out his hand: "Congratulations."

All the way back, Tyler's words "we need you in there" echoed in my brain, like a song that gets stuck in your head. Yet I didn't really have a title and I was "detailed" to the press office. As soon as the driver got me back, I got out at the Southwest gate. I walked toward the Ellipse, and got my cell phone out to call Bob. I had to make sure I wasn't crazy.

"Bob, I need you to check my thinking. I just rode up to Camp David with Tyler. Crane is out—of the White House. Moving to the campaign. They aren't bringing anyone new in. Tyler is detailing me to the press operation. Wants me to be his eyes and ears. But, Goodington will still be at the White House." Saying it out loud made it sound even more confusing.

"You're still alive. Way to go!"

"Thanks. Yes. True. But—I'm not sure how to say this. Does it seem like I'm cannon fodder?"

"Possibly." Bob coughed into the phone. "Sorry. So, did he say, 'Jack, I want you to be my eyes and ears, and by the way, don't piss anyone off?"

"No. He said, I need you in there. Do what you did at State."

''Ok. So what did you do at State? You played nice, right?"

"Not exactly. I brought them around to my way of thinking . . ."

"There you are. That's it." Bob let out a long yawn. "It sounds like he wants to get that operation out of Crane's clutches. Classic White House infighting. By the way, the Chief of Staff does usually win."

"But what are they fighting about? Not just my job. Tyler can hire anyone he wants."

"The President's ear, most likely. That's what it usually is. One of them wants to push him in a particular direction and the other is throwing his body in front of it."

"I don't want to wander out over any land mines, that's all."

"Of course. Just watch your step. Time will tell."

"Or maybe . . . not just time . . . Thanks, Bob." I thought of Linda. If I could find out where the land mines were from her, it could save me. I spun around and hurried back to the Southwest Gate.

If I was going to take on Goodington, I had to make sure I was up to speed on everything. Economic policy, health care, energy. I resolved to work the Fourth of July weekend and bone up. Most of what I could say to the press was long standing policy, of course, and I knew all that. I watched for breaking news all weekend and was lucky. It was relatively quiet. On Saturday afternoon I was at my desk flipping through my briefing books one more time, when Sarah called. She said there were developments in Lixubistan, and asked if I wanted a briefing. I invited her over and cleared her in.

She looked like a child peering out from behind my massive door as she pushed it open. It was the weekend so we dressed down a bit and I realized I had never seen her in jeans. Nice. I was surprised that she hadn't asked to bring her usual entourage. She even said hello and smiled at me.

I motioned her to my couch and sat across from her in a wing chair. She handed me a SECRET cable. She must have known my clearance had finally come through. "You might want to read this, and then I'll fill you in on the rest."

I skimmed the four pages. "So they are creating a human rights commission? Great. That ought to sell big. Who's on it?"

"Well, there's a mix. A number of former government types, academics, press officials."

"Okay . . ." I nodded encouragingly.

"There's another development, Jack." She pressed her lips together and sighed. "You might remember, they've been talking about new power generation for some time. You probably remember from the earlier briefings . . ." She was looking through her papers for something.

"Sure." I nodded. I checked my watch while she looked through her papers. I wondered if she would have lunch with me in the Mess, or whether it was too late.

"They're saying, you know, the usual. It will raise the standard of living. Make possible the electrification of homes, farms and the construction of some manufacturing plants. Now they are beginning the actual design and bidding process."

"Okay. Sounds good. I forget the name of that river." I thumbed through the cable, looking for the river name.

"It isn't hydroelectric, Jack." She looked right at me. "It's nuclear."

"Oh shit. This could be news. Real news."

"Exactly." She shook her head and her blonde hair flipped back and forth. "This is the third world. The developing world, of course. They say hydroelectric wouldn't provide nearly as much power and that it would take just as long to build. They keep telling us that this will help the people more than any single thing that we could do."

"Right. Sure, whatever. But the important point is, the

press hates nuclear. They are suspicious of it."

She tilted her head slightly and pressed her lips tight.

"Am I sensing that you are not okay with this, Sarah?"

She didn't answer, glanced off to the side.

"Okay. Understandable. Let's see if we can sort it out." I handed her back the cable. "Who gets the contracts?"

She reeled off several names, several high profile CEOs. "But most likely, the only company that is big enough to do this and do it right is General Power. But all of the CEOs are big contributors, of course." Another tight-lipped, worried half-smile.

"Sure. To both sides, most likely?"

She nodded. "True."

"And jobs. Do you have the numbers? How many jobs will this create for us?"

"A lot." She flipped through the papers and gave me those numbers, seemed to relax a little.

"Okay. Here's the big one, Sarah. What happens if we don't get involved? How many other countries are perfectly capable of helping them build it?"

"I don't think I have a list. Not by country. Let me think. Germany, for sure. Maybe France, maybe Japan. I have the foreign companies."

"The point is, if we don't do it, someone else will, right?" I thought of every possible angle and she had an answer. Finally, I put down the papers. "Has the President been briefed on this yet?"

"Not yet, but today or tomorrow."

"So he knows nothing about it?"

"No, no, no. He doesn't know some of these latest developments, but the basic policy—last year there was an interagency task force to work out our policy. And we agreed in principal to help with power generation. But that was a year ago."

"Interagency task force. That's like war games with rubber bullets, right? Okay. So let me guess. Who's against this? Inside the administration."

"Well, Defense and Energy are not against it, *per se.* They would like more time to run through their concerns about nuclear proliferation . . . which, if we follow their timetable, we could take as long as three or four years." When she said this, for an instant, I again became so distracted by her, looking at her eyes, I almost didn't hear her.

". . . meanwhile, they still go nuclear except our companies are cut out and we lose our influence to moderate them."

"But you say this has been aired out in front of the President?"

"Well, yes, but that was last year."

"And they lost?"

"I wouldn't say that. The policy was never carried out."

I closed the cable and handed it back to her. "This is really helpful, Sarah. Thank you. Do you think this is going to make it into the press any time soon?"

"Well, I think that could depend on your old boss, Jack."

"Good point."

She slid her papers back in her slim briefcase and got a business card out. "I'm going to put my mobile number on this, Jack. If you want to, you can call me to see if there are updates. It isn't secure, but I can let you know if anything is going on." She handed me the card then stood up and took a step closer to the door.

"Thanks." I looked at the card then slipped it in my pocket. "Are you seeing your fiancé tonight?" I put my hands over my heart.

"I told you, we are not engaged." She smiled. "Yes I'm seeing Carl. He has a dinner we need to attend."

I nodded. She wasn't fooled. She knew I was just trying to find out if they were still together.

Chapter Fourteen

I was fully prepared for the briefing on Monday. I would get there early and be close to the podium. Everyone was expecting Goodington, of course, since Crane had left him in charge. He would wait until the press had assembled and glide up to the podium. But I planned to make one of my creative announcements and then proceed with the briefing. Unfortunately, one thing I was not quite prepared for was Scott Goodington already standing at the podium.

The briefing room was set up in such a way that you can't exactly peek in the door or slip in unnoticed. I walked in, saw Scott and retreated smoothly to a position along the wall. Unless you were right there, checking my face, I'm not sure you would have thought I was affected at all. After he had been talking for a few minutes, in came Linda behind me, looking like she might pounce and devour him any minute.

Goodington didn't see her and went on well enough through the President's schedule, but then a question came about Lixubistan. I swear I had nothing to do with it. It was exquisite.

"Scott, does the President think Lixubistan has satisfied our human rights concern with this new commission?"

Scott's eyes fell to his notebook, and he realized as he had his thumbs in it that he would look like an idiot trying to look up the answer. "I don't have anything on that."

Three more Lixubistan questions, and I thought he

might fall to his knees in tears before he would glance over, turn the thing over to me. So I took a few steps toward the podium, not sure what he would do. Would he look defiantly at me, refuse to budge? Or step back?

He stepped back. I straightened up, smiled and said. "Jack Abbott. Let me address what we know on those last few questions."

I talked about the villagers, about the decades of unrest. I looked down thoughtfully then went into "the progress we think we've made on human rights, on the rule of law . . ." I went on, spouting a few facts I remembered from Sarah and adding, "What we have to remember of course is that Lixubistan is a sovereign nation, with their own traditions, many of which go back at least as far as our western values and traditions . . ."

These were hard-hearted press people. I wasn't going to bring tears to their eyes, but the truth was, I just about brought them to my own.

". . . It makes sense to engage this government, give them a chance to get their act together." I almost saw their heads nodding.

The nuclear cat was out of the bag, too. A short, red-haired reporter asked, "Jack, some of the LLF are saying the nuclear power plant will be a platform for developing nuclear weapons . . ."

I shook my head meaningfully. "This administration would never, never facilitate the development of any nuclear facility in the world without providing first that there will be safeguards and verification. What Lixubistan needs more than anything is power. They certainly don't need, or we believe, want, nuclear weapons. But any agreement will require verification, inspections. We expect this endeavor to be so successful, Lixubistan may even be able to export excess power to neighbors."

I realized later I was out a little in front of the State Department on some of that, but you know, I sensed it, I felt it in the room, that this was what they were looking for. And clearly it would have to be part of any agreement.

As I was about to finish, I got a final question. "Jack, how is the President doing?"

I nodded and beamed. Stepped back up to the podium and held both sides. "The President has a bit more chemo. He has come through the initial weeks with minimal side effects. He says he feels stronger every day and is looking forward to the Convention. And let me add, he looks great." Another easy, confident smile, and I stepped away from the podium.

As I turned, I caught Linda's face as she slipped out of the briefing room. She was holding back a smile, trying to keep it from a grin. She cut her eyes toward me and tilted her head in a subtle nod. I think the fact that I had taken over from Scott was huge. He didn't show up at the briefing for the rest of the week.

On Friday, I got home at about 10 p.m. I had three phone messages from Bob, all containing escalating profanity and abuse, culminating with: "Hey big shot. If you ever check your fucking messages, call us back. Evan has John's boat on Sunday. Since we can't take you any place because you're so fucking famous, why don't you meet us and we can cruise up the river for the afternoon."

I was going to have to work on Saturday but I thought I could take some time on Sunday. I called them back and got directions to the boat before I went to bed.

John kept the boat in Southwest Washington. Sometimes he went with his son, Paul, who was just starting high school. Evan had taken it out a few times, usually with his girlfriend.

I pulled into the parking lot, just off Maine Avenue as Bob was pushing a huge wheeled cooler toward the dock.

"Abbott. Great. Take this to the boat. I have another cooler in the car."

"Jesus, Bob. We're just going for the day, right?"

Evan was already on the boat, filling it up with gas. It was small enough to handle, Chris Craft, about 26 foot, but big enough to have some shade and a small cabin where Bob could take a nap. John could have had a 75-foot yacht, of course, and a crew to go with it. But that wasn't his style. We got underway and once we were clear of the marina, Evan opened it up until we got around Roosevelt Island. On the shady side of the island we pulled close to shore and dropped the anchor.

Evan handed me a sub and a can of Heineken. "So do you have your room yet at the Convention?"

Bob sat up. "Hey, I bet you have a suite, right? That could be good." He looked at Evan and winked.

I unrolled my sub while I was trying to think of a good answer, Bob went on, "And by the way, which parties are you going to get us into?"

My Heineken was ice cold and I cracked it open. "Actually, I'm not positive I'm going."

They stared at me.

"Somebody has to stay in the White House and run that show, right?" I stole a glance at each of them to see if they were buying it. "But if I do, you're in, of course. I mean, unless the Secret Service sees you."

"Not sure if you're going? What kind of bullshit is that, the fucking White House Press Secretary not going to the Convention?"

My mouth was full of sub. I shrugged. "Press Secretary? I'm not even Acting Press Secretary. Look, I just don't know. I haven't heard anything yet. I don't want to rock the boat, right? Isn't that what you guys keep telling me?"

"Did he really say that, Bob?" Evan had a cold beer from the cooler and he touched Bob's arm with it. Bob didn't jump. He just slowly turned his head to Evan and thanked him.

Evan went on, "Don't worry about it, Jack. Maybe they want you to handle the White House." He exchanged a look with Bob—like he didn't want me to know I was terminal. "After all, they have the campaign staff, right?"

They let it drop, but I didn't. I started to worry. Surely I wasn't going to be left behind. But why didn't I already know? Maybe it wasn't decided yet, or if it was, maybe I still had a chance. No way would I sit in Washington and watch the Convention on TV. In late afternoon, we went back to the marina. The coolers were much lighter.

Monday morning, I learned that not everyone was thrilled with my press briefings. Edmund Nichols, former Secretary of State, called from China. He asked if I had read the reports on human rights, on nuclear. "You know, Jack, some of us talking to the President have been trying to chart a less strident course of support for the Lixi government."

I was stretched out on my sofa, inbox contents on my lap, sorting, reading. His tone made me sit up. "But that's not what I hear from the State Department." I caught myself and went on, "and that's not what the President decided, as you know."

"No. I don't know. Tell me, when you last spoke to him about this, that he didn't suggest we leverage our support in return for elections?"

I swallowed. Since I never talked to him about this, for all I knew Nichols was right. "I don't make policy, sir. I'm just the messenger. I'll certainly relay your concerns to the President." Before I blew him off, I realized I was going to get hit with this shit in my briefing before long and I better figure out what I was going to say. So I knew I had to listen. "I realize they aren't exactly Boy Scouts."

"Thugs. They are no better than common criminals. They do not share our values."

"But, do we have to share their values, sir? I mean, isn't that a little ethnocentric of us?"

"I'm not talking about Santa Claus here, Jack. I'm talking about respect for human life. Let alone human rights."

He went on for twenty minutes. I began to have my doubts, but not so much about the policy. I thought about how they might be letting me crawl out on a limb, farther and farther from our policy and the President. So I really needed to see the President. Not just to clear this up, to make sure I am on the right branch—but so I could say, definitively, what the President actually said. And I needed to know before I opened my mouth again and got us in even deeper. It was still early. I had just enough time to slip in to see the President. Get a quick word from him, before the daily briefing began.

I hurried over to the West Wing and ran up the back stairs. It was a chance to make sure that nobody had moved into the Press Secretary's Office, which was right next to the Briefing Room. Linda was in the hall, just outside of the staff entrance to the Oval. Blocking the door, actually. She looked up from her papers and smiled at me. "Hi Jack."

"Hi. I was hoping to catch you." A slight exaggeration. I was hoping to avoid her. "I need to talk to the President," I told her, with a bit of urgency and an unusually solemn look. Access to the President was essential, after all, to good press relations. Everyone knows this. They had to let me see him.

"Jack, he's going over his acceptance speech. He's exhausted and already about an hour behind schedule. What's going on?" She lost her smile.

"Rehearsing? Shouldn't I be in there?"

"No." She shook her head. She went on in a low voice: "They're still fighting about what gets in. And it's way too long, as usual. He can't give a ninety minute speech."

"Ninety minutes? At a Convention? Are you kidding?"

"No. I'll try to get you in when he reads it. What did you want to see him for?" She nodded toward her office and I followed her.

"The Lixubistan problem. I need five minutes. Only five. Guaranteed." I sighed and waited for the "are you serious, nobody gives a rat's ass about that" lecture.

Inside her office, her assistant wasn't there. She closed the door. "Actually Jack, he's resting."

Resting, meaning taking a nap? I wasn't going to ask. "Okay. How about Tyler?"

The way she looked at me, I knew I wasn't going to see

the President or even Tyler. I might as well just tell her. "Look, Edmund Nichols just scolded me for saying the President's mind is made up about letting them go nuclear." I sat on the far end of the couch and tried to look comfortable. "I need to know whether I went too far. Whether I need to dial it back."

She perched on the arm of the couch but didn't answer.

"So am I off the reservation on this? I mean, it sounds like there's an interagency fight going on. And I just boxed us in. Supported the bastards running the government. I mean. I don't want to give them an excuse to get me fired."

I thought she was going to roll her eyes, but she just nodded patiently. "You're fine, Jack. Don't worry about it."

I took a breath and it helped to calm me. "I am worried about it. State is telling me it is decided but apparently that is not true. And Nichols—he pretty much accused me of causing more deaths." I listened to myself, surprised at how upset I sounded.

"He's good, isn't he? So this is what the big leagues are like, Jack." She stood up and went behind her desk. "I know how it looks. But think. Nothing is really going to happen until after the election. The contracts, the international approvals for the nuclear power plant, the loans, they're going to take months. If we ding it now, they'll just go to the Germans or French or somebody else." She paused, looking for a glimmer of understanding in my eyes. "The final approvals won't go until after the election," she said again. "Like a year after. So the worst thing we can do now is change course and send them in a different direction."

"But don't you think I better cool it a little? If we end up reversing course, it will look like we were very foolish or maybe like we lied." I didn't mean for my voice to go up when I said that, but it did and she noticed.

"No. It would send the wrong signal. We are trying to work with Germany and the others so nobody will help those guys. But the best thing would be if we agree to build it—then we have control over it, the security, the timing, everything.

We can't afford to piss off the Lixis until we reach some kind of understanding. And if Europe thinks they can cut us out and make a deal with the Lixis, we've got nothing—no leverage and no contracts. So what you said is great. Perfect." She leaned back a moment and looked at me. "I never had a chance to offer my congratulations, by the way."

"Thanks." I shrugged. I couldn't think of a way to bring up going to the Convention. It was completely unrelated. I had to punt. "I was going to call you, actually." I watched her carefully. I'm pretty good at spotting an opening. ". . . to see if you want to go have a celebratory drink."

"Sure," she said, almost like she was surprised. She went to her desk and tapped her computer. "When?"

"I don't know. What about tonight?"

"I think so." She nodded, thinking. "Sure. Late, of course."

"Of course. I'll be in my office. Call me when you're ready."

I left her office just as the door to the President's study opened. Two of the doctors stepped into the hall and hurried toward the elevator. I nodded at them and took the stairs.

By eight o'clock I began to think about a new plan. She might cancel tonight and I would need a fallback. But apparently, like me, she had no food at her house, and she also needed a ride home. Her car was in the shop so I picked her up in the West Exec lot. There were only a few cars left on the street outside the West Wing, and I was sure the uniformed Secret Service standing at the entrance took notice of the two of us together. She climbed into my car and I decided I might just appreciate the company and stop thinking so hard.

She wanted to go to Old Town again so she could make it an early night. Parking was a bitch, but we found a spot around the corner from her place and walked to another nearby establishment she knew. There was a line out the door, so we went to the bar. She got a martini, which blew me away. I was expecting a soft drink, or maybe a glass of wine.

So I got one, too.

It wasn't too noisy and you could never be sure what the bartender was overhearing so I spoke softly and close to her ear. "So what was the Convention like last time? I assume you went."

A question out of left field. The bartender dealt the napkins and slid our drinks toward us. When he stepped away, she took a sip. "It was pretty crazy. The Vice President problem . . ."

"Yeah. It was a crazy time for us, too. Are you still mad at John Cook?" I pulled my martini closer but kept my eyes on her.

"No. Not at all. I mean, he seems like a decent guy. I was pretty mad at him for a while, I admit. But the scandal—I mean, he was cleared. It wasn't his fault."

I nodded. "Exactly. So I guess that's one problem you won't have this time."

"No. Not as long as, you know, everyone else behaves. You know who I mean."

Again, I nodded sympathetically. "I have gotten pretty good at helping with that, don't you think?"

She smiled. Like now she figured out why I asked her to have a drink. "Yes. You are a regular Mr. Fixit."

"I was hoping to go. I don't want to beat around the bush about it. I mean, you know I'm a good soldier and all that."

"I think you should go." She shifted on her chair and touched the base of her martini with her fingers. "But it's still a few weeks away. Tyler will make those decisions last minute, you know? Depending on the crisis du jour."

"Can you think of anything I can do to improve my chances?"

"Hmmm. I was going to make a joke about kidnapping, or locking someone in the attic, but really, on reflection, that would cause too many headlines." She fondled the base of her glass with her long fingers and I felt like she might purr at any moment. She eased her face closer to me and asked "Are you okay about today, Jack? About Nichols and all that?"

Was it just friendly concern, or was she vetting me? "Of course. I had to make sure I had some rough idea what I was talking about."

"You'll go far in this town, with that approach."

I chuckled agreeably and inched my chair closer to hers. I was feeling comfortable enough to push a little further. "So what was the big fight about?"

She leaned toward me again. "Oh the usual—little things. Who would ride on Air Force One and where they would sit. What time of day to do an event."

"Or how to handle the cancer announcement?"

Her eyes looked away, looked at her glass as she slid her hand around the stem and lifted it.

I went on, carefully, "Or whether to dump Cunningham?"

She put her drink down and shook her head. "No, Jack. Think. How could we dump him? What would happen if we did?"

I shrugged. "Good point. He would cut your throats. Say he was forced out for refusing to go along with the 'cover up.'"

She didn't answer, but I could tell I was on the right track.

"So, that means we're stuck with him. He's bulletproof. Or dumpster-proof."

We had ordered some appetizers and more drinks. The waiter brought the food and fussed with our silverware, napkins and condiments. Finally he went to the other end of the bar. "I saw two of the cancer doctors in the hall, leaving the President's study. What was that about?"

"Oh, you know doctors. They test everything. If he blows his nose, I swear they test the tissue."

"I take it he's still doing well. Which is what I am telling everyone, so it must be true."

She raised her eyebrows and let out an easy laugh. "You are the Spin Doctor. If you say it, it must be true. So, here's to the Acting Press Secretary." She said it softly, leaning toward me again, but lifting her glass, clinking it lightly, almost noiselessly on mine. "You may not have the title yet, but you are doing the job." She took a sip and put her glass down, watching me like a cat. "Are you hearing from old friends? People who knew you when?"

It was true. I grinned. "My high school called yesterday. They want me to come speak to the students."

She nodded. "That's great. Isn't that like a fantasy of some kind?"

"Sure. Definitely."

After a few martinis, I was convinced there was no more beautiful woman in the world. We split the check and left through the crowd, which was still going strong. I wondered why I had never realized she was so sexy before. She wasn't dressed in a provocative way; it was how she walked, talked, moved. We made our way down the uneven brick sidewalk. I should have been feeling a lot more relaxed. But I was thinking hard how I was going to get her to invite me in. We got to her door and she didn't wait for me to say goodnight or push my way in. She slid her arm around my neck and pulled me down to kiss her. I'm not sure what she meant by that. It was just long and wet enough that I couldn't write it off as friendly. I hesitated a split second then kissed her again. So she would know she had been kissed.

And then, I thought—I was pretty sure—she would invite me in. We would have to work out how we were going to handle a workplace romance. Whether to keep everything secret. But her eyes were on something behind me, something coming down the street.

"Jack. There's a cab. You should catch it. You don't want to drive home tonight."

I glanced down the street and saw the cab, crawling down the street looking for a fare. She waved and, holding my hand, pulled me after her, down her steps toward the curb. The taxi stopped and I got in.

Chapter Fifteen

I woke up back in my apartment, thank God. It was still early. What was I thinking? Christ, my head hurt. I think I was still a little drunk. I remembered, as I went down to the garage to look for my car, that I had taken a cab home. Which meant my car was still over near Linda's. It would take me an hour or two to go get the car and get to the office, so instead, I took a cab to work.

I wasn't sure if I stepped over the line—kissing her. I thought it was mutual, but I wasn't sure and I was afraid I had pissed her off. If I called her, that wouldn't tell me anything. So I went over to her office, unannounced. I could think of a reason on the way. I would be able to tell if I was in trouble by eye contact and body language.

She was rushing down the hall and saw me coming up the steps. "Jack, why aren't you over at State? Lixubistan is falling apart." Linda's eyes narrowed. "Didn't they invite you?" She looked at her watch. "You need to get over there and make sure they stay with the program."

Goddamn Lixubistan. While I tried to stammer out an answer she waved me to follow her into her office and she clicked on her TV. "Did you see this?"

Breaking news. All over the cable news, even networks. Breaking heads in Lixubistan.

"Jack, if this mess gets out of hand, you can forget the Convention."

"What do you want me to . . . ?"

She ignored me and went on, "And Harrow. He's talking about more hearings. We don't need that in the middle of the Convention. You need to think of something. You need to take care of this, Jack. So don't even talk to me about the Convention until this goes away."

"But . . ."

She wasn't listening. "Here's what Tyler will say: Jack Abbott? Isn't he supposed to be handling Lixubistan?"

I backed out of her office and hurried to over to State. I was late but I got there in time to hear Prixell summarize the new information: The insurgents, led by the Lixubistan Liberation Front had more human rights violations than Attila and worse table manners. They were linked with terrorists. They had no intention of working with us. If they took over, we were cut out, and the nuclear technology we would give as part of the nuclear power project would fall into their hands. And if we worked with the government, there was a good chance we could foster reform from the inside. In other words, State stayed with the story put out by the bastards that were actually running the government.

Here's what I knew. The bastards running the government were at least as bad as the so called rebels. However, the smart money had them holding on to power, at least without any major intervention from us. Which wasn't going to happen. The government would stay in power and a price would be paid if we encouraged the rebels. So it wasn't about the policy, it was about the politics. My job was to make it a non-issue, which wouldn't be that hard if the U.S. had one voice. As long as there was no real dissension about our policy. But as usual, Congressman Greg Harrow did not get it. He was not on board. He was planning to hold the hearings during his own party's Convention.

It seemed like a week but it was only Tuesday when Sarah called. Harrow's committee was going to vote to allow him to subpoena information from State. I never thought he could get them to do it but apparently, he got the other party to go along. He wasn't going to need any votes from our side.

Back in my office, I flipped on UNS and there was more news. I had the "mute" on but the pictures didn't need any sound. It was the Lixubian army: You couldn't mistake those uniforms. Normal people turn away from this kind of story, or perhaps change the channel. In my job, I had to watch. I had to see what the questions were going to be about at the briefing. I sat down and put my hand to my forehead, hung up the phone. There was a close-up of a young kid, perhaps 16 years old, tee shirt and jeans, being dragged by two heavily armed soldiers. His face was contorted by pain, anguish, fear, or perhaps sadness. My stomach tightened. Then the obligatory dropping and clubbing him—into unconscious or beyond. The camera shook and moved on. It wasn't long before Willie came in without knocking, from congressional affairs, and said Harrow was calling for hearings again—which I already knew of course. I pictured his red-headed girlfriend in his office screaming and crying, and him trying to do something.

State came to my office the next morning to brief me again. They claimed the guy I saw on TV was actually a guerrilla leader who had just thrown a bomb into a group of soldiers, killing five. He was chased, caught and told to lie down. He refused. The guerillas advanced again and they had to move him. This was the footage UNS had. They were trying to move him and he resisted, told to lie down and he wouldn't. I thought about this story and whether the press was going to buy it. Not sure I could pull it off.

As the group left the briefing, I pulled Sarah to the side in the hallway and leaned in close. "Is that really what happened? Because the truth might make a better story."

She shook her head. "I don't know. Frankly, I'm not sure we know what that is anymore." She blinked her big blue eyes at me. "Listen Jack. This is what we have from our people, and it's essentially straight from the government. I can see as well as you can, those soldiers went too far." Her eyes flickered for an instant. "But that's what happens when they are at war."

"I'm beginning to doubt—I'm not sure I can keep the cork in the bottle at this point, you know? I mean, people have eyes, right?"

"Nobody cared about this issue before Harrow, Jack. There are lots of problems in the world. Plenty of dictators who abuse their people. If Harrow would just, I don't know, go back to his district or something."

It was panic time. I called Bob and asked him to meet me for a drink, but he said he had started without me and to come over. I met him at a little dive close to our building. It was a classic student hangout. As non-students, we were invisible. The students were busy looking cool, eyeing each other, and we could get a drink and steal a glance at the occasional cute coed. But tonight the place was deserted. The first summer term was over and they had fled the city. The later it got, the worse everything looked to me.

I sucked down my drink. "Harrow is going to screw me. They blame every breath he takes on me. Like he's my Frankenstein monster."

Bob stared at me. I wasn't sure whether he was already too drunk to listen or not, but I went on anyway: "Harrow hit us with a subpoena on Lixubistan. He's cooking up hearings and we're going to look bad, you know. The President. The whole party. But Harrow doesn't give a shit. He's looking for some kind of headline, a little vindication from the press."

Bob said, almost growling, "All the dirt on that guy, all his shenanigans over the years, why hasn't any of it ever come out?"

"You tell me. He's charmed or something. Something else bumps the story off the front page. Nothing he's done is a really big story. I mean, how can you document his alcoholism or the fact that he's psychotic? What I don't understand is why everybody went crazy over John Cook's problems but nobody seems to care about Harrow."

"Dirt shows up more on white than gray, you know." Bob tried to sip his drink, but it was empty. "You aren't the only one who hates him, you know."

"I don't actually hate anybody."

"Uh huh."

"But if these hearings get out of control, it's over for me."

"No way. After all the trouble we went to? To get you in there? Harrow?" Bob snorted, then began coughing. He swirled his empty glass and tried to drink it again. His eyes seemed unfocused and I waved to the waiter to bring the check. I never saw him like this and I wanted to get him out before I had to carry him.

Two days later, I didn't have time to read the Post before I got to the office. I switched on the TV and reached for the news clips. The lead story on every network was Harrow: "Congressman accused of improprieties. Named in harassment suit. Sexual assault."

I knew a lot of dirt about Harrow, but this was new. Five years earlier, Harrow was drunk at a party and groped one of the other guests. Unfortunately for Harrow, he was so drunk he didn't see the woman's husband was right there. He smashed his fist into Harrow's face, requiring a call to 9-1-1. The ambulance took Harrow to the hospital and he even missed a couple of votes. At the time, all parties wanted this kept quiet. But now, the woman was mad and wanted to go public. She had heard about a couple of other incidents Harrow was involved in, her husband had passed away and it had always pissed her off that Harrow could get away with something like that. So the first story contained a lot of "alleges." Harrow never needed a flack more than now. That was Friday. It played all weekend. Drip drip drip. By Monday night, Harrow was immersed in it. There were witnesses, eager waiters, reluctant friends.

Of course, I thought this was the answer to my prayers. Harrow was sidelined, maybe permanently. May even have to resign. Not that I wanted any credit for it. But then, I didn't know what Crane was up to.

Monday night, Linda came into my office and closed the

door behind her. Her face was taut. I thought maybe someone had died. Someone almost did.

She stayed in position, leaning her back against the door. "Crane went to Dexter a little while ago. Told him he didn't want to be associated with your 'tactics.'"

"What are you talking about?"

"You know. Harrow," She said in a loud whisper.

I stared at her. "Harrow? What about Harrow?"

"Come on, Jack." She moved toward me. "I know I told you to fix it, but I never thought . . ." she trailed off, shaking her head.

"My God, Linda. I had nothing, nothing whatsoever, to do with Harrow's mess." I stood up, afraid, I guess, that she was going to leave before I could explain.

"Keep your voice down."

"If I were going to pull something like that, leaking a story on Harrow, would I let it lead back to me? No way. I would be the chief suspect. But that's not the main reason I wouldn't have done it. You may not believe I could have a thing called loyalty, but that sort of trick is not done. I mean if I wanted to smear the guy, why wait until now?"

A long pause. "Good question."

I think she may have believed me. But it didn't matter. She went on, still almost whispering, "Stay out of the briefing room." She turned and started toward the door.

"Linda, wait."

She stopped and looked over her shoulder at me.

"I'm not kidding. I didn't do it. I didn't even know about this. I swear. Give me a chance to prove it, somehow."

"Jack, I'd like to believe you. But I remember how much you impressed upon me your desire to go to the Convention."

"I still do. But I didn't do it."

"Don't hold your breath. Tyler can only save your ass so many times, you know?"

She left and I dropped into my chair. I had to prove I didn't do it. It couldn't be that hard—I could just find a way to talk to the woman who was causing the trouble for Harrow.

She might tell me who got her to come forward. And that's when it popped into my head: Was this Bob's handiwork? Was it Bob? Bob didn't go in for scandal either, but he was pretty mad about Harrow.

The more I thought about it, the more it became clear to me. Perhaps he thought he would rather have a friend in the White House than a friend who used to be in the White House who is now looking for a job. Shock gave way to outrage. I had to do something, maybe get him to admit it at least. But couldn't bring myself to ask him straight out, so I called Evan.

I laid out the problem for Evan. He laughed. "Jack, you dork, you must be the only guy in town who hasn't seen the color of the money from the Lixi lobby. They even have Filchock and Butterfield on their payroll."

"Those sleaze mongers?" Filchock and Butterfield had an unusual Washington practice, mainly lobbying. They were former prosecutors known for their extreme tactics—and results.

"Exactly."

"So you're saying Bob had nothing to do with it?"

"Did he talk to them? I don't know. But I'm surprised it hasn't been reported in the press that the Lixis are trying to nail Harrow. Figuratively, of course. This scandal is perfect— Nobody listened to him before, but now, he'll hear the giggles in the hallway. They'll be laughing in his face next week."

If everybody in town knew it, Crane certainly knew it. He was trying to flush me with this, even though he knew I had nothing to do with it.

The other question: Did State know the Lixis were doing this? Did they help? I was in solitary confinement, so to speak. I figured I had nothing to lose by calling Linda. Maybe she could fix things with Tyler before he pulled the plug on me. Anyway I wanted to make sure they were fully aware of what was happening with this little tar baby. She took my call, which was a good sign. She told me they had a briefing on Lixubistan this afternoon and a follow up in the morning.

"I'd like to sit in," I told her.

"I'm not sure that's a good idea. Let me talk to Tyler."

I was afraid she would hang up. "Wait. Make sure you ask them about Filchock and Butterfield."

"What about them?"

"They're the ones who screwed Harrow. Not yours truly."

"Really."

"Really truly. As I told you, I had nothing to do with it. Apparently, the Lixi government hired them. And—this is the best part—what are the odds that Crane knew this?"

She didn't answer but I had her attention. ". . . And tried to screw Tyler by nailing me. That's the way I read it."

She sighed.

"So, what do you think?"

"I'm not sure, but I think you may have just saved your own ass."

I exhaled, but not out loud. "Good. That's a start. How about grabbing a drink or a bite to eat tonight so you can apologize for being so mean to me?"

That one took her by surprise and she actually laughed. "I can't eat until after the Convention."

"Is that like Lent, or something?"

"No, it's like, we're up to our necks in shit."

I nodded, trying to think of a fallback position. "I guess you have the Mess. You don't need me to bring you a sandwich."

"I guess not. That's nice, though."

I felt a little stronger, took another breath. "What do you think the chances are of my going?"

Long pause. "Not good. I'm sorry Jack. I wouldn't push it. The campaign staff can handle it, and maybe we can get things back to normal after the Convention. If you don't do anything else crazy."

Chapter Sixteen

I thought it might look a little strange to the press that I wasn't at the Convention. I joked that somebody had to stay home and mind the store and Tyler decided it would be me. During the first days of the Convention, I spent a lot of time frowning and rushing through the hall as though something important was going on that only I could handle. But mostly the press ignored the White House. The real news was elsewhere.

Bob and Evan were at the Convention. Most of the press office staff were stuck in Washington with me. Crane took his campaign press staff. The President was only there for three days. We were bombarded with all kinds of requests at first, various backgrounders, facts about the trade deficit, etc. I farmed them out to various staffers. Goodington handled most of them.

When the President went down, our office was quiet. But you know what they say—the lull before the storm. I wasn't going to watch the Convention in my apartment. That would be like wearing a t-shirt that said "I am a loser. Nobody needs me, I have nothing to do."

Instead, I made a production of bringing TVs into the waiting area of the press office. We made popcorn in the microwave and had a couple of cases of beer and soda brought in. Scott left at six along as did a number of other staffers. A few stayed, including Donna, the receptionist.

How it could happen when it has happened so many

times before still baffles me. Human nature, I guess. The last night of the Convention, the night of Dexter's big speech, when he was to accept the party's nomination, they lost control of the schedule.

Everyone wanted to be heir to Dexter and in order to showcase their talents, droned on into the evening hours. And then he finally began, after a very long ovation. But the speechwriting machine had gone off track and Dexter's speech was at least twice as long as it should have been. And he almost didn't make it through.

The press reports had him dying. Was Dexter up to the job? Was he terminal? Film at eleven . . .

Like millions of Americans, I saw the whole thing. All that happened, really, was, he leaned hard on one elbow, like he was in a subway train that took a sharp curve, and one knee buckled for an instant. He seemed to go pale, paler than usual and it was a full twenty seconds before he could pull out his smile, wink, take a desperate sip of water and go on talking. It was a horror movie and he was the talking corpse.

The press went nuts and there was nobody from Crane's shop, including Crane, anywhere to be seen. The networks didn't even carry the speech. But when Dexter faltered, they interrupted their programs with breathless reports while showing the footage over and over again. They reported Dexter was under a doctor's care.

I tried to call Tyler for the go-ahead to do something: Maybe put out a statement or at least coordinate with Crane. Before I could get through, Linda called me on another line.

"Jack, Crane just quit. Tyler wants you. Get a driver, go to the airport and get your ass down here."

Now they needed me. Now was my chance. "Wait a minute. Isn't Dexter going to Camp David?"

"Yeah. But we need somebody to talk to the press, smooth things over about Crane."

I know you can't really say this about women anymore, but the truth is, she sounded almost hysterical. Not that I blame her. "Linda. Tell me what happened."

"Just get here, Jack. It doesn't matter what happened." I heard her take a breath and she added, "I told you. Crane just quit. He told the press before Dexter, so he could get his spin on it, I guess. Announced he'd stay a few days to help with the transition." She stopped, I thought she was going to hang up. Then I heard her say "I'll tell you the rest when you get here." And she hung up.

Not okay. I called her back. "I need to talk to Tyler. It will take me two or three hours, at best to get down there. This thing is a brush fire now. If we say nothing for three hours, it will be a national disaster."

"Tyler said come."

"Listen to me. This is a leak right now. Nobody has anything on Crane resigning. Crane must have embargoed his announcement until morning because it isn't in any of the stories. This isn't the time to hole up and talk strategy. Everyone will jump to the wrong conclusion. Anyway, the Convention is over. I can draw off the pack, move the story back here, maybe turn it off. The people who are already here in town can cover it. I get the spin out *we* want. Then I come down or meet you at Camp David. Whatever."

"I'll get Tyler and we'll call you back."

I was in my office, working on a statement when she called back about ten minutes later. "He said good, go ahead."

"Really. No instructions?"

"Nope. Just said, 'Jack can handle it.'"

"Great. How about a few facts to sprinkle in, like, what the hell happened?"

She sighed impatiently, like she had to go to the bathroom. "The President got overheated, that's all. He's recovering from cancer, after all."

"Shit, Linda, I can make up something better than that. What do the doctors say? I'm going to need a doctor or two."

"They're checking Dexter right now.

"Oh, shit."

"They're going to say he's okay, of course. I'm telling

you, he just got overheated and tired."

"And what about Crane? What is he telling everyone?"

"Not a goddamn thing. Let them draw their own conclusion, I guess he thinks. Obviously he doesn't want the President to win." She sounded so sincere, so wounded.

"Duh."

"Jack, why would he embargo his announcement until morning?"

"The President usually announces when people leave. You know. So maybe Dexter is giving him a hard time about leaving. And maybe he's trying to control the story. And maybe, he's trying to look like he's distancing himself from the fainting event."

"Of course"

"Okay. Stand by. No statements out of your end. Everybody talks to us. Watch the news. And please . . . no freelancing. No friendly leaks. If his condition changes, call me first. Don't make me a liar."

The speech was late to begin with and now it was just before midnight. I had to get something in the all-night cable news and make sure the big papers were careful before they pronounced him dead. I faxed a short statement to the networks, wire services and news channels to stop the bleeding. I'm sure Tyler wanted to control every word but he knew he couldn't. I worked the phones, and I used everything I had. I didn't kill it completely, but I did manage to point out that the President was still recovering from some of the treatments, and that they were going to look silly if they overplayed it. I had the TV on all night and I never heard a mention of the Crane resignation. Nobody from his operation. Nothing.

I told Donna to alert the press corps there would be a briefing at eight a.m. That way I would preempt all the morning talk shows and get something out before the stock market opened. The morning shows might even want to interview me for a few minutes. I went home to change and throw some underwear and some shirts into a bag so I could meet the President and Tyler at Camp David after it was all finished. As I packed, UNS was hinting at the Crane story. They were wetting their pants, saying: "UNS has learned a high level Dexter campaign official is expected to resign today." Crane's name was added at 6:00 am. Crane said he had told Dexter long ago he was only staying as long as the Convention and wished Dexter well. The immediate speculation was that Dexter had fired him for flubbing the Convention. No fingerprints on that one.

Nobody ever quits in Washington.

I drafted a statement for Dexter saying how much he appreciated Crane's hard work, et cetera, bla bla bla. When I got back to my office, I gave it to Donna to put in a press release to be distributed at my briefing. No, I wasn't going to run it by the President or Tyler. Because it didn't matter what they thought about it: We had to get a little something out there for the press to nibble on, and it could not smack of bitterness. How many days would it take for me to get Tyler to agree to a statement complimenting Crane?

Balls out. That's how this had to be. It would either work, or they would fire me before the sun set.

At eight o'clock, I went through the door with my hair combed, my tie a little straighter than usual. I walked slowly. And I smiled. Not a grin, not a smirk, not really that happy looking—just a sort of vacant, all's well with the world smile. As in, what's all the hub-bub?

"First, the President is doing fine. Doctors are doing some tests because they suspect he caught a bug of some sort. I hate to admit it, but several of us on the staff have had it, and I won't list the symptoms here for you in polite company. Anyway, the President has a slight temperature, and is resting this morning. As soon as I get the results of the tests, I will let you know. Obviously, there may have to be some adjustments to the schedule, and I will also let you know about these, as soon as I have that information.

"Next, I am releasing a statement from the President

about the resignation of David Crane. As many of you know, this was not unexpected."

Then I did the *Today Show*. I told them how much I had learned from David Crane. It was true. I learned how to stay out of his way, how to go around him whenever possible and I had learned he must truly hate Dexter to do this to him at this particular moment. I could speak with great feeling. And I was able to talk quite convincingly about Dexter and his cancer, I think. Because I could point out that I had seen this sort of thing before. I spouted the facts, such as the survival rates when there is early detection, and I know my voice and face reflected the sincerity with which I believed these things. Dexter was not my father. I was uplinked to the other network morning shows, then did some of the cables. I was on all day long, giving interviews, backgrounders, doing my damnedest to be personable.

My words calmed the nation. Think of it.

I was in the zone. I don't think I made one misstep. I'm not saying that they believed me with all their heart, but I had calmed the world down. Now, I just had to hope the ensuing days wouldn't make me a fool—or worse: a liar.

The rest of the day I kept up the pace. My staff kept me informed about the news coverage.

Friday night, it was dark when I left for Camp David. I dozed in the car and didn't wake up until we were almost there. I wasn't sure where I should go—find Linda, or Tyler. The guards at the gatehouse were waiting for me. They told the driver to "take me up to Aspen."

I jolted awake. That was where the President stayed. Since his wife passed away, maybe Tyler stayed there, too? Or maybe we were just meeting there? I thought Dexter might be at the Eucalyptus cabin, which was an infirmary. But if he was still having tests, he wouldn't be meeting with me anyway. Before we drove off, I leaned up and asked, "Where's Linda Saracen?"

With a hesitation of a moment, while he looked me over, "Witch Hazel."

We drove through the gate. I asked the driver "Which one is Witch Hazel?"

"Closest to Aspen. Small but close."

We drove up to Aspen and I could see a silhouetted figure taking a sip from a short glass on the screened porch. It was Tyler. When I closed the car door, he saw me and waved me in. "Drink, Jack?"

"Sure." I eyed the glass he was holding to see what he was having. I didn't want to look like a wimp. "Anything is fine. Whatever you've got there." Tyler poured me a scotch, saw my eyes go to the water pitcher and splashed a little in. He handed it to me without a word.

Tyler leaned forward, elbows resting on knees, in a chair made out of twigs and branches twisted together in a disturbing tangle. "You did a good job today, Jack."

"Thank you, sir."

He eased back into his chair and went on: "Seriously, you did a good job handling . . . everything." He nodded at the other chair, next to him.

I moved self-consciously to the chair and sat.

"We want to put out a statement tomorrow, you can figure out the timing, and announce that you will be named Acting Press Secretary." Tyler reached over, hand extended. "Congratulations, Jack."

"Thank you, sir." I went into a half stand so I could reach over and shake his hand. He wasn't asking. He knew I would accept. All the questions I had formed, the cogent points I had planned to share at such a moment were like bubbles in the champagne. All I could do was smile, trying not to grin, not to look too pleased. "Is the President resting?"

Tyler swallowed a sip, savored it a moment and nodded. "Yeah. He's over at Walter Reed resting right now."

I somehow controlled my eyes from popping wide open and before I could say anything Tyler went on in a toasty, familiar intonation: "You know. The President sneezes, we have to have a few tests. He should be back here by bedtime. Tomorrow morning at the latest."

The fact that I had spent the day telling the press nothing of the kind was exploding in my head and it was hard to hear his words. In a tiny, non-threatening voice I managed: "Will we get the results of the tests tonight? The press is going to want to know exactly which tests and the results, like always."

Tyler shrugged. "I'm not sure. We should be able to get some kind of doctor's statement, I think. But we don't need to release that he went to Walter Reed last night."

I swallowed. "Are you saying we just omit the visit to Walter Reed?"

"Not necessarily. No. I mean, he has to have tests somewhere, right?"

"Right. Good point. I did tell them all day long that he had tests. Nobody actually asked where he spent the night."

Tyler looked at me and nodded thoughtfully.

"It's nice Walter Reed is so close, isn't it?" I drained my drink and eyed the bottle, wondering if Tyler was going to give me a refill or if I should get up and get it myself. "Do you have any read on possible schedule changes yet?"

Tyler shook his head. "The schedule is already pretty light. We can make a few more cancellations, just as you hinted we would do today. Keep the schedule very limited for a week or so. The other convention is coming up. The country, the press anyway, expects us go almost dark during their convention."

I nodded back, trying to process everything and figure out what I should do, start screaming or what. Stay calm, I told myself. Think. I decided to change the subject with some probing questions. "Okay. Good. I also wanted to ask you for a candid read on the Lixubistan policy. There's a lot of dissension on it. I want to make sure I don't push us out there too far in support of the Lixis going nuclear if we're going to wind up backing off from them after the election."

"Isn't State handling this?" Tyler was looking around, distracted and sounding a little annoyed.

"Uh huh. State is all over it. And so is Cunningham." I knew this would make his bushy eyebrows go up and it did.

"He's more supportive of Lixubistan than, say, England, I think."

He stared at me for a second or two, then waved his hand dismissively. "It doesn't matter. That shit can wait, Jack. Let's get the man reelected, and we'll be able to get rid of those bastards and put things right."

I shrugged. "I'm just worried about the nuclear issue. You know. Isn't it going to be tough to reverse ourselves after we've been in bed with them for another year?"

"Why? Why does it get any harder? We're just giving them plenty of self-determination rope. You know. We have to give them a chance to work out their own problems. Right?" He sipped his scotch and made a tight face. "The nuclear deal isn't going anyplace Jack. I promise you. Dexter will never stand for that. But you have to be realistic. Look how divisive it would be to stop this thing right now. After the election, that's when we'll have the leverage. This is big league diplomacy, Jack. We have to let it play out. This is the kind of thing you can't get diverted on. I know I don't have to remind you that you don't want to get involved in setting policy."

No, but I'm the one you send out in the shitstorm to defend it, even when it's idiotic. But I couldn't say that so I nodded obediently. "Going back to the press organization, sir. Is the press operation in the campaign still intact?"

His eyes narrowed and a nasty smile spread on his lips. "Mackenzie is coming in for the rest of the campaign to take charge there. I think we can make sure we have better coordination, Jack. Better for everyone." He tilted his head in a jaunty, familiar pose, sort of conspiratorial. "You can fire Goodington, if you want to. The whole thing will be over in ten short weeks and Mackenzie will go back to his firm."

There wasn't much else to say. At least it was something I wanted to hear. I put down my glass to leave and as I started toward the door, David Crane smashed it open with his fist. It swung past my face, just missing my nose. Apparently his pass hadn't been pulled yet. Probably never expected him to show up.

Instead of his usual icy demeanor, his eyes were wild, his hair was windblown, sticking straight up. Was he drunk? "Where's the President?" He spun around like maybe we were hiding him behind the door. "I want to see him."

"How did you get in here?" Tyler stood up, rattled at first. "How can you show your face?" Tyler's face reddened, but his voice was controlled. "You thought it was going to make him quit, didn't you? Fuck up the Convention. Humiliation on national TV. It didn't work so you thought quitting would do it." I knew that somewhere, there was a panic button Tyler could push, but for some reason, he didn't. Maybe better to keep this private.

Crane aimed himself at the cabin doorway, as though he would find the President in his bedroom. Over his shoulder he sputtered, "What kind of friend would send someone to his death just to hold onto power for a few more months? It's all going to come out, you know. He should have stepped aside, gotten treatment. Not put the country through his long and tragic death. Look what you're doing to his legacy."

Tyler took a step toward him. "He has gotten treatment. What are you, clairvoyant? Do you know when we're all going to die? We all are, you know."

Crane reeled and glared at Tyler. I couldn't imagine David Crane punching Tyler, but I was afraid I was about to see it. "The campaign is going to kill him." He pointed in the air with his finger, then at me. "Even your hack flack knows that."

Tyler turned his back on him and eased into his chair. "The President doesn't want to see you. Get out or I'll have you escorted out by the Marines."

He gaped at Tyler for a moment, then turned toward the door. In a restrained, low voice, he growled, "There will be no recovery from your bad advice this time, Phil."

Crane slammed the door on his way out and Tyler stared at it for several moments, like it might burst open again. Then he turned from me without a word and took a few steps, a deep breath, and turned around again, this time with sad smile. "I've been fighting that bastard for years. I'll never understand him."

I nodded like I had some idea what he was talking about, waited, hoping he would go on. But after several moments of silence, I stood up. "I guess I'll be going back, sir, if there isn't anything else." I really didn't want to spend the night.

"Right. Thanks, Jack. And again, good job."

I walked down the hill, not really knowing where to go. Linda came out of her cabin and called to me: "Jack, did you already meet with Tyler?"

I nodded.

She hurried after me. "I thought you were staying."

I stopped walking. "I think I should get back. I can keep the press briefed better from the White House."

"Good point. Hey, I think congratulations are in order . . . Mr. Acting Press Secretary."

We started walking again, slowly. "Thanks." I squeaked at her, "So guess who dropped by my meeting?"

"I heard. I could hear the yelling when I was on my way up. I went back in to wait for the smoke to clear."

"That was smart. Don't get caught in the crossfire. So what's it all about? What's up with Crane?" I stopped again, because I wanted to see her face when she answered.

She just looked at me, expecting me to crack a joke, I guess. I went on, whispering: "Tell me the truth, Linda. What happened? Why is Crane out?"

She waved a mosquito away from her face. "Come on, didn't you hear?"

"No. Tell me, damn it." I could feel a mosquito bite on my ankle, right through my sock. "He's been telling the President to pull out all along, hasn't he?"

She looked at me like she wasn't sure whether I was kidding.

"Oh my God. Oh shit. Why didn't I see that? He was ready for the President to pull out."

"If he runs. Tyler thinks he'll die if he doesn't run. Pretty basic, huh."

"But if Crane is right, we're actually electing Cunningham."

She shook her head. "He isn't right. Come on Jack. Dexter isn't going to die, Jack. He's beating the cancer."

"Are you sure?"

"No. Of course not. Come on, Jack. Okay, so we're all going to die. But do I think Dexter can serve out his term? Yes." She turned and took a few steps, then waited for me.

I followed, slowly. ". . . Because I might spin, but I don't cover up. I don't lie. I never, never lie. I thought we were clear on that."

"No, no way, Jack. No cover up. No smoking gun."

We got to the car, but the driver wasn't there yet. I kept thinking about Walter Reed. Linda must know he was there, too, but no point in asking a direct question. I crossed my arms and leaned back on the car. "But you've seen Dexter. He looks bad."

The driver came out of the darkness and opened his door. "Ready, Jack?"

I nodded.

Linda whispered:"He's tired. Just tired. Who wouldn't be? After a few days, he'll be better." She put her hand on my arm. "It looks like you are in good shape for the second term. I'm glad. You deserve it."

Chapter Seventeen

The press bought it. Oh, sure, there was a little lingering suspicion, but they had nothing concrete, and they basically had to give it up. It turns out I wasn't the only one Crane had been nasty to. There were quite a few reporters who were pretty eager to connect the dots in a rather unflattering way about Crane, with very little imagination required on my part.

On the other hand, I was able to give them tidbits, off the record of course, about how Dexter dropped by my room while I was in the bathroom—scared me to death when I came out. How he had beaten me at cards. They bought it all. I just wanted to reassure them, to put everyone at ease. And it was off the record. But it would inform their reporting. It was important they understand that I was tight with the President, or I would have no credibility.

After the initial fright that the President was really ill again, he was able to appear a few days later, looking ruddy cheeked and vibrant. There was a surge in the polls. Then, there were the post-mortem stories, which some might call puff-pieces on yours truly.

That's right. Long gushy pieces interviewing my friends and colleagues about how my cool handling of the crisis contrasted with Crane's arrogance and lack of concern for "THE PEOPLE." Crane didn't come off so well, I'm afraid. On the other hand, I was something between Mother Theresa's nephew and Walter Cronkite. Members of the press were quoted anonymously, of course, saying things like,

"Jack is a straight shooter," and "Abbott gets high marks from the press for his candor and humor." Comments which, from the press, verge on the orgasmic.

It started with a piece in the *Wall Street Journal*. The way the *WSJ* had it, I single-handedly grabbed the controls of the campaign and stopped it from crashing.

The next day, the wire services ran more stories, several paragraphs about Dexter's health problems and how I had capably managed what could have been a disaster. The town was abuzz with my prowess: The talk shows, the papers, the politicians all treated the health issue like it was now old news, like I had reduced it to divorce or religion or a shameful ethnic joke with my indignation. Deep in every article was the reference to my father and his own tragic death and how that had informed my handling of Dexter's cancer.

Dexter had already scheduled a week at his ranch after the Convention. He was so far ahead in the polls, and the other party's Convention was coming up. He would hit the campaign trail on Labor Day weekend. But it was going to be a pretty light schedule. Frankly, the idea of not keeping up the campaign worried me. But while he was resting up at his ranch, I stayed in Washington. It was a quiet week with nothing on the schedule and no bad news. That's how I was able to sneak away for an afternoon to give a talk at my high school. They were dedicating a new wing and had invited me to be the keynote speaker.

It was surreal to me, but the fact is, at that point in history, that nanosecond of time, I was the man. I was famous. People were starting to recognize me. Who knew how long it would last? And even if I was only Acting Press Secretary, that was big for the little town I grew up in. I was almost there, stopped at the light just before the school parking lot when Linda called. "Lixubistan is coming unraveled. You need to get back here right away."

"What happened?"

"Some official has been shot by the guerillas. Not the President, but somebody associated with the government. It's on the news."

"Is State handling it?"

"Sure, right now."

"Okay. Unless you want to send a helicopter for me, I can't get back before three hours or so." I thought a minute. "You don't want me out there on this anyway. It will make it look even worse. I'll get back as soon as I can."

She was satisfied and calmed down but I knew she wanted me to cut this little fantasy as short as possible.

I wheeled into the parking lot of Linton High School and wondered if the fence looked so rusty or whether the sidewalk had this many cracks in it when I went here. The new wing was the same color brick, but the windows were bigger and outlined in blue. They must have given the old part a little face lift too, because the entrance had a new dark blue roof over it, and the surrounding windows now had blue trim. I floated in on a cloud. I had a few notes in my pocket, but hadn't worried about what the hell I was going to say. Now, with each step I took, I began to doubt what I could possibly tell them that would interest high school kids.

Three students were standing under the blue roof, waiting for me. I shook their hands and they walked me to the alcove outside the auditorium. The principal, the superintendent, a couple of the teachers who used to glare at me, the mayor, some school board members. I felt like a rock star. They all wanted me, wanted to connect. I followed the delegation on stage and when I cleared the curtain, the kids stood up and cheered. They stood there yelling, clapping, while the principal showed me to the right seat, center stage.

The principal had a long, rambling introduction. I can't tell you exactly what he said except that I wasn't completely sure he was talking about me until he got to the end and said my name.

Again they cheered. Applause is a good drug. I pulled out my notes, smiled and they quieted down. What do you say to yourself, your young self, your pre-college, mostly unformed self? "To thine own self be true?" or maybe "do unto others before they do unto you?" What you are thinking about the whole time, of course, is what you wish you had known. Mostly, you say vapid stuff like be determined, hold to your dream.

I placed my notes on the podium but never looked at them. I told them about my father, how he built up a business after my mother died, added a couple of his quips. I was pretty cocky up until then but when I started on that sentence it was like something reached up and tightened its fingers around my throat. When I said his name, I got this blazing image that he might be seeing me there. Then I had absolutely no control. It just about freaked me out. There wasn't a thing I could do but stop, look down and wait. But that didn't work either, because my eyes filled up and I had to actually wipe them.

They liked that part. Yeah. They stood and cheered at the end and everything.

I didn't talk that long, and, of course, I had to stay to take a few questions.

The first kid, a tall, skinny blonde girl, bangs in her eyes, asked me what it was like to work in the White House. I tried not to sigh or roll my eyes. I said things like, "very exciting, endlessly interesting, very hard work." I was going to have to get out of here soon, before the clock struck twelve.

Then, zing. "Mr. Abbott. Have you ever lied or been asked to lie? And what would you do if you had to lie?"

Time for the totally sincere face. I had some trouble putting it on, but I don't think they noticed. "The quick answer to that is no, I haven't. Nobody has asked me to. There are times when you can't tell everything you know about something, of course. Like a military action, or some internal strategy. But there's a big difference between withholding information and lying." I paused and added, "If the press ever thought I was lying to them, I would lose all credibility." I answered the question, but the words were still echoing in my head, so much I could hardly hear the next question:

"Have you ever disagreed with a policy of the President's?"

I was able to smile. A relaxed, patronizing smile. "There may have been times when I have disagreed with some minor aspect of the President's policy. But I agree with him on the big stuff."

". . . But what if you didn't? Could you work for someone who wanted to do things you don't agree with?"

I shook my head purposefully: "No, I don't believe I could. By the way, I think that's a very good question. I'm going to be able to take one more, then I'm afraid I have to leave."

"We found your old yearbook here, in the library . . . from when you were a senior. It says your favorite quotation was, 'Our lives begin to end the day we become silent about things that matter,' by Martin Luther King, Jr. Can you tell us why you chose this quotation and if it is still your favorite?"

Ah yes. My Martin Luther King period. I memorized him. Gandhi was another favorite. "Truth never damages a cause that is just" popped into my head but I didn't say it. I smiled thoughtfully. "I think you can see from that choice why I was drawn to public service." I paused, decided to leave it at that. "And yes, of course I still enjoy quotations. I think that one is as good as any I might recite for you here."

The principal was at my side, thanked the students, then whisked me to a reception in his office. I met everyone, and it took me almost an hour to get to the door. Of course, I didn't try very hard. I didn't want to leave, ever. I tried to shake every hand, but they were still in line when I finally had to go. I had to drive back by myself, and no matter how loud I put the music, I couldn't get King and Gandhi out of my head. I stuck in my earphone and called the office to check my messages.

When I got back to Washington, Sarah was waiting in the OEOB press office. I was Acting Press Secretary—I hadn't formally moved into the Press Office. I motioned Sarah to go with me to my office. She had on a cream colored suit and when she looked at me with those blue orbs . . . She still had an effect on me, but I tried not to show it. "Ah, Miss Gorrell. Bringing me more tidings of barbarism from Lixubistan?"I held the door for her. "What have those rascals done now?"

In the hall, she stopped and whispered. "The rebels car-bombed the Chief Justice."

Even I really couldn't make light of this, although a little black humor usually helps. She gave me all the particulars, and I even focused on them and not her lips. The government was going to make another crackdown, of course. But they would be careful to keep it under control, not like the dreadful over-use of power we have seen in the past. Of course.

We finished our business on the way to my office, but she followed me inside anyway and waited just inside the door.

I had given up hitting on her, but I was beginning to think about it, the way she stood there, taking me in. Finally, she said, "Jack. I was wondering if we could have dinner sometime."

Hmmm. Dinner, not just drinks, not a meeting. "Is something up?" I asked.

"We just need to catch up. I could use your advice on something." She was so unblinking, so sincere.

"How about tonight?" I smiled my most innocent, benign smile. Like, no big deal. "The President is still away, so it would be good for me. Otherwise, I'm not sure . . ."

"Perfect." She didn't want to meet in some discreet, quiet restaurant, but the Old Ebbitt. "It's close and quick, right?" She shrugged.

Instantly I thought about Linda, about how she had made it clear we were only going to be friends. And Sarah— when did I stop being attracted to her? We agreed to meet late, nine o'clock.

As soon as she left, as I was sorting through my in-box for time bombs, flipping the news channels there was a meek knock on my door.

Scott Goodington pushed his face through the opening. And the face was oddly unfamiliar, without the usual sneer.

"Do you have a minute, Jack?" He was so subservient.

"You know the answer to that, Scott, but come in anyway."

He tried to smile.

"What's up?"

He couldn't talk. He let out a long exhale. I waited, trying not to laugh. Finally, "I was just wondering. Um. Do you know what Tyler's plans for me are now?"

I shrugged. I wasn't in the mood to fire him. "Not really."

"Well, I mean," he exhaled a long breath. "I know I haven't been that helpful to you. It was like we were playing some kind of nasty game."

"We?"

"I mean Crane. You know."

"Ohhhh"

He swallowed, afraid to look at me, like I was the sun and I was so bright I hurt his eyes. "Does Tyler want me out?"

I really couldn't believe this. The guy who had been trying to get me fired was in here begging for his job.

Before I could answer, he went on: "I don't know if you know, but my wife and I are expecting our first child in a couple of months."

"No, I didn't. Congratulations."

He shrugged. "Thanks. I'll cut to the chase. Should I look? It's a bitch of a time to look for a job, you know . . . right before the election."

"Yeah. I do know." I paused, for dramatic emphasis. Then I surprised myself. "Scott, Tyler hasn't said a word. I don't know if I have any say, but I hope you'll stay. How could we possibly replace you so close to the election?" Easy, I thought. I could get a new plant for my desk.

The air started coming out of him. He closed his eyes. "Thanks, Jack."

"I'm not one to hold a grudge. Anyway, you have all the contacts on the campaign, right? I want you to keep me in the loop about what's going on. And with Cunningham."

When I said Cunningham's name, he drooped again. Then he shook his head. "Of course. I can do that." He shook his head. "Do you ever wonder—are we doing the right thing?"

"What? What do you mean?" He couldn't mean he had the same concerns I did . . .

He stared at the floor briefly. "I had finally gotten away from him, you know. But I can do it."

This intrigued me. "I'm curious, Scott. What is it about him? I can never quite put my finger on it."

"Oh, I don't know. There's that self-righteous side, you know, where he's supposed to be so honest and everything." He pressed his lips together and looked up at the ceiling, then went on: "But personally, the way he is with staff, the way he analyzes issues, behind the scenes, for that matter," Scott went on getting softer, perhaps avoiding my eyes. "He's just such a bastard."

I shrugged. "I'm not exactly in his inner circle."

"Yes, of course. Neither am I. I mean they're all egomaniacs, right? But he is so petty, yelling at everyone, picking somebody out to blame. Berating them. Asking who they've been talking to, who they used to work for . . ."

At this point, I couldn't really see where this was going and I was thinking about seeing Sarah, so I was only half listening. "Well, don't worry about it." I stood up and put my hand on his shoulder, easing him toward the door. "You'll still be on the press staff. I just want you to keep looping them in." I put out my hand, as in, *'No hard feelings, let's be friends.'*

He looked down at my hand and for an instant had a smirk. Only an instant, but I saw it. Then he grasped my hand and thanked me again. I was almost sorry I hadn't canned him.

As I was leaving for the Old Ebbitt, Evan called. He and

Bob had already congratulated me earlier in the week. "So when are you giving us our White House tour? Bob wants to know. Can we come over?"

"I can't tonight. How about tomorrow?" I thought about Sarah. "Let's make it late in the day. I think I am going to be busy in the morning."

"Oh, really." Evan paused, like he was trying to think of a snappy comeback. "Okay. You can tell us all about her later."

"Right. Okay. I have to run. Come over tomorrow at four. I'll show you around, then we can get a drink somewhere. I'll buy. I'm going to put you on with Donna and you can tell her what she needs to know so you can get cleared in. Hopefully the FBI doesn't have your profile yet. Or Bob's."

After Evan's phone call I left for the Old Ebbitt. I had plenty to think about. I wondered if I could tell Sarah about my high school. Or would those dreamy blue eyes glaze over. Linda had understood. Maybe I could slip in a reference, something offhanded. Like no big deal. The Old Ebbitt had a line out the door, waiting for a table. I nudged past the crowd and inside, veered right to the legendary massive mahogany bar, and got a beer. Sarah was there a few minutes later and ordered a glass of wine. It was crowded and noisy and there were no stools. We leaned close together and talked. "So what's been going on?" I asked.

She whispered a quick update on the Lixi situation in my ear. After all, it was probably classified.

"General Power is over in Lixubistan meeting with them. At the airport."

"What? How can that be? I thought we were dragging our feet."

She stood close and kept putting her hands on me, brushing off my coat, patting my arm.

"Yes, well things have changed. We think it is worth exploring. They are insisting they need a deal to show to their people. Stability. You know. So we can get our companies in there, or watch the Germans steal the show."

I had drained about half of my beer when maître d tapped me on the shoulder and asked if I would like a table. That had never happened before in my life. We followed him to a table.

Was it my imagination, or were people looking at me? Staring at me? I've been out with good looking women and I know that's what happens, but as we crossed the restaurant, it really seemed like they were looking at me. Like they knew who I was.

Sometimes, I've gotten a pretty good table there, nice and quiet, out of the way, but they never called me by name before. Sarah noticed it too, I think, but she didn't say anything. We sat down and ordered a second drink.

The waiter left us alone and I sipped my beer. "So have you set a date yet?"

Her smile vanished and she dropped her eyes. "No, actually we broke it off."

"Oh. I'm sorry." I paused, watching her. "Actually I'm not *that* sorry."

Was she going to smile or perhaps shed a tear? I was pretty sure I had put my foot in it until she looked up and said, "Actually, Jack, I hold you responsible, at least in part."

I felt a warmth breaking, a nervous sweat, but I didn't let it show.

Her eyes went around the room, "All the time spent on White House briefings, keeping you informed. We were just spending less time together."

I nodded sympathetically, of course.

Sarah went on, ". . . Being in the White House, working at the highest levels . . ." She paused, and glanced down and gave a reluctant nod. "Working with you. It made me rethink everything. And what you said, about this being an opportunity for me . . ."

"Uh huh." I didn't want to interrupt her. I liked where this was going.

"I couldn't believe it when you called me, you know. I

didn't know what in the world happened to you. I didn't even know you left Harrow's staff."

"I wanted to call you." I shrugged. "It seemed so pitiful, being out of work. Not the best way to impress a beautiful woman."

She gave me a shy smile on that one. "That's silly. I would have been relieved you weren't with that buffoon."

"Buffoon. God, that is just the word. I hear his reelection doesn't look so good."

"Did you have anything to do with those articles?" she whispered. "You must have known all about it. His drinking and everything."

I shook my head. It was a little disturbing nobody believed me on this. "I didn't. I do know half dozen or so other stories that aren't even out yet." I waved the waiter over so we could order. "I feel sorry for his staff. There are some very good people there."

"If you say so," she said with a cynical half-smile that I had never found that attractive.

We both ordered some food and two more drinks. I thought the waiter was going to pull up a chair and join us. When he finally left, I went back to Harrow: "I have to tell you though. I think Lixubistan is about the best issue Harrow ever found to demagogue."

"Really." She smiled and tilted her head a little like she didn't quite understand.

"You have to admit, our policy is getting pretty hard to carry on with a straight face." I took the last sip out of my beer. "Except that it isn't funny, of course."

"I can handle the policy, knowing how it fits in with the bigger picture."

Now it was my turn for the cynical twist of the mouth.

"Come on, you know . . . regional politics, gradual building of allies and democratic principles."

"Still, I'll feel a lot better when the election is out of the way. Maybe the policy will be reassessed." I watched her to see if she knew anything about what Linda had told me.

"What are you talking about? Is that what the National Security Advisor is saying?" she said with a squint.

"You know. A lot of people are pushing for more reform to be tied to trade and aid. Like Nichols, for one."

She shook her head, smiling again. "Oh. Nobody listens to him, Jack."

I took that one without flinching. "So how did you become an expert on Lixubistan, anyway? Surely there isn't a Lixubian Studies major?"

"No, of course not. I was Russian Studies. But the Russia desk is . . ." she waved her arms, "full, you know. Lixubistan seemed like a good spot. Of course I would like to go back to Russia. That's one thing I was wondering. Do you think there is room in the White House, maybe a detail to the National Security Advisor or something? Lixubistan is pretty hot right now."

"Who knows? I can look into it, if you like."

She opened her luminous eyes and offered the most sincere smile. "That would be so nice, Jack."

I nodded agreeably and reached for my drink even though it was empty.

With her left hand, she swept a wisp of hair back from her face, then raked a couple of fingers back through her silky mane and I was thinking for a moment how I'd like to do that, too, for starters. She leaned in on her elbows, a warm smile spread on her lovely mouth. "That was a great story in the *Post* yesterday."

"Thanks. I didn't write it, of course, so I don't know why I'm thanking you."

"Seriously, it was really impressive what you did. For the President . . . the country."

"Thanks. Just doing my job, as the saying goes."

I have no idea what I ate. I just know it went down fast and I got the check as quickly as I could. I couldn't wait to see how this evening was going to end.

My car was still at the White House, safely under guard, and after a couple of drinks, it didn't seem like a good idea to drive. We took a cab to her place. It was a sticky-warm Washington night and in the cab she sat close to me. But I didn't mind the heat. All night long, I had been getting signals and not knowing for sure how to read them. Oh, I know she was flirting. But was she baiting me, ready to slap me if I touched her? There I was with her face a few inches from mine. I resolved to be patient and she leaned up, ran her fingers around the back of my neck and up into my hair and kissed me. Maybe it was the fact that I had wanted to kiss her again, since the night we were caught in the rain, but it seemed like Madame Bovary could have taken a few lessons from Sarah. Unfortunately, the cab stopped at her place and we had to get out.

I admired the watercolors on her wall, the folk art she had from Lixubistan, nicely displayed by the stair. I had a line on the tip of my tongue, but I wasn't going to make the mistake of blowing this and I held back.

She went to the kitchen and took out a bottle of wine from a rack under the counter. "I don't have any beer. Do you want some wine, or maybe a cup of coffee?"

"What are you having?"

"Mmm. Wine I think. So, do you want some, too?" She handed me the bottle and the bottle opener.

"Sure." I expertly unscrewed the cork and poured us two glasses.

So we sat on the couch and very soon picked up where we left off in the cab. And as I say, I don't know much about women, but I am pretty sure when they unzip your pants, it does mean something. You can't really read too much into it.

I knew exactly what I was getting into. No illusions. I saw it coming, and I knew that my brain was going to catch up with the rest of my body if I didn't move fast.

My mind plodded along: *She doesn't even like me. If she did, we would have been doing this months ago. She is here because she thinks I can help her career. Or because she thinks I'm important now.* Oh, yeah, this didn't just pop into my head. The thought had been floating around in there all evening. What I couldn't decide was whether this was entirely bad or even slightly distasteful. Doesn't it happen to doctors and actors all the time? Women want you because of who you are? Isn't that true to some extent with all men? Isn't it in the primal nature of women to want to mate with someone powerful?

There was a certain amount of time involved because my mind also had to figure out how to get the buttons on her shirt undone, how to get upstairs without tripping, how to get the rest of her clothes off. But she helped and I have to say, it isn't possible to lust after someone for months and be disappointed. It was intense. I was able to park certain thoughts until we were both extremely hot and that's when the stray revelation, nothing to do with her really, made its way into the ballpark. I was there, breathlessly humping her and it was like I looked *it* in the eye. Partly what she said at the Old Ebbitt. What Goodington had said earlier. Partly what I already knew in my soul. Nothing was going to change after the election. We were going to approve the nuclear contract, probably help with financing. The voices of dissent had been quieted or gone to the other side. Dexter was either going to die or be too weak to make any changes. Lixubistan was screwed. It would be years before they got another chance to topple the government. Lixubistan was screwed and I was on top. Dexter was going to die, and I was the one telling the nation he was fine. Cunningham was going to be President, thanks to me.

I am relieved to say, I was able to hit my usual home run, and it was a grand slam, of course, despite these revelations.

After, we were there next to each other, and she began to talk again about being detailed to the White House after the election. I had wanted—desperately ached for this woman for months. I liked to think it was about more than just the way she looked. But now, all I really wanted was to get out of there. I was becoming anxious, strangely agitated. About how I'd been out there, explaining it, defending it, believing the whole time it was going to be changed, reassured that behind the scenes, we were lining up a better policy. The magnitude of the betrayal was sinking in. I was the one who told the story and left out the truth. Willingly. Eagerly, even. And she liked me better because I did it. She thought it was fine. I barely heard her words now. All I could think was thank God we weren't at my place—I would have to figure a way to get rid of her. So of course I didn't stay the night. I made excuses and went outside to call for a cab on my cell.

I was extremely tired and probably still a little drunk when I got home. But I couldn't go to sleep. The fishing box on my kitchen table was closed and latched. I hadn't opened it since I brought it over. I thought about finding one of those fishing weights in it, something I could put in my pocket, and have when I was stressed out, to make me think of the cabin. I opened the latch and started taking everything out. Neat little trays of lures, corroded from the salt water but still perfectly good. Tiny jars of salt pork, used for bait.

In the bottom, under the tray of lures, there were scraps of paper. Probably shopping lists, receipts. I didn't need to see his handwriting right now so I left them. But when I tried to put the tray back, it had to go just so, and it wouldn't fit. I put the tray back on the table and pulled out the scraps of paper. A receipt for a half-dozen peeler crabs, gas for the outboard. I unfolded each one and put it aside. On the bottom, I found a note in his handwriting.

It was not a receipt. Not a shopping list. It was a note. To me.

> *Dear Jack,*
>
> *I'm sorry. I can't call you and say goodbye, I just can't. I'm going to leave another note, a note for the police, which you've probably already read.*
>
> *You know I love you, son. I know it was hard for you. It must have been. I thought about it for weeks, right after they told me about the cancer. Advanced they said. They*

> *wanted me to do radiation and chemo, and
> that would have meant dragging you over from
> Washington, and for what? I couldn't go
> through any more hell—and then a death you
> wouldn't wish on your worst enemy. When I
> remembered about the bridge, and how they
> keep it quiet, I knew what to do. Because the
> last thing in the world I wanted to do was
> embarrass you. God knows I've done enough
> of that. You're a good son. I love you.*
>   *Dad*

It is still hard for me to admit, even to myself, that it wasn't actually cancer that killed my father. It was the fact that he drove to the West-bound span of the Bay Bridge at three a.m., parked his car next to the suspension tower, climbed the rails and jumped. Of course, like most things in life, I had thought mainly about how it affected me. I had assumed he was taking one last shot at causing me as much embarrassment as possible, killing himself in such a public way. I had known for years, from a friend on the Maryland State Police, that they don't publicize the jumpers. But I had no idea he knew. I didn't realize he knew about the hush policy and that in fact, he took himself out in the most discrete way possible: no mess for me to clean up, and I was free to invent whatever story I wanted for my Washington life. His body was found right away, they notified me, and I took care of the arrangements.

I didn't want to admit it, or even think about it. And I didn't have to lie about it, except to myself, or even work very hard to put a spin on it. I just said, "colon cancer." For the most part, nobody would pry into the details. Even friends. They sense you don't want to talk about it and they leave you alone. I figured the church would have a fit about burying him in the churchyard, so I hit on the idea of spreading his ashes, still putting his name on the stone next to my mother's. I was even afraid my secret would somehow affect my security clearance. That they might have doubted my mental stability or accused me of somehow covering up his death.

I have to admit, I cried. I put my head down on that table and cried, and when I woke it was still dark. I grabbed my keys and went to the car, not sure what to do or where to go.

But of course, I drove back to the cabin.

Chapter Eighteen

When I got to the cabin, it was still dark. The air was warm and clammy, like a thunderstorm might blow across the bay any minute. I sat at the end of the dock and leaned on one of the pilings. I was so tired, I couldn't be sure I was thinking right. Was I just telling lies all along? Were they using me because no big-time press person would stand for the lack of access to the President? The chilling idea that it wasn't all inadvertent—that I was being used because of my father's cancer. Was Linda part of it? I felt like I was in a nightmare I couldn't wake up from. I kept thinking about being on top of Sarah, and realizing, my God, what I was part of. She was having me. They were all having me.

The mosquitoes became unbearable and I went inside. I had unfinished business. I reached into the top of the cupboard, in the back. Out of sight. I felt for the Jack Daniels bottle. The bottom stuck to the ancient linoleum on the shelf and some of it pulled off with the bottle. I thought it was so funny, so perfect at the time, to put his ashes in it. They wanted to charge me for an expensive urn. I was so mad at him, I had thought about flushing the ashes. I intended to release them to the Bay, but I couldn't bring myself even to look at the bottle. I thought about how my father had tried to shield me. Protect me. I thought he was trying to embarrass me, and I had hated him for it. I thought about all of his ruminations about being more trouble than he was worth and how I had silently agreed with him.

I took the bottle with me to the bedroom, put it on the dresser, curled up and fell asleep. When I woke, the sun was up. I doused myself in bug spray and went back out on the dock. There was a slight breeze. The peaks of water caught the sun and I stared at the hypnotic, shimmering waves. I guess sleep had helped me to calm down a little, and began to realize, maybe I was off the deep end. All I could think about was Dad's note. A flood of feelings, forgiveness, sadness, love and memories of our contentious years washed over me. And more tears came. I let it go for a few minutes, until I felt the sun burning me and realized I was sweating. I was desperately thirsty and I went in the cabin. I drank a couple of glasses of water and got a quick shower. Then I locked up and drove back to Washington.

I had to be wrong. I was just tired and it looked worse than it really was. I crossed the bridge and I resolved to pull myself together. I had what I always dreamed of. I was Acting White House Press Secretary. And Dad would be proud. I wasn't going to blow it. My place was to explain and advocate. Inform the public. The other party was about to have its convention and everything I had questioned, all my secret doubts would be aired out by them. That was their job. Not mine.

As I drove back, I thought about calling Evan and Bob and making an excuse. I didn't feel like hanging out, and I definitely didn't want to give them a feel-good tour of the White House. But I couldn't bring myself to make the call and when I got to OEOB and saw them coming through the metal detectors, I even thought they might help me get my mind off things.

The Secret Service guards handed them VISITOR passes on chains to hang around their necks and they hurried over to me.

We started walking, our footsteps echoing in the empty halls. I wanted to slow them down, let them appreciate the old, weird interior of the OEOB. "Do you want to see my office or go straight to the West Wing?"

They exchanged looks. There was nothing special about my office, not compared to the West Wing, after all.

They followed me through the hall to the OEOB West Exec exit. We crossed the pavement, enclosed at each end by iron gates, to the canopied West Wing entrance. The Secret Service nodded approval and I escorted them inside. They followed me up the stairway and into the press briefing room. I took Evan's picture behind the podium. Bob took a seat and asked impertinent and obscene questions in various imitations of the network reporters and he made me laugh. I was glad they were there after all.

There were some reporters in the back and when they heard us they came rushing out. I assured them nothing was going on. I got them out of the briefing room and tried to get a brisk pace going, past the press secretary's office. They kept moving, nodding, elbowing each other. They seemed to get the idea, in the noiseless, odorless environment, almost churchlike, that they should behave and they followed me quietly. We came to the cabinet room, the doorway blocked by a half door. They each stuck their head in the doorway, then hurried to catch up. When we got to the Oval, they stopped walking. Evan stepped to the opening first, looking first to the left, taking a wide sweep around the room, then stepping back. Then Bob stepped up. He was still grinning, but his eyes had a look I had never seen. Not on him at least. Evan made an excuse to look again, and whispered a question. I don't know what they were looking at. It looked exactly like all the pictures. No stacks of files on the desk. No balled up paper on the floor. Not even footprints on the rug. It wasn't that the President didn't use it. But as soon as he left, the papers were whisked away and everything was restored. So you could look around the room, take in the molding, the color of the rug. You could see a few pictures on the credenza, behind the desk. But you couldn't see behind the curtain. Still, it was something to see the curtain. In person.

While Evan took his turn looking in, Linda came out of

her office. "Jack. I thought I heard your voice."

I wondered how much she had heard and was a touch embarrassed for a moment. "Hi, Linda. Let me introduce two friends of mine: Bob Carson and Evan Brett."

"Nice to meet you." She shook Bob's hand then Evan's. "Are you from out of town?"

I thought Evan might wet himself, so I answered. "Sort of. They work on the Hill."

She laughed agreeably.

I remembered Sarah's revelation. "I need to talk to you, Linda. About something I heard last night."

"Really. Come on in." She motioned toward her office. "Evan and Bob can check out the Roosevelt Room while we talk."

"Are you sure you can trust them in there?"

"Sure. The furniture is bolted down, like at the Holiday Inn . . . And, there are secret cameras." She flashed a half grin.

Before they moved on toward the Roosevelt Room, out of the corner of my eye I saw Bob step to the doorway of the Oval again and drink in another long look before he followed Evan.

Linda closed her door. "Your friends seem like a lot of fun. I'm glad. You need a break."

"They are. Too much. But listen, I'll make this quick. Last night I heard that General Power is meeting with the Lixubians at the airport." I watched for her reaction but there wasn't any. "Did you know about that?"

She went behind her desk and sat down. "Yes, Jack. I mean, it has been in the works. We talked about this. We can't just stonewall them. We have to play along. If we aren't meeting with them, there are plenty of other companies, companies which have very supportive governments . . ."

I took a couple of steps toward her. "So now that genie is out of the bottle. I don't see how it can be stopped. Can you?"

"Sure." She shrugged, shook her head, then went on,

trying to sound patient. "If we need to. We need to be in the tent. Otherwise, they won't listen to us. We will lose our influence."

I leaned on her desk and almost whispered. I wasn't sure if you can hear through the walls, or if someone might be outside the door. "Are you sure Cunningham isn't involved in this? It sounds like the kind of thing . . ."

But she was shaking her head. "Come on, Jack. You know we would never allow that. He might think he's in control. But that just keeps him, you know . . . busy."

I felt a little better. I straightened up and reminded myself that Bob and Evan were waiting. "But what am I going to say to the press? You know they will get wind of this. If the President ever has another press conference, I don't see how he answers this."

She nodded, like she was agreeing, but she was really just reasoning with me. "For one thing, Jack, nothing has happened yet. Just a meeting. There aren't any contracts. That's what you say to the press."

I had pushed it as far as I could. At least they were aware of it. I was afraid it might be Cunningham, once again shooting off his mouth, but apparently they were keeping him on a short leash.

We finished our White House tour and Evan wanted to go to the rooftop of the District Hotel. Bob would have preferred the dive near his condo, but Evan wouldn't hear of it.

We got a great table and could see the top of the White House, just past the Treasury Department. Our drinks came fast, along with appetizers we didn't order and a very solicitous maître d.

"I'm beginning to think this wasn't such a bad idea, Evan." Bob raised his glass. "A toast. To our friend, the household word."

"And what is that word?" I thought I might as well give him the straight line, and I waited for the joke.

Evan nodded. "Seriously, Jack. You were awesome. I

was really proud of you."

Bob didn't say anything, but clinked glasses with Evan.

"Thanks. I wouldn't be here if . . ." My phone went off. It was Sarah and she wanted me to come over. I made some excuses about having to catch up my laundry.

While I talked to her—as discretely as possible—Bob and Evan exchanged leers. When I got off, Bob whispered, "Don't tell me, was that the lovely you had a meeting with in the White House."

"Linda? No." They waited while I debated what to tell them, since I wasn't sure how I felt about Sarah at this point. "You remember Sarah, from the State Department?"

Bob looked at Evan. "Gorgeous blonde. He's doing laundry. Last month she wouldn't return his calls."

"Yeah, so who was that woman in the White House? Linda? Oh my God, Jack. Tell me you aren't seeing her, too."

"I'm not."

"But you blew off a woman to do your laundry? Are you nuts?"

Bob shook his head. "No Evan. He blew her off to hang out with us. He lied about his laundry."

"So when does he come back?" Evan whispered. We all knew who "he" was, of course.

"After they finish up their convention. It's bad form to campaign while they have their convention." We all knew who "they" was, too. "He's going to stay at the ranch, maybe do a couple of events from there. Come back a week or so after Labor Day."

Our waiter came by and took our empty plate of appetizers and slid another in front of us. "The chef wants you to sample these shrimp satays. We're thinking about putting them on the menu." He glanced nervously at the maître d', who was nearby, with his arms clasped behind his back, watching him.

"Wow, thank you." I said. "We will be ready for another round of drinks in a few minutes, but one thing: My dad here . . ." I nodded at Bob. ". . . will be very angry if you don't give him the check. Isn't that right Dad?"

Bob put down his drink. "Sure. Usually your mom pays, but she's away in prison, of course."

The waiter caught on that we were kidding around, and smiled appreciatively.

Evan obliged and stuffed a shrimp in his mouth. "God, these are great," he said with his mouth full.

The waiter backed away smiling and the maître d' disappeared from the doorway.

Bob rested an elbow on the table and leaned toward me. "So you are actually running things, day to day?"

"Pretty much. Not the campaign events, of course. But I do the gaggle. We pretty much go dark during their convention."

Bob shook his head. "After the primaries, I can't believe all they have left is Sam Oakton."

Evan washed down his shrimp with some beer. "Damn, that was spicy. So Jack, what will happen after the election? Have you got a shot?"

I shrugged. "Damned if I know. You know how unpredictable things are. I think I'll get to stay on at least." I thought about the President's health and let down my guard for a moment. "But I'm . . ." I caught myself.

"But what?" Evan took another shrimp.

I sighed. Surely I could level with these two. I needed to talk to someone. "I'm a little worried about him, I guess you could say. We're playing a pretty dangerous game with Lixubistan. If Cunningham took over . . . well, I think we all know that's not the only thing he would screw up."

Evan had his drink, which was nearly empty, in his hand and put it down. "What do you mean, you're worried about him?"

I wanted to tell them about my doubts. About the tests at Walter Reed. The results I never saw. I didn't see why he should have passed out at the Convention."

Evan leaned in. "How does he look in person, up

close?"

I couldn't bring myself to say that I hadn't seen him up close and in person since before the Convention. Way before.

"The doc says he's okay, right?" Bob waved at the waiter and made the circle motion, to signal another round. "What, are you a doctor now?"

"When my Dad . . ." I started to tell them how he never looked like the President, and he was stage four, but my voice cracked.

There was silence for a moment, then Bob said softly, "Jack, you know, you could be too close to this."

Evan nodded. "Yeah." He picked up another shrimp. "You have been a total professional. Everybody has been talking about it, Jack. You're a star. It must be difficult, considering your experience with your father."

"Agreed. Consummate professional." Bob shook his head. "I mean, you never know how things can shake out after the election, but you have done . . ." He caught himself, not wanting to sound too enthusiastic, I think, and the waiter showed up with another round.

We didn't stay out late for once and it did feel good to have a few drinks. I wish it would have helped relieve my worries.

Chapter Nineteen

Sarah called as I was getting ready for bed. She suggested we meet after work the next day. I wasn't as infatuated with her as I had been, but I have to admit there was still a strong attraction. I was relieved I hadn't blown it with her.

I got to the office around seven on Monday morning. A little late for the White House, but the President was away. Scott Goodington was waiting for me just outside my office.

"Jack, I don't know if you heard. Meeting over at State today on Lixubistan."

I unlocked my office door. "Nope."

He followed me inside. "Do you want me to take it, or are you still doing Lixubistan?"

It hadn't dawned on me that one of the bright spots for me would be that I could palm off Lixubistan on someone else. "Yes. Thanks, Scott." It occurred to me that something big must have gone down or there would be no need for a meeting. "What happened?"

"Nothing. The Vice President called it. Or his office, anyway."

Uh oh. "Let me know what happens as soon as you get back, okay?"

He agreed and left. The day flew by, and I was thinking about Sarah and where we would meet when I realized I hadn't heard from Goodington. I decided to go to his office and find out what went on at State. He met me in the hall. "Was the Lixubistan meeting cancelled?"

"No. Unfortunately. But I had another meeting after. Sorry Jack."

I bit my lip. No point in scolding him. "What happened?"

He sighed. "You mean other than losing two hours of my life that I'll never get back?" Another dramatic sigh.

"That's why we get the big money, right?"

"Right," he smiled uncomfortably. "It was a fucking disaster. Anyway, the upshot seemed to be, the Vice President is up in arms because they aren't getting the intelligence reports in his office quickly enough."

I was tempted to get him to cut to the chase right there in the hall, but I knew better than that. "Come on in," I nodded toward my office.

"You didn't miss anything, let me reassure you, Jack." He followed me and sat down on the couch, like I would sit in the wing chair next to him, so I did.

"Who was there?"

"Interagency group. Defense and Energy. I have their names written down. Pretty obscure. Assistant Secretaries, I think. " He shook his head.

"Who from State?"

"Just who you'd think. Ralph Prixell, and Sarah Gorrell." After he said her name, he smiled. I was afraid he was going to wink. "Some guys from the National Security Adviser's office."

"Who from Cunningham's office?"

He frowned at me, like he was puzzled. "What do you mean? He came and brought his chief of staff."

"He as in Cunningham?"

Goodington nodded. "I told you—he called the meeting." He stood up. "This isn't my area, Jack. You've been handling it and I'm not sure I can give you the details. But you need to talk to State." His eyebrows went up again. "You need to get a full download from Sarah. Otherwise, that's pretty much all I know. I told my wife I'd be home in time for Lamaze class."

"Oh well. Sorry to hold you up." I went back to my desk and saw that I had a message from Sarah. She was going to meet me at the restaurant, a small cafe, which was near her house.

I met her in front, as she was coming down the street from her place. She had changed into white slacks and a scoop neck top. I couldn't take my eyes off her, and didn't exactly have to force myself to kiss hello. We got a table and some drinks and I was looking forward to walking her home.

She scooted her chair close and tucked her hair behind her ear. "What did Scott tell you about the meeting?"

"Not too much." Damn Lixubistan. I looked around. There was a couple with a small child near us, but they were occupied with entertaining him. I went on quietly: "Said there was a complaint about his office not getting information? Said I needed a full download from you."

"That's right." She nodded. "I don't think he should have talked to Energy and DoD that way. They looked really shaken after the meeting."

She explained that Defense said, and Energy backed them up, that they were worried about conversion. She said, "Cunningham told them, 'They're going to do nuclear.' He said it like he was talking to a preschooler. Then he said, 'We can be part of it or we can sit by and watch German companies get the contracts.' In front of everyone."

The waitress plopped a basket of rolls in the middle of the table and Sarah waited for her to leave before she went on: "Then Prixell said, 'We can work with them to preclude conversion.'"

I tasted the wine. "Sure. Like that ever works."

"But listen to this, Jack." She touched my hand. "You won't believe it. Cunningham interrupted and said, 'So what if they do? God, I'm so sick of hearing that same tired bleating about this. I mean, so what?'" She paused for emphasis and looked at me, then went on: "Everyone around the table stared at him, not sure we heard right. Finally, Prixell spoke, 'You mean, we will be able to *stop* any conversion . . .'" She picked up her wine. I started to interrupt, but she held out her hand to stop me and went on: "Then Cunningham yelled 'No Ralph!' He caught himself and lowered his voice. He said, 'I mean, *so what* if they convert it to weapons. First of all, it will take years—it will take years to build the reactor and years for them to figure out what to do, how to convert it. *Think* people.'"

We were startled by a scream from the next table. The curly headed darling had thrown his sippy cup on the floor. The parents cooed and cajoled him and finally we could hear ourselves.

I tried to keep calm. She looked like she wasn't done. "Did he leave after that?"

"No. If only. He shook his head, as if he were totally disgusted, almost amused by our shortsightedness, our apparent stupidity."

"How did everyone react?"

She shrugged. "We were quiet after that. Not believing we heard right, I think. But listen, there's more: He started again, he said, 'Their neighbors have nuclear. Everyone knows this. The fact is, if they have it too, it will make the region more stable, not less. So, maybe it's not a bad thing. You really have to think outside the box a little bit.'"

I gasped. "Oh my God. Are you sure? This is pretty crazy, even for him."

"I don't know." She pushed the bread over to the far side of the table and picked up her glass again. "I kept watching for a smile, for some indication he wasn't serious."

My evening was definitely over. Damage control. "Did you talk to anybody after the meeting? What are the chances of a leak?"

"I don't know. They're all political, I think. None of them are career."

"And it isn't like he told them to do something, right?"

"He said he wants everything cleared through his office from now on."

"Okay. What about the General Power meeting? You

must have had embassy people there."

"It was routine. Not high level. Although they want a follow up."

I nodded, but was only half listening. I was thinking about how to handle the leaks out of DoD and Energy, if it got out that the VP was flailing.

"But that isn't the biggest news." She touched my hand again, slid her elbow on the table and whispered in my ear. "I'm supposed to start planning a trip for him for right after the election."

With her breath on my ear I shut my eyes. "This can't be happening."

"I know. I have to figure a way out of this. Have you thought any more about the detail idea? If I am at the White House, I won't have to do this. Plus, I can be closer," she met my eyes and paused, "if there is a crisis."

I caught the eye of the waitress and waived her over. "I haven't really had a chance." Headlines flashed before my eyes: *Vice President Favors Nukes for Lixubistan.* "Sarah, I have to go back. I have to let them know about this. Can we get together later in the week?"

The waitress glided to our table. "Your food is almost ready, sir. Do you want another round of drinks?"

"No. Sorry. I have a family emergency. I need to get the check." I looked at Sarah.

She slid back her chair. "Can you make the food to-go?"

The waitress nodded and left. Sarah didn't look happy. I gave her a peck on the cheek and told her I'd call her later.

I left the restaurant and called Linda from my car. She wasn't at her desk but the White House operators tracked her down.

"Jack, I'm on my way home. What's the matter?"

I was stopped at a light. "There are some developments about . . ." I remembered that our phones weren't secure. "Did you hear about a meeting today?"

"No. I guess not. Since I don't know what you are talking about."

"I'll cut to the chase. I'm afraid there's going to be a leak."

She suggested I stop by to brief her, which was fine with me. I aimed toward Virginia. It would take me at least thirty minutes to get to her house, but I didn't want to go back to the office either.

When I got there, she had already changed. She had on running shorts and a t-shirt and her angular form and long legs were pale. I wondered about the last time she was outside in the daytime.

"Okay, what's going on, Jack." She sat on the edge of a side chair in her tiny living room.

I perched lightly on her leather couch. "Cunningham went off the page. Started talking about Lixubistan. Wants to go there after the election. Told State to set it up." I shifted and the leather creaked. "And here's the best: the nuclear reactor. He told a room full of staffers from God knows where that it wouldn't be a bad thing if they developed a weapon."

"Shit. You misunderstood or something."

I shook my head. "Nope. I wasn't there. So what I'm worried about, first of all, is leaks. Like I said, there were several people there from DoD, Energy. State."

She stood and paced toward the kitchen and got her phone, then came back, then reversed again.

I went on. "It probably won't. We think they are all politicals. But what if it does? What if he says this on his next campaign stop? Or interview?"

"I'm going to have to let Tyler know about this." She looked at her phone, then at me. "I think he's still in the air. I can call him but not from here." She ran her hand over her forehead. "Before I freak out, let's think a minute. What can we do, Jack? You're the spin doctor."

"If they leak it, simple: Cut him off at the knees. Simply say that the remarks were obviously misunderstood and that the Vice President is fully supportive of our policy. Reiterate that he is not going to Lixubistan. Refer them to State for further elucidation of the policy." I thought a moment. "Of course, that would make the leakers happy. If they do it."

"That sounds pretty good." She lit on the chair arm again. "We don't want to say anything on this, if we don't have to right now. Let's get through the election."

"Right. But Linda, even if nobody leaks—don't we have a problem here?"

"Of course. I'm going to get it all to Tyler, don't worry. But I don't need to bother Tyler with this tonight. I can brief him in our morning meeting." She stood up. "It's good you are on top of this, Jack." She tucked her phone in the pocket of her shorts. "Want a beer or something?"

"Sure. Is that a trick question?" I thought about how I had left Sarah in the restaurant, how I said I'd call her. I stood and went toward the door. "But, I think you were going for a run when I got here. Maybe another time."

I was relieved that Linda hadn't tried to explain Cunningham's behavior but I could tell they weren't going to do anything about it and that was eating me up. I knew my place as the flack, but that didn't stop me from worrying about what really happened at Walter Reed and maybe even more, about what I had done. And why wasn't the President campaigning? He made a few stops, Florida, Michigan, Pennsylvania, Ohio, but they were controlled. Single shot, give a speech to a huge crowd, have dinner with a small group of contributors, then leave the state. In Florida they scheduled a round of golf. Of course it had to be cancelled because of thunderstorms. Wouldn't they have known what the weather was going to be? Was that planned? All in all, I knew I'd feel better when I saw him in person, and could know he wasn't on a hospital bed dying.

The next day, on my way into the West Wing to see Linda, I was startled to see Shawn Peterson, head of the President's Secret Service detail. So, the President must be in the White House, or at least in Washington. But it seemed strange that I didn't see the helicopter land. I was relieved and hurried up the stairs to find out what Tyler said about the latest Cunningham fiasco and met her in the hall. She had a stack of notebooks and papers and was hurrying toward Tyler's office, which must mean he was back, too.

"When did the President get here?"

"Hi, Jack. What?"

"I just saw Shawn Peterson."

"Really? What's he doing here?" She squinted at me, then went on, "Tyler is here today, going back to the President tomorrow."

I sighed, maybe shook my head.

"What's the problem, Jack?" She took my arm and turned me around. We walked together, slow steps, in the other direction.

I leaned toward her and whispered. "Isn't it a little unusual not to be campaigning now?" I caught myself and added. "I'm not sure how to explain that to the press and still play down any health issues."

She shrugged. "Haven't you ever heard of going fishing, Jack? Why campaign when you are still twenty or more points ahead in the polls, coming out of your opponent's convention?"

"Yeah. I've heard of it. Very funny." I gave her arm a soft punch. "Not that anyone will buy it. Seriously, is he okay? I mean, with Cunningham running around . . . doing God knows what?"

"Of course." We stopped outside the Press Secretary's office. "Why haven't you moved in, Jack? It would be so much closer. And closer to the Briefing Room."

We did another about-face and walked in the other direction. "It isn't done. Looks bad. Uppity. Must be humble for the press. Pride goeth before a fall."

"Wow, I didn't know you could quote the Bible."

"More a paraphrase. Actually, I'm quoting my fourth grade teacher. She told me that all the time." I looked for a smile, and she obliged with a small one. The other thing is—I don't have the job yet. Remember? I'm Acting. I'm not sure why that is. I don't know what else I need to do to prove myself." I guess it had been gnawing on me over the past few days and I couldn't hold it in any more. It was fine to put a good spin on it for my friends, but the more I thought about it, the madder I got.

She didn't answer. She just looked at me, thinking, I guess.

I went on, down to business: "So what did Tyler say?"

"About?" Her pace slowed. "Oh. Cunningham. I hate to tell you, Jack. He's used to this kind of thing."

"Will he let the President know? I'm concerned a reporter might hear something and ask questions about it. On a campaign stop."

"Good point." She sped up again. "I'm not sure, but I'll mention it. The reporters are not going to get that close for a while, so don't worry about it."

I nodded, and hurried to catch up with her. "So you never said. How's he doing?"

"Okay I think. I haven't seen him, but I hear he's getting a lot of rest. Hard to do that around here. Tyler is going back to the ranch tomorrow."

"I'm just, you know—concerned. Trying to keep a lid on things. I want to get in front of any health updates, for example."

She nodded slowly. "Okay. Good. We'll keep you informed, of course."

I went back to my office feeling even worse, having had my hopes raised by the sighting of the Secret Service. And I have to admit, it was pretty clear that they were, to put it nicely, holding back some information. Was the President back in Washington, at Walter Reed again? I pulled up some footage of the campaign appearances and watched it, pausing on the close-ups. He looked happy, smiling. He could still project the energy. But thinner. Gaunt? Was that too much of a leap?

The daily chaos of the White House kept me busy, although the campaign was carrying a lot of the burden of the day to day message. We were tasked with keeping the brush fires around the world—and around town, for that matter—from burning out of control. I had been spending the little bit of free time I had with Sarah, so I asked Evan and Bob to meet me for a drink. We met on the Senate side, so Evan could slip out and join us. The Senate was racing to finish the spending bills before the new fiscal year began on October 1st. Also, they wanted to recess so they could go home and campaign.

Bob insisted we go to the Monocle, between the Dirksen Senate Office Building and Union Station. He said he used to go back when we were toddlers and hadn't been in years. He secured a corner table in the bar, which wasn't crowded. Evan got there right after me, sweating and breathless from his short walk. "Hey, before I forget. I think I may be able to get some World Series tickets if the Orioles make it."

Bob's eyebrows went up. "Putting aside that it is bad luck to even talk about this, how much?"

"Free, I think." Our drinks came and Evan took a long gulp. "I don't know. Who cares?"

"Great. I'm in." Bob looked over at me. "Jack. The Orioles . . . Hello?"

I didn't want to talk about the Orioles, but I knew better than to explode all my concerns on them right away. "Of course I'm in."

"What's the matter with you, Jack? The Orioles. Be happy."

"Who isn't happy?"

"Oh, I get it. Heavy hangs the head that wears the crown. Am I right? Affairs of state have you worried?" Bob stirred his drink.

Evan frowned. "What's the matter, Jack?"

My eyes closed almost involuntarily. "Cunningham. You wouldn't believe what . . ." I remembered the meeting was classified. "He's been saying some crazy shit in meetings. If it gets leaked . . ."

"Is this about Lixubistan?" Evan whispered. "Nobody cares, Jack. You worry too much."

Bob leaned on the table. "Come on, Jack. He's the Vice President." He took another sip. "Nobody cares. And, I mean, you keep telling us, the President's health is fine . . ." Bob got up and started for the Men's.

"I'm not sure."

He glanced at me over his shoulder and shook his head.

"Anyway, you can't tell from the way someone looks." I tasted my beer.

The bartender, a lanky brunette, brought a bowl of bar snacks over. Evan was momentarily flummoxed when she smiled at him.

When she was back behind the bar, he whispered. "You're unbelievable." Evan lifted his mug to his lips but put it back down. "You aren't the chief of staff, Jack. You do the press. That's it. You aren't a doctor. Okay, you know something about cancer, more than any of us want to know. But you don't know what his prognosis is."

Bob slid back into his chair. "Oh God. Prognosis. Now we must be worried the President is going to croak."

"Okay, you can think it's a joke, but how would you like to be the flack out there lying your ass off every day."

Bob shook his head. "I don't believe it. I respect your creativity too much."

"Very funny. You know what I'm saying. When you have to push something you disagree with or at least aren't sure about, how hard do you go?"

Bob put down his glass and pointed a finger at me. "That and that alone is why you're making the big money, son."

I looked at Evan. He shrugged and smiled.

I didn't really believe the President was at death's door, but for the sake of argument, I went on: "Are you serious? I mean, what if he's terminal? You know? What if he's not going to live out a second term?"

Bob's eyes blinked at the unintentional word play but

none of us smiled and I went on: "Maybe not a year?"

Bob gazed into his drink. "You'll be toast, of course. So will I. Just like if we lost. Evan will be buying."

"And Cunningham will be President."

Bob shrugged.

"God knows what that man would do . . . How hard?"

Bob lifted his glass and downed the few drops left in his drink. Then he leaned toward me, close, like he didn't want anybody to see him slap me. "As hard as you have to." He paused and then said slowly through his teeth, punching me in the chest with his finger as he said each word: "That-is-what-you-take-the-money-to-do. If you want to stop making the money—then quit. They aren't paying you because you are good looking."

There wasn't much point in arguing, especially since I wasn't sure I disagreed, but I couldn't stop myself: "But don't I owe it to them to put up a little resistance? A red flag?"

Evan crossed his arms on the table. "Well, have you said anything? What does he say when you ask these questions?"

The bartender came over, exchanged nods and waves with us and brought another round.

"I haven't said anything. Not really." I couldn't bear to mention the fact that I had no access to the President. That I had actually only met with him a few times for a few minutes. "I guess that's the question, really. Shouldn't I at least suggest they should disclose more? Question our policy in Lixubistan?"

Bob answered. "Sure. You can do that if you want and maybe live through it." He took a sip. "Let me ask you this, Dr. Abbott. Do you want to be Press Secretary in the second term or have you had enough?"

Had enough? God no. It almost made me break into a sweat. I was born for this job. I would do it underwater. I would do it naked. Could I do it and lie? Um. I'm not lying, really. They may be giving me lies and I may be repeating them. It isn't the same in my book. "Okay. Okay. Okay. " I looked at Bob. "But you wouldn't say anything? Just do what you're told?"

"Come on, Jack. No bullshit. Get creative. You can push this a little bit without putting your ass on the line."

I gulped the cold foamy brew. So maybe I had overreacted. I was beginning to convince myself I had. Maybe they were right. Hey, I'm not a doctor. I'm not a foreign policy wonk, right? I just do the press. I get paid to explain. And to be fair, shouldn't I give Tyler the courtesy of answering my concerns? After all, the press asks for medical updates every day. It wasn't like it was my doubts I had to represent. The President's medical records, what happened at Walter Reed, the Lixubistan human rights angle, the nuclear weapons fears. I needed guidance, right? Just looking for my marching orders. Not trying to steer the boat. If I was any good, I could convince them. I could walk the tightrope, back off if necessary and make sure they weren't mad at me. Because I did want the job.

Chapter Twenty

On the way home, I played the chess game in my head. If I wanted to see Tyler, I would need to talk to Linda. She would ask what I wanted, would tell me not to worry about it, or would somehow delay me. Getting in to see Dexter would be even harder, especially if I went through proper channels. But, I kept reminding myself, fortifying myself, that I had the title of Acting Press Secretary, and they usually have access, make it a condition of the job. Tyler wasn't going to let me in by myself and he wasn't going to take me in to talk about the President's health. We had never talked about access. I never made demands about it, because my foothold in the job was so tenuous. But I was Acting Press Secretary. How could he fire me for meeting with the President?

Sometimes Tyler went over to meet with campaign staff while the President had his seven a.m. security briefing. Getting some time alone with the President was nearly impossible and I thought this would be my best shot. I told Doreen that I needed a moment. I said I wished Tyler were there, but that this was important and it would only take five minutes. When the door opened and the national security people left, the President saw me standing in the doorway.

"Come on in, Jack." Dexter waved me in to the Oval. He was at the desk. Was that look in his eyes amusement? He took me in with an expert glance and knew I was so nervous I could barely speak. He could turn on the usual charm until my jaws thawed out, or he could glare at me and run the risk of me soiling myself.

He got up from the desk and went toward the study. "Let's go in here, Jack. Coffee?" I followed him to the study.

I had been so wired up, so prepared to give him my pitch, but now I couldn't quite answer. The President was going to get me some coffee.

"What do you want Jack?" He nodded toward the Filipino steward at the end of the room.

"Nothing, thank you." I squeaked.

"José, I'd like some coffee please. None of that decaf crap, either."

"Yes, sir." José grinned conspiratorially and nodded.

I looked at Dexter's face, his coloring and the way he moved. He was a skeleton. He was tan but somehow his color was off. Pasty. His eyes had a yellow tinge, like you see in alcoholics. Or sick people.

"Have a seat, Jack." Dexter said to me then turned to José, "Bring Jack some coffee, and something to eat. How do you like your coffee?"

"Black, sir." I don't know why I said that. I can barely drink it with a half cup of milk and three sugars. I sat and waited for him to sit across from me in what was obviously his favorite chair. Just to the side of the Oval Office, through the door I could see the flags and the Remington sculptures and the massive Roosevelt desk with its carving and out the window, the Rose Garden and it was so surreal that I was sitting here, getting ready to tell this man to put all this in jeopardy.

Dexter sat next to me and sipped his coffee. "What's the latest on what the market will do when the unemployment figures come out?"

We all knew ahead of time, of course, about the various economic numbers. What we didn't know was how Wall Street was going to react. "The last I heard, there is no consensus. What Oakton will say—that's another matter."

Dexter gave me a bored nod.

José brought me my coffee in a dainty china cup and

saucer. I didn't touch it. I took a breath and went ahead. "I'm worried about Cunningham, sir." I winced, realizing I should have called him "the Vice President."

He didn't know where I was going with this and he just watched me.

"The Vice President has involved himself in foreign policy, in areas I'm not sure you are briefed on. He made some statements on Lixubistan at an interagency meeting the other day. Very disturbing. Especially if they are leaked, of course."

He had the day's clips on his lap and his eyes scanned them. "What did he say?"

"He said it would be good if Lixubistan got nuclear weapons." He stopped reading and looked at me. I went on. "I don't want to be guilty of spinning this. He was asked why we weren't worried about Lixubistan converting the nuclear program to build weapons. He said we shouldn't worry about it—it would be a good thing."

Dexter didn't say anything but gave a tired exhale. Without looking up he said, "I know you aren't going to ask me to dump the Vice President, Jack."

"Of course not. But I am worried what it will do to your legacy if . . ." my mouth went totally dry ". . . if it turns out the cancer comes back, if it looks like you withheld health information, and Cunningham ends up taking the reins . . ."

Dexter looked at me a long time. I waited for him to answer. "That isn't going to happen, Jack." Before I could say anything he went on, getting a little agitated: "But even if you are right, what are you saying I should do? Do you think I should withdraw? If I withdraw now, Cunningham is the nominee. I mean, the Convention is over."

"I'm not asking you to withdraw. Just tell the truth." My throat caught as those words came out and hung in the air. "I didn't mean . . ."

Dexter's expression didn't change much, but his eyes opened slightly like I had just pinched him.

"What I'm saying sir, is, I think you can get reelected,

even if you share more about your health with the voters. You can say that you need more treatment, but that your prognosis is very good."

"Aren't we already saying that? I'm surprised at you, Jack. Surely you know that the press corps will be all over me, getting conflicting opinions from every doctor from chiropractors to psychologists. Everyone debating my chances. My survival becoming the ultimate issue in the campaign. And Cunningham. He becomes enough of an issue to lose the election for us. Isn't it better to put the niceties aside and get our business done? We can put policies in place after the election. He's not going to be able to unravel . . ."

While he was talking, Tyler came in, glaring at me across the room with a look that would melt glass. "Jack. What brings you in here this morning?" Then without waiting for me to answer, he turned his back toward me and started talking to the President.

I stood up, waiting to be dismissed. Tyler turned toward me again. "You're done," he said, and I felt my knees go soft. I was able to walk out, but I swear, I was choking.

You're done. Holy shit. I went back to my office, and when I got there, I already had a message from Tyler: "Get back over here. Now."

I went back over, a Niagara Falls of sweat. Tyler nodded me in, unsmiling, and he sat in one of his guest chairs. I moved toward the other and he looked at it, not speaking, signaling I should sit down.

He sat there, gazing at the floor. A long time. He sighed, a long time. I started to speak, intending to grovel and apologize, but he interrupted. "Jack, I know you aren't stupid. You know we didn't hire you looking for that quality. So I'm going to level with you. I talked to you about loyalty and you said you were here for the long haul . . ."

I found myself lacking any personal courage whatsoever, nodding eagerly.

"You are worried about our legacy, about what we are

doing. Okay. I want you to think about our choices here. Can you support Oakton? Do you think he'd make a good president?"

"Well, no." I knew what to say. I shook my head for emphasis.

He threw the papers in his hand across the desk. "Come on, Jack. It isn't just about the man. They would bring all their people in. Think what they could do to the government."

"I know. It isn't just about the President . . ."

He went on like he didn't hear me. "Okay, suppose the President stepped aside in deference to the Vice President. Is that a good idea, thinking only of the country's best interest?"

"Oh God, no." I didn't' even have to try on that one. "The V . . ."

Tyler held up his hand, "No, I'm not going to ask you to note the shortcomings of the Vice President."

"Good. We could be here all day. In fact . . ."

He interrupted again. "So let's see, we are left with a President with a health problem. One that is cured a great deal of the time."

"No. That's not what I'm saying. That's not what I'm worried about. What I am worried about is the appearance of a cover-up. I think we can be more forthcoming and still win."

"Cover up?" Tyler exploded. "How can you say that?" He seemed honestly exasperated, in disagreement, not just pissed off at me. "You disclosed it yourself. You held up pictures of his goddamn colon."

"But what about Walter Reed? The night after the Convention. And there must be more detail. More than the one paragraph updates you're giving me." I couldn't say that I wasn't sure they had told me the truth about his condition. I had no hard evidence. "We need to get the doctors together for another briefing. There are rumblings, you know. Nobody wants to be irresponsible and report the rumors, but you know, somebody will, and soon, unless we quash it with information."

He had his arms folded and looked like he heard me. I

had him listening so I went on: "And if I may, sir, feeling as you do about Cunningham, why is he still on the ticket? I know you wanted his support during the cancer announcement, but the President was so far ahead in the polls . . ."

"I wish he weren't. But he is." He leaned toward me and rested his elbows on his knees. "Now, I am going to tell you this in confidence . . ." He lowered his voice to a gruff whisper. "Cunningham is under investigation by the Justice Department. There is a long list of activities he has been involved in, and they believe they are close to an indictment. If we pulled him off the ticket before the Convention, it was going to blow up the investigation. And, it was going to look like we may have tolerated some of his activities, known about them. That would be hard to overcome in a few short weeks. Remember the Chinese. Remember the other sensitive negotiations we are handling. We are making history here. After the election, he will be indicted. Removed."

"Really?"

"Yes, and you know who the President wants to replace him with? Your friend John Cook."

If he had swatted me with a baseball bat, I wouldn't have been any more disoriented. I managed: "Does John know this?"

"NO. Nobody knows it. I'm trusting you with a lot. But there will *never* be a President Cunningham. For Godsake, you can be sure of that."

A moment later, he got a call and I left. I was a little lightheaded. I was so relieved, so elated. I was sure I had overreacted on Lixubistan and the President's health: He could get some treatment and be perfectly fine. The idea that Cunningham would be out, how John Cook could step in, in his rightful place. It seemed improbable, but maybe it could happen. It had to happen.

Chapter Twenty-one

The perils of the near famous: I couldn't go out in Washington without being recognized. So I definitely couldn't go to a bar to meet a friend and wait, by myself. Not if I wanted to stay by myself. Chances are, someone would recognize me and maybe want to chat. I even had a few ask for an autograph. So I was a little distressed when I went to the Old Ebbitt to meet Sarah, and she wasn't there yet. But they took care of me, got me a table and fended off the public.

I wasn't looking forward to seeing her. I knew she would harangue me again about a detail to the White House. I wasn't sure I could help her, even if I wanted to. But she was driving me crazy. I planned to tell her that I was going to be awfully busy for the next several weeks and that we might not be able to see each other. In other words, the polite brush off. The waiter brought me my beer and I wondered whether I could have a quick drink with Sarah, then go back to the White House to see Linda. I wanted to ask her if she knew about what Tyler had told me: The Cunningham investigation. After my initial elation when Tyler told me about it, my doubts were creeping back in. Indictment of Cunningham now seemed fantastic. Too good to be true.

Sarah was only a little late. It seemed as though all eyes followed her to my table, unable to turn away, probably wondering if she was an actress or TV personality. We had progressed to cheek kisses in public, and she barely said hello. Before I could launch into my kindly let down, she leaned toward me, the top buttons of her shirt open, I noticed, just hinting at her porcelain cleavage. "Jack, I have wonderful news."

"What?" I signaled the waiter to get her drink order.

She ordered and watched until he moved far enough away.

"Ralph thinks he can get me the detail to the White House." A triumphant smile spread on her lips.

"No kidding." I smiled back. Good news but unlikely. There would be more detail coming and might not be so wonderful. "Whose office? "

"That's the thing. It's a secret, of course." She lowered her voice and held the edge of the table as she shifted in her chair. "At first I wasn't thrilled with the idea, but Ralph pointed out, it's where I'm needed the most. Especially if he's going to go there in a few months."

I blinked. "The Vice President?"

She nodded. "I know what you think, but from my point of view, this could be a great career move. And Ralph believes I can have influence on other foreign policy, that it could even lead to a top advisor role.

"No doubt." I tried to look serious an even bit my lip. "But Sarah . . .you know, the Vice President doesn't exactly like me."

Her eyes dropped to the table. "Yes, I know."

The waiter brought her wine. I debated asking for the check, whether that was rushing things too much.

As soon as he left, I took a drink of my beer, downed most of it. "Sarah, this is a tremendous opportunity. I can see that. If he finds out you and I are good friends, it could hurt your chances. Almost certainly."

"I know. I'm not sure how to say this, Jack, but it might be best if we don't see each other for a while." She reached over and took my hand in hers. "I hope you understand."

I bit my lip again, trying not to crack a smile. "I think you're right, Sarah. Hate to say it, but it would be best for now."

Over her head, I saw a familiar looking silhouette come through the door. Willie Lavas. Some others I had seen in his office followed. And then, Linda. Willie was coming toward me. Sarah still had my hand, caressing it under hers. She was still leaned in close, and she was still speaking softly, probably telling me about more of her career plans. Willie saw me and stopped at the table. I wanted my hand back, but didn't want to be too obvious.

"Jack. How are you?" I stood and we shook hands, after I eased mine away from Sarah. But Linda saw. I caught her eye for an instant, then she wouldn't look at me. Finally she smiled and waved, as Willie and the group eyed Sarah but didn't wait to be introduced, kept going to a table.

As they paraded by, I saw Sarah sneak a look at her watch. I know I had planned to give her the brush off, but it seemed pretty clear that she never really had any feelings for me and it did cut into me. I sucked down the rest of my beer and motioned for the check. I think Sarah thought I was upset. I was planning to put her in a cab and slide into Willie's group.

While we waited for the check, I couldn't resist a few last digs about Lixubistan. "I have to confess, Sarah, I'm a little surprised that you have become so comfortable with our policy. Of supporting those people . . . And given some of the more extreme statements of the Vice President . . ."

Her smile vanished. "That's why he needs me, Jack. To keep him better informed. Look at the realities of our national interests, of what we know about the difficulties, the impossibility really, of getting involved with regime change."

"I'm just saying, look at the facts . . . Look at what these people are doing."

"The facts? The facts are what we say they are, Jack. You of all people should know that. There is a legitimate national interest here, and you should try to remember that."

She grabbed her purse and stood up, eyeing me, perhaps trying to decide if I was a lost cause. Out of the corner of my eye, I saw Linda leave. If I hurried, I might be able to talk to her. So I followed Sarah, who now thought I was trying to make up with her. She got a cab and gave me a goodbye wave. Linda was nowhere to be seen. I rushed around the corner in time to see another taxi, with Linda in it, pulling away from the curb.

I thought about grabbing another cab and following Linda home. Did she know anything about what Tyler had told me? Cunningham getting dumped? Or were they lying to me and was she part of it? And briefly, I let myself entertain the idea that I didn't like the way she looked at me with Sarah.

But racing to her house in a cab might have seemed a little nuts to her, so I went back to the White House, got my car and headed home. I pulled into the underground garage and into a space, but I didn't get out. I had to see her. I drove back out of the dark garage and over to Old Towne. I wasn't going to be able to sleep without asking her if she knew about the investigation. And all the questions I didn't have time to think of in Tyler's office. Like, is there a chance this could break before the election? Do we need to be ready?

I didn't hurry. I wasn't sure what to do when I got there. You don't just show up at someone's house unannounced these days. There was a parking space down the street from her place. And what if someone else was there? It didn't occur to me until I was parked. I dialed the White House operators. "This is Jack Abbott."

"Good Evening, Mr. Abbott."

"Good evening. I need to reach Linda Saracen."

"Yes, sir."

I waited. I could see her car. Where could she be?

"I'm sorry, Mr. Abbott. There is no answer. Would you like us to keep trying?"

"No, thank you. I'll try again later."

The light was dim but it was not yet dark. I could try a simple knock on the door. But what if she was seeing someone. What if, oh my God, Tyler was there? Or Willie?

Maybe she was seeing Willie. I got out of the car. If I walked by the house, maybe I could see if there was a light anywhere. Maybe she was on the back patio. I was almost in front of her steps when I spotted her about a block away.

She was alone, coming back from a run.

"Jack, what's the matter?" She looked worried. No cracks, no niceties. After all why would I show up on her doorstep unless someone had died or something? Her face was wet with sweat and flushed pink. She had on loose running clothes and they stuck to her sweaty form.

"I'm sorry. I didn't mean to ambush you, but I need to talk to you."

She didn't look very pleased with the idea, but I didn't budge.

"Okay. Come in. Can this wait for ten minutes while I get a shower, or do we need to talk right here on the sidewalk?"

I followed her double-knotted running shoes up the front steps and in the door. "Go ahead." I felt like such an idiot. "I'll watch your TV, okay?"

She yelled something back, it may have been fuck yourself, or make yourself at home, I'm not sure. I sat on her couch and flipped on the TV, muted the sound. She came back in a few minutes, hair in a towel, no makeup, still radiant from the run. "What happened to blondie? The State Department babe?"

"Sarah? She's just a friend."

She whooped out a laugh. "Just a friend. I saw her hanging on you. I thought she was going to climb into your drink." She sat on the end of the couch, leaned back so she could look at me. She stretched her legs out between us and her bare feet just about touched me.

"No." I made an innocent face. "She wouldn't fit through the straw."

She crossed her ankles. "So what's up, Jack?"

I was thrown off by her crack about Sarah. I didn't know where to begin. "So, what do you know about the

Cunningham investigation?"

"Come again?"

"Tyler told me Justice is closing in on him."

She patted her hair with the towel. "Okay. I guess Tyler told you so you might as well know the rest. Yes, it's true."

I wanted to believe her. I liked hearing it, whether it was true or not.

She went on, " . . . three years, at least. Almost as soon as we got in."

"He said the indictment was imminent."

She nodded. "That's true. They could indict him any time. But, they want it to be airtight, you know? Hermetically sealed. We don't want the country twisting in a two year trial. They'll spring it on him and he's going to have to resign to get a deal."

I nodded. Tried not to notice her legs. "So does Cunningham know about it?"

"Not officially. But he has to know." She shrugged. "It hasn't exactly helped relations between him and the President."

"Yeah. It explains a lot. So how long to make it airtight? How much longer?"

She went to her kitchen and brought back two Bass Ales and handed me one. "I don't know, Jack. I'm not sure they do." She put her beer on the table. "What else? I can tell there's something else you want to know."

I thought I had a better poker face. I nodded. "Crane. Did he want to release this? Or what? What was all that about? Really."

"Oh, God knows what he would say." She stood up, started for the kitchen and talked to me over her shoulder. "I already told you. He wanted Dexter to pull out. Retire. And Cunningham. He didn't care what happened to him. He didn't want to be hanging around, holding the bag, I guess." She got a pair of beer glasses, and put one on the table next to me. On a coaster.

"He may have had a point there." I poured half the beer,

waited for the foam to go down and took a drink. "You sound like you don't miss him."

"Seriously, Jack. Who could miss him?" She held her glass at an angle and poured the beer slowly, filling it perfectly with a neat, foamy head, not too thick, on top. Then she took a sip.

"I don't know, but he sure has a great reputation."

She put her beer on the end table and perched on the end of the couch again. "You have a reputation that Crane will never have. The press actually likes you. They respect you. You are professional but you are a person. They have a sense that you understand them." Her fingers wrapped around the bottom of the beer glass, but her eyes were on me. "Back when you teared up, when you talked about your father's cancer. People got that you are for real." She lifted the glass and held it in both hands. "When you took over after the Convention, you calmed the nation. Think of the panic if we had to scramble around to get the word out that Dexter was fine. The financial markets would have taken a hit—the uncertainty that could have created. I'm not exaggerating. People would have lost their jobs. That's what I care about, Jack. Keeping the country running. Not disrupting it with months of uncertainty—investigations. And no, we don't run the financial markets, but we have to try not to mess them up." She took a long sip of her beer and put it down again. "Sorry. I am wound up." She picked the damp towel up and folded it in half.

I watched her face. Her body language. Her eyes. Could she be this good an actress? "So what did Cunningham do exactly?"

"Oh, where do I start?" She slid to the seat of the couch and turned to face me. "Contractors working on his house. Sweetheart deals for land purchases. That's how he got rich, by the way. Then there are the companies that fly him around . . . you name it."

"So, I guess I still don't get why is it taking so long? It sounds like they just have to connect the dots. Show a few bank transfers and bang: They have him."

"If only. Remember, he isn't as stupid as he sometimes appears. Transfers go to his wife, his brother in law. It's a tangle. But they are close."

"Funny it hasn't leaked, don't you think?"

She frowned. "Don't get any ideas, Jack. It would lead straight back to you. And worse, it could ruin the whole thing."

"I'm not the type who leaks." I smiled angelically. "This sounds pretty good. I am relieved, if nothing else, that Tyler and the President seem appropriately horrified by the idea of Cunningham becoming President."

"Absolutely. The President didn't want to be sedated for his operation so they wouldn't have to transfer power to him."

"That says it all. I just wish he looked better. He looks like shit." I gulped some beer. "I don't remember my father looking like he does, and he was stage four."

She looked at me, tight lipped. "I'm so sorry about your dad, Jack. I think the President is just tired."

"Do you really think they can get Cunningham to resign? I can't imagine he would do that."

I drained my beer and she stood up and started for the kitchen. "How about another one?" she asked, without looking at me.

I thought a moment, not sure how to take the suggestion. She had answered my questions. "Don't you want me to run along now? I'm sorry I barged in."

She stopped. "It's okay, Jack." She turned toward me. "There aren't that many people I can let my hair down with." She took a few steps toward the door. "I'm glad you stopped by."

It looked like I missed my window of opportunity, so I stood up.

We moved toward each other and the door. "Maybe we can do this again, not during the week. After the election."

"Sure." I decided to go for a cheek kiss. Not to look too pushy. She slid her hand around the back of my neck and pulled me back in for a real kiss. A long one. Then she clicked open the door. I clicked it shut. She opened it again. I moved through it on cue and we said goodnight. It seemed like I was growing on her. I wondered if after the election things might get interesting.

Chapter Twenty-two

The next day slipped by and I went home late, as usual, and alone, as usual. I saw I had a call from another cell phone. I checked my messages, expecting, hoping perhaps, to hear Linda's voice.

Not this time. "Jack, it's Martin. Listen, I really need to talk to you."

It took me a second to realize it wasn't a White House staffer or reporter, but the Chief of Staff of my old boss, Harrow. Poor Martin. He must have finally gotten the boot. I called the number he left, which was not the office number.

He answered on one ring.

"Martin, it's Jack. What's up?"

"Jack, thanks for calling back."

"Of course. Are you okay?"

He sounded like that was a weird question. "Sure. I'm fine. Listen. I need to talk to you. Um . . . Could we meet?"

"Martin, what the hell is it? Did Harrow fire you?"

"No. It's just that I have some information for you. I just need like, ten minutes or so. But I don't want to come to your office. I know that would compromise you."

"Okay. I'm not coming to yours. Even if I wanted to, it would take too long. There's too much going on to be away for that long."

"Right. I understand."

Both of us pondered the problem silently for a moment.

"Okay, what if I drive over, call you when I get as close

as I can . . ."

"Sure. That should work. We can pull over, talk. How about eleven? Tomorrow morning."

"Okay."

"And aim for 17th and Constitution. Call me on my cell when you get there and I'll walk over. You can get a block closer, but you might not be able to pull over. Martin, what kind of car do you have?"

"Lincoln Towne Car. Black."

"Right. Okay. I'll know how to spot you." I closed the phone and went to bed.

In the morning, it hit me as I got a shower. Harrow had a Lincoln. Martin must be borrowing it. Probably supposed to take it to buy gas or get it washed.

I got to work early and when it was close to eleven, I was glad for the chance to go for a walk. I figured Martin was trying to get a job, trying to get away from Harrow. He needed to talk, not just a phone call, maybe hand me his résumé. It was a pain in the ass that he was so paranoid. But Harrow really could be such a vindictive SOB. I couldn't blame him and of course I would help him. I mean, Christ, Harrow had him out gassing his car. What kind of job was that? My cell phone rang and a moment later, I saw the car, which pulled over to the corner where I stood.

The windows were tinted, and frankly, I really wasn't looking that hard. I opened the door, smiling, and Martin had a sort of worried but agreeable grin back at me. An instant later or almost simultaneously I noticed the back seat. I was already sliding in the front, smiling, and now I had this feeling I was being kidnapped. I didn't close the door, debating whether to get out again. Because in the back seat was Congressman Greg Harrow and his redheaded girlfriend.

I was speechless. I just stared at Martin. Then I thought, why not be civil? "Are we dropping you two somewhere?" Okay, maybe that wasn't completely civil.

"Jack, we just want to talk. I knew if I told you, you would never meet with us. Come on . . . Ten minutes."

"You got that right, Martin," I said without really looking at them. Okay, what the hell, I thought. Get it over with.

Martin put his blinker on, ready to pull out.

"Wait a sec, Martin. Just stay here. We don't really need to drive around, right? I really do only have ten minutes."

Martin glanced around at Harrow, who said nothing. Martin shrugged and put the car back in park, turned off the signal. "Jack, we want you to have the full story. You aren't getting it from State."

I suppressed a roll of the eyes.

Harrow was silent.

Martin went on: "Our government is covering up their atrocities, Jack. I'm not talking about marginal activity."

The anger was bubbling up inside me. Martin gets me out here on a ruse—I come because of our friendship. He's being forced to do it by Harrow, who sits like a thug, like some gangster in the back seat. I interrupted. "Martin, it sure is good to see you. I have to say, I don't think your sources are any better than mine, and I don't want to sit here and be lectured, I opened the door, and the redhead started to speak—yell, actually.

"You are no better than a butcher!"

I'm used to a fair amount of flack, but this took me aback. "Excuse me?" I asked. "This from a terrorist? Or are you just a supporter of terrorists?"

"Your country is letting the murderers get nuclear weapons—they are helping them in fact. Don't you care about this?"

"So are we supposed to shut down every nuclear reactor in the world, is that it?"

"That's just the beginning. They are going village by village and murdering the men. Men and boys." At this she started to weep.

I know I should have jumped out then. Harrow had his hand on her arm, and I actually looked at him for the first time. He had lost about twenty pounds, he was shrunken and at the same time puffy and pink, especially his face, like he was drinking even more heavily than usual. His eyes were embedded deep in his face, red and now also watery. If he didn't have such a good haircut or nice coat, he could pass for a homeless man, begging on the street. I fought it hard, but I was feeling sorry for him. I clicked the door shut.

His raspy voice started, "Jack. I know we've had our differences . . ." He shook his head, "Her brother, her father." The redhead held up her hand like now she was composed but Harrow went on, anger building in his voice. "And, she's had her life threatened, you know. We were probably followed here."

"I'm sorry," she squeaked. "I'm sorry, Jack. I have no right to yell at you."

"It's okay. I'm used to it."

She handed me a fat brown accordion folder.

"I don't know what I can do, since, as you point out, our State Department is already way out there on this. I can't actually make policy, you know?" I opened the folder, thinking it might have something that would set off the metal detector if I tried to take it back to the White House. Like a bomb. I thumbed through it: a neat stack of reports, photos. "Can I ask a question? Why isn't, say, the United Nations, or some other group doing anything on this?"

Martin answered: "Unfortunately, most groups, and countries for that matter, wait until long after the atrocities have been committed before they find the courage to do anything."

"I guess I'm not really clear on what I can do with this. I have nothing to do with policy."

"You are our only hope," she whispered.

"Oh. Okay." I looked at Harrow again, seeing the concern on his face and I had a small flash of what I must have seen to have taken the job with him in the first place, those long years ago.

I waited another moment but nobody said anything. I started to get out of the car again. "Good to see you, Martin." The redhead handed me two photos. Tears spilled out of her eyes and she didn't say anything.

"Her family," Harrow said softly. "Thank you for coming, Jack . . . Apologize for the false pretenses."

I nodded at them and got out, hoisting the huge folder under one arm, carrying the pictures in my other hand. I had about two blocks to go. I thought I heard the car pull out behind me and after I crossed the street, I saw a trash can up ahead. I looked around carefully and couldn't see the car but couldn't tell for sure if it had pulled out or not. I shifted the folder as I got close to the trash can. But I couldn't do it. The pictures were stuck to my hand and I wanted to toss them in. I couldn't look at them. What the hell was I going to do with them? Take them back to my office I guess. Keep them for a few days then throw them away. I slid the pictures in my coat pocket and got my badge out. I was coming up to the southwest gate.

I got back to my office, closed the door and went to my desk. I had a mountain of information to digest. But I couldn't concentrate. I was haunted by her face, her expression. The pictures. It was real, not a video or a press report. I knew I needed to shake it off. This wasn't my problem. State was handling it. We couldn't scold the government in public, or in private for that matter, and not hurt our companies. And even that was an over-simplification. The last thing Lixubistan needed was a decade of instability while they work out who has the biggest guns. I knew all that, and yet, I couldn't stop caring, worrying about the people in the photos, and their families. Wondering if there is a limit to what we can let happen.

I called Linda. "This morning I got these pictures." I slid them out of my pocket and laid them on my desk. "This woman . . . Harrow's friend, the redhead. She said they were her family. These appalling, nauseating pictures of what happened to them."

"How do you know they aren't fakes?" She sounded impatient. "Please tell me you aren't losing it, Jack. How do you know who they were? Couldn't they have been killed by the rebels? Maybe they weren't even dead."

"They were dead. Unless you know of some way to live without a head."

"Oh, please. Jack, you really have to get a grip. You do press. You are not Secretary of State. I mean, can you handle it, Jack?" I could hear her breath. In a softer tone, she went on: "You can't overreact on every issue. Or try to inject yourself. Come on, Jack. Only a few more weeks."

She was right and I knew it. I took some deep breaths and went on with my reading, my conference call with the campaign, the gaggle and the back to back meetings. Around six I was called over to Tyler's office. I wondered what could be so important that Linda wouldn't just tell me. I wished I hadn't called her about Lixubistan earlier in the day sounding like such a wimp.

Tyler greeted me with a warm smile and waved me to the couch. He got up from his desk, took off his reading glasses, laid them on a stack of papers and sat in the chair opposite me on the couch. "Jack, you probably already know I've been interviewed for several backgrounders on the way the Convention was handled. And the cancer announcement. Two different journalists are writing books about the campaign, and clearly, you are going to come off as one of the big heroes."

"Thanks." I knew that wasn't why he called me over, but I reflexively started to offer some denials for the sake of modesty.

Tyler waved me off. "Right. You realize, they are going to study what you did, how you handled your job, in colleges and universities across the land. Justifiably."

"I'm not sure about that."

He smiled at my modesty, and went on: "I wanted to have a conversation with you about how things are going to be after the election. How we want to run things. People are already starting to speculate, you know." He kept eye contact, eyes like drills. "You are on the young side to do this job. I know you have done a lot of public service, and haven't had a chance to make your way in the private sector. Make some real money."

I swallowed. Was I getting cut loose, and he was trying to tell me he was doing a favor. "That's true." I discretely tried to breathe. Deep breaths. "Are you bringing Mackenzie, or someone from his shop in?"

"No. That's what I wanted to talk to you about. The President wants you, Jack." He paused to let the words sink in. "He wants to give you full rein. Mackenzie does want to go back to the private sector, but that's not the point. You earned it. You have done a tremendous job." Then he smiled at me, waited for me to answer.

What was I going to say? "Thank you. That's great, sir." I smiled broadly, trying to think. I wanted to ask about access to . . . no—insist—on access to the President. "I'm glad . . ."

He interrupted: "Before I forget, the President wants you to go with him to the World Series Saturday night. Opening game."

I nodded my head very slowly, like there might be a punch line. I'm not really sure what I did or how I looked but I kept thinking he was going to tell me it was some kind of quasi campaign event, and I would have to hold hands with two hundred old fraternity brothers of the President. But he didn't. He got a very amused smile watching me process what he said with my little brain and that just added to the suspicion he was going to say "gotcha" any minute.

"That would be great." I nodded, but not too eagerly—I didn't want to seem too anxious. I was floored. But I managed to remember what had been keeping me awake at night. Any second he was going to stand up and walk me to the door.

Right on cue, he stood.

I stood too, and looked him in the eye. "Before I forget, sir, I did want to remind you of my concerns . . ." I watched to see how he would receive this.

He was almost to the door, but he stopped and looked at

me again. "Of course," he nodded earnestly.

"I really need some more detail on the President's condition. And Lixubistan. We need to make clear what our intentions are there. I know all about the contracts. But you have a PR nightmare in the making over there."

"Done and done. I've thought about what you said—I think you make a good point, Jack. And, I think the President should make a statement about our human rights concerns there."

I nodded, surprised the words "human rights" had come from his lips.

"Listen, the advance people will be in touch about the game." He put his hand on my shoulder and walked me toward the door.

When I got back to my office there was a message to meet Evan and Bob for a drink that night at the bar near my apartment. I finished up as fast as I could and left after eight. I was relieved. I knew I couldn't tell them too much but I felt like celebrating.

Evan wasn't there yet, but Bob was waiting, scotch in hand when I arrived, about 8:15 p.m. The bar was pretty empty, as I had hoped it would be. I got a beer and we took our drinks to a table off to the side of the bar. I wanted to wait for Evan to tell the big news, so I made small talk, which wasn't easy with Bob. "Bob. Last time we got together, you turned the fire hose on me, remember?

Bob squinted at me but didn't answer.

"Just wanted to say thanks." I scooted my chair forward. "I'm beginning to get it, I think."

Bob gave me a bored look. A clever, cutting remark was on the tip of his tongue. Evan joined us just as I was draining my beer. We got another round and Evan asked for a menu. "Did you guys order any food?" Evan asked, probably not expecting an answer.

"Sure. We had steak dinners while we waited for you," Bob said with a big disingenuous smile.

"Oh. Well, I'm hungry. I'm going to get a burger or something," Evan said and went to the bar.

"Get some nachos," Bob called.

I sucked on my beer and waited for him to come back to the table.

Evan carried his beer back and dragged the chair out with his foot. Before I could say anything, he folded his hands. "I think you two should buy my drinks." He waited, sipping his beer through a smug smile: "I got them."

Bob actually grinned. "No shit. Where are they?"

"Behind the dugout on the first base side."

Bob's grin spread. I thought his face might break.

"In a box. Of course."

Bob's eyes closed and he threw his head back and yelled. "Yes!"

Evan looked over at me, waiting for me to do handsprings. "What's the matter, Jack?"

Bob stopped laughing and stared at me.

"Nothing. I mean, that's great, Evan. The thing is, I have to. Um. I've been asked to . . ." I realized it hadn't been released that the President was going to the game. "I don't think I'm going to be able to go."

"Why not?"

"I have to go, um, someplace."

There was a long silence while they worked it out. "With the President?" Evan's lips were parted. Eyes wide.

Bob leaned in and whispered. "Is the President going to the game, Jack?"

"Shhhh!" I patted the air.

Evan's eyes were as big as the worn out coasters on the table. "Holy shit. Are you going to the fucking World Series game with the President?"

"I have something I have to do. That's all I can say. If it has something to do with the President's schedule, you two know that would be classified."

Bob shook his head. "Do you believe this guy, Evan? A few months ago, he's out of work, out of money. Now he's dumping us to go to the World Series with the President."

"I guess you've been able to resolve your concerns about the Vice President then, Jack?" Evan exchanged smirks with Bob.

I guess I tried not to smile. I looked down at my beer and tried.

"He knows something, Evan."

"Is that true, Jack? Come on. No holding out."

I shrugged. Tried to look casual. "I got the job. After the election." They looked at me, puzzled expressions, and I waited a moment, then went on. "Press Secretary."

"You dumb bastard. You mean you've been sitting there holding that in all this time."

Evan raised his beer and tapped mine. "Congratulations Jack. You deserve it. You earned it."

Bob clinked his glass on mine, still shaking his head. "I'm impressed. Worried about the nation, but, I have to hand it to you . . ."

"And I do know something else. I shouldn't tell you, but I have to tell somebody. About Cunningham." I watched their faces. They leaned in.

"Under investigation," I whispered.

There was a pause, then Bob sat back and laughed. "Who told you that?"

"Shhhhh. I'm not at liberty to say."

Evan leaned in, whispering. "Who's doing it?"

I looked around. The bartender was at the other end. "Justice. And nobody knows this."

"I bet they don't." Bob had a very annoying smirk. He crossed his arms.

I didn't like the way he said that. "What do you mean?"

"Nothing." He shook his head. "Nobody knows? Cut me a break. That's the oldest rumor in town, right after Betsy Ross slept with George Washington."

Evan asked, "Is that true? I never heard that."

Bob looked at Evan and shook his head. "He's a smart son of a bitch. They've never been able to get him on anything."

"I thought they vetted him when they picked him. They picked him over John Cook because he was supposed to be Mr. Clean."

"That's what I said. He's smart. Nothing sticks."

"You're shitting me, Bob."

"I wish I were."

The bartender brought over Evan's burger and the nachos. I wasn't hungry anymore.

Chapter Twenty-three

The odds were, I might not get much of a chance for face time with the President at the game. I knew that. I probably would not get a chance to nudge him toward more disclosure, to open up to me, or even to somehow restrain Cunningham. But I thought, worst case, I could cement my position, get them to trust me more. To like me. And that could pay off later. I would have been crazy not to go.

Let's face it, as a lifelong Orioles fan, I was excited enough they were in the World Series. We were going to drive up to the game early. The President would arrive separately. Probably helicopter in.

I drove over with Tyler in a government car. He seemed more solicitous than usual, but still pretty distant, flipping through work the whole way over. I couldn't really find an opening to bring up Cunningham again. It was strange to see him out of a suit. I wondered if he had someone run out to the store and buy him a polo shirt for the occasion.

We pulled up to the VIP entrance to Camden Yards, which was crawling with Secret Service and police. One of our advance guys walked us to an elevator I never knew existed. The area had been secured for the President and the Secret Service already had a presence along the curved hallway. When we got to the box, an agent handed us small pins to put on our shirts to show that we were allowed to be close to the President. The smell of barbeque filled the box. The rest of the food was in covered chafing dishes. Crab cakes, and the usual ballpark fare, plus a large bowl of salad. Tyler picked up a plate and helped himself to a crab cake and some coleslaw. The air conditioning felt good because it was unusually warm for October, although the evening would be cooler. I pushed through the doors to the seats in the box and checked out the field. The lights glared over us and beyond, I could see the blimp hovering. We were late for batting practice. The groundskeepers were grooming the field, running around the bases pulling straw mats behind them to smooth out the footprints. The excitement in the stands was building. The vendors were strapping on their boxes of food or drink. People in the stands craned their necks looking back at me, to see if I might be recognizable or important looking. I looked down to the right, off the first base line for a glimpse of Bob and Evan, but the stands were filling up and I couldn't make them out in the sea of orange.

Back inside I could see that nobody else had arrived. Tyler was sitting on the couch eating, and the agents were standing near the door. I slid the glass door open and went in, trying to decide whether to eat or wait. I decided to follow Tyler's example, filled up a plate and sat across from him. "Who else is coming?" I asked.

"We kept it small, Jack. This is one event the President actually enjoys and we didn't feel like we wanted to make him work that hard. Just a little fun for all of us. For you, after all your hard work . . ." he said, pushing some coleslaw with his fork.

I nodded appreciatively.

Just before the opening game ceremony, his Secret Service detail, the military aide, with the well-known nuclear football, the White House Photographer, David Rossi and a couple of other aides burst into the room. A moment later, surrounded by more agents, the President followed. He came through the door, smiling and crumbled to the couch next to Tyler. His face was flushed, but not in a healthy way. He was breathing hard. An aide handed him a glass of ice water but he waived it off. He sat with his eyes closed. Another aide stood at the doors, watching the field. "They're getting ready to start, sir."

The President stood up, like someone was inflating him with an air hose. He started toward the doors, looking around. "Come on, Jack," he said. The aide slid open the doors and he went out with me behind him. The agents had positioned themselves around the perimeter of the outer box and most likely had counterparts all around the stadium. I followed the President and stood a few feet behind him, off to the side. He moved down the center aisle to the edge of the box. As soon as he was in position, they put the camera on him, and he was on the Jumbotron screen, smiling and waving. The crowd reacted with a thunderous ovation that lasted several minutes. The stands twinkled with flashes going off, and the twinkling continued on and on. Did those holding the cameras not know the flashes were useless at this distance or did they not know how to turn them off? Or were they a kind of visual applause the President must get all the time and never, never tire of. Finally he gave another wave and stepped up to sit in the second row of seats, on the aisle. He pointed at me and nodded to the chair next to him. I slipped quickly into the chair, and when I looked up at the Jumbotron again, there I was. I hoped Evan and Bob were looking. Maybe they would snap a picture.

Up close, his smile was real but his face was strained and tired.

We watched the opening ceremony and Rossi came out and took some photos of us. After a few minutes, an aide tapped him on the shoulder and he slowly rose to go back inside. He sat in a comfortable chair in the corner and I could see one of the owners of the Orioles come in and shake his hand. He stood up and Rossi crouched nearby, taking pictures. Tyler flanked the door, shook hands and chatted. I could see others waiting in the hall.

There was a procession of VIPs who stopped by the box. In between, the President closed his eyes and rested, or watched the game on the TV monitors.

One of the aides came out and sat on the other side of me. The air cooled but the rain held off. And it was a great game. Gabriel pitched the first six innings, then they put Clayton in to close. Randall's streak continued as he homered his first at bat. They were tied in the eighth inning, with Reed on first and Randall up to bat. I was sure we were going to see history: He was going for Mickey Mantle's World Series home run record. He had fifteen now. But then, he did the unexpected. A sacrifice bunt. The crowd was stunned. But it worked. Reed rounded second and made it to third while Randall was out at first. Thomas was up next and hit a fly to the right field corner, caught just inside of the foul line. Reed tagged up and slid into home. Safe.

The crowd roared. While I was watching, I didn't see the President come back out and stand next to me, this time with an Orioles hat on. We were all standing and the President was on camera again, waved, doffed his hat. When the Braves were up, Dexter put his hand on my shoulder, "Jack, I have to go back. There are thunderstorms over Washington so we have to motorcade. You can stay and ride back with the others or you can go now with me."

I couldn't believe Tyler was actually going to stay and watch the game, that he was going to let me ride by myself with the President. I wondered if it could be part of an elaborate plan to schmooze me, but the idea seemed far-fetched. I was going to ride back alone with the President. My doubts and concerns and reservations seemed like a touch of indigestion.

As we walked to the limo, and I thought it might be the chance I was waiting for. The driver held the door for the President and he got in the limo. I went around to the other side, opened the door and crouched to get in. Should I sit in the fold down backward facing seats, and be across from him? Before I could decide, the President motioned to the seat next to him. The driver closed my door and got in the front. The Secret Service lead agent, Sean Peterson, sat in front with the driver. The glass panel was up. Total privacy. The motorcade started and the President turned down the interior lights. He reclined his seat slightly. I wondered if he was going to sleep all the way back to the White House. But he pushed some buttons and asked the driver to put the game on. A TV screen rose from the console. The Braves were still up, only one out. By the time we cleared the Baltimore beltway, it was over. Orioles had the first game.

It was dim in the car and the position of his seat made it hard to see his face. I thought his eyes were closed and I assumed he was drifting off to sleep. But he was awake. "Great game. I can't believe Randall made that play. That was really something. Sacrificing yourself for the team."

I looked over. He faced straight ahead, not toward me, and his eyes were open. "I hope he comes back next year. He should have another year or two, I think," he said softly.

"He still seems to have it. As long as he takes care of himself." I straightened out my legs. "It would be pretty hard to let go of the sound of those crowds cheering."

"I'm sure," he agreed. I could hear the leather on his seat groan as he turned his head toward me. "Phil tells me he's talked to you about staying on after the election."

"Yes, sir."

"I'm glad to hear it. There's one more bump in the road we will need you to handle. Although I don't expect it to be an issue until after the election."

"Cunningham? And the scandal? What's the timing?"

I heard him exhale, maybe a sigh. "We still don't know. The investigation is progressing, but he has been very careful, as you would expect." Then his voice became very soft and sympathetic. "Jack, I know you have first-hand experience with illness, with your father . . ."

So the bump was going to be his health, as I feared. I interrupted. "Sir, I haven't been completely honest about my father, I'm afraid." Dexter's eyes closed, yet I knew he was still listening. I went on, ". . . My father didn't die from cancer."

I could see his eyes open. "I know," He said. "That's

one of the things that impressed us about you. A lot of people don't know how to keep a secret. Especially in this town."

I waited, almost dazed by the idea that they knew. They knew everything.

He looked down a moment, then turned in his seat so he could look straight into my eyes. "That isn't it, Jack. I wish it were." He sighed again. "I have a heart problem. It's completely manageable, they tell me." He paused. "I had a procedure after the Convention. Angioplasty. And I am being treated with drugs right now. After the election, I might need a bypass. I'm sure you already know dozens of men who have had this done and go on to live a long life. My prognosis is no different. I assure you. It turns out that's why I passed out at the Convention."

I think I managed to keep my mouth from dropping open. I didn't answer, I just looked back into his eyes, and let it sink in. I couldn't speak.

"Are you alright?" the President smiled.

I tried to breathe. It brought back when my father told me he had cancer. When I found my voice I mumbled, "I think we need to release this." But I said it so softly, he couldn't hear me. So I said it again, louder.

"No. Jack we're not going to," he said, shaking his head. "Here's why. There is no guarantee that if we do that, the public will have time to understand that this is not a serious health problem. I am a little tired, but I promise you, I am fine now." He eased back into his seat and closed his eyes again, but just for a moment. "If we release it, given the problems with our vice president, I think there is a serious chance we could drop in the polls and not be able to overcome it. Particularly since I have to take it a little easy. I mean, I can campaign, but I can't do any of these 24-hour blitzes and such."

"We have the cover of the cancer. You already have a fairly light schedule."

"Yes. I know. And believe me, Jack, I thought long and hard about running. Maybe I made a mistake in not pulling out a year ago. I was beginning these talks with the Chinese. I felt then, as I do now, that if I can straighten out our relationship with them, and put things on a right path, that will be good for the country and an important legacy. And I also knew, if I pulled out, there was a very large chance, because of my popularity, that Cunningham would have gotten the nomination and cruised into the job on my coattails."

"I see your point. But couldn't you just dump him? Just tell him he's off the ticket?"

"Slippery slope, Jack. If I did that, I'd have to have a reason. The investigation would come out and I would be tainted by it. My presidency would have been colored by scandal. After all I've worked for, my life's work would be minimized in favor of a description about Cunningham's shenanigans. And whether or not we covered it up."

"I guess that answers the question of why not get a leak out of Justice."

"Exactly. Think what that would do to my legacy. I would spend whatever time I have left in office answering questions about how long I have known about the investigation."

We rode in silence in the dim light. I squinted to see his face, and let out a long breath. "But there is another way this could play out. Allegations of a massive cover-up of your health problems. We don't want that. All the good things would be overshadowed by this. Your health issues will come out after the election and it will be clear that this was withheld."

"No." He shrugged. "It won't. I'll check into Walter Reed for tests, and it will be explained that I need a bypass. Happens all the time. Cunningham will resign, be led out the backdoor and forgotten. And remember Jack, there is no law against keeping my health information private."

The car pulled up to a stop by the White House entrance. An aide opened the door. Dexter held up a finger and he closed it again.

"But what if? What if something happens on the

operating table? We don't want to think of this, but what if you don't make it?" I swallowed. I hated to be so direct. "They don't have Cunningham yet and from what I hear, I'm not sure they will be able to nail him." I shook my head. "President Cunningham. Can you live with that? Can you live through a second term, knowing that you earned it by . . ." I chose my words carefully . . . "withholding this information from the American people. And if Cunningham is not indicted, you will not get rid of him. He could get the nomination in four years and follow you into office himself."

The aide opened the door again. "Sorry sir, there's a call for you inside."

The President patted me on the knee. "Thanks, Jack. It was fun."

"Thank you, Mr. President."

I climbed out the other side and went to my car.

It was after midnight when I got home. I tossed and turned for a while. Maybe the President was right. Angioplasty is no big deal. Bypass surgery is very common. It explained so much: why he looked so tired, for example. I woke up early and couldn't stop thinking about it. It was clearer than ever, painfully so, why I was hired, why I was there. But it is true that I never realized until then what I had done. How I had spun my own life. And my own father's death. I never thought of it that way. And I was in on this, now. They expected me to keep on spinning. I was on the inside, like it or not.

In the morning Evan called to say that he had John's boat for one more Sunday before the end of the season. I wanted to tell someone, but I knew I shouldn't. So I shouldn't go, because I wasn't going to be able to resist. Evan said it would be a little chilly out on the water, but I said I'd go.

The sun was out when we started and I felt its warmth despite the cool air. We went upriver, under the bridges to the far side of Theodore Roosevelt Island and Evan let down the anchor. Bob opened a beer and handed it to me. The trees had turned and we could see a few hikers on the Island.

We talked about the game, and the time slipped by. They wanted details on my night. I told them about the box, about the ride up with Tyler. They teased me about being on the Jumbotron.

"Did you go back with Tyler?"

I shook my head. "I rode back with the President. Alone. But I almost wish I hadn't."

Stunned silence. Then Evan looked at Bob, "He's kidding, right?"

Bob put his hand to his eyes, like he had a headache. "I don't think so."

"I found something out. The other shoe has dropped. It isn't just cancer. There's something else . . ." I couldn't decide what to tell them or whether to just tell them what I knew. "I'm trying to figure out if I have to do something or say something."

"Say something? Do something?" Bob said, mocking me.

"I'm not joking, you know . . ."

Bob held up his hand. "Don't tell us what it is, Jack. Don't."

"I have a conscience, believe it or not . . ."

Bob shook his head and held his hand out to stop me from going on. "I'm sure you do. Good for you. But remember, you also have a job. A job you would have cut your nuts off to have a few months ago." Then he bore down on me: With the meanest voice I ever heard coming out of his head, he went on, "They trust you. You told them you were loyal. John Cook personally vouched for your loyalty. So, wait until the last hour of the last day you want to work there, Jack. That's when to say something. Do something. No." He shook his head for emphasis. "The last minute you want to work as a flack for anyone, anywhere. Do you think for an instant they are going to change direction now because you are squeamish?" He squinted at me like I just pissed on his shoe. "If you think there is anything you can say that will convince them, when they are twelve points ahead in the polls, to shoot themselves in the foot, you are fucking nuts. You will be out. They will freeze dry you until they can roll you out into a ditch someplace in the middle of the night. And nobody is going to care and nobody is going to say, 'Poor Jack, he just tried to do what is right.'"

"Okay." I wanted him to stop but he went on.

"Forget ever eating lunch in this town again. They will poison the air you breathe. Your name will be synonymous with traitor." He paused. "Your friends, Jack. What about us? What about John Cook? How many powerful friends do you have who can take on Tyler? Your friends won't be able to save you and you know, why the hell should we? So if you want to self-destruct, go ahead . . . And you know every word of this already."

His words hung in the air. I sat in silence, in conflict with myself but unconvinced.

Evan was a little more sympathetic, but not much. "Jack, it might be uncomfortable. But I agree. It's about loyalty. You got this information in confidence. They trusted you."

"And I trusted them. I mean, there are certain lines you assume your boss won't cross."

"But can you violate their trust?" Evan took a breath, shaking his head. "Even if everything you think might happen comes true, you are like the priest or the lawyer. You work for them, you have gained their trust. That's the greater betrayal, if you ask me."

"Evan, it's me who's lied. My mouth. My face. My words. I'm a person, too. I have a conscience."

Evan folded his arms and looked at Bob, who couldn't wait to chime in. "Yeah. But didn't you rent it out?"

A low blow. I looked at Evan. "Is that what John would say?"

"I don't know. Maybe. One thing I do know, John wouldn't tell you to do anything pointless. He's a little more pragmatic these days. There's no point in going public if nobody will corroborate your story."

Bob nodded. "The only person who might back you up is the traitor Crane. I suppose you could join up with him."

A speedboat went by and we started rocking in the wake. Evan's bottle spilled and he scrambled to clean it up. It was time to go back anyway, and I was glad. I couldn't wait to get to the marina. They were both still mad at me. I couldn't shake the feeling that I was making a huge mistake. I didn't know what I was going to do but by the time I got back to my place, I had resolved to become my father's son again.

After my anger cooled, I had to admit they had a point: There was no point in just going public. Sure, I could get the President's health into the headlines, but they would just bring out some doctors to refute whatever I said. The remaining story would be on whether I had some nefarious motive for spreading lies about the President, or whether I had simply cracked up. Either way, I would be done in Washington. But Bob's sarcastic reminder about Crane rang in my ears. What if I could convince Crane to join forces with me. If two of us raised questions on the President's health, we would be listened to. I decided to chance it.

Of course it was not like Crane was going to take my call. Maybe I would have to run into him. Ambush him, if you will. But first I would do the polite thing and call. I told his assistant I wanted to see him. She called back and told me to come by his office the next day.

The idea of going public was unnerving, to say the least, but with Crane's experience and credibility, it could work. Crane had been a bastard to me, but he was good. I never said he wasn't good.

I took a cab from the White House to his office on 19th Street. He didn't keep me waiting this time. His secretary recognized me and alerted him right away that I was there.

"What's on your mind, Jack?" He was pushed back in his chair, appraising me.

I sat in the chair across from him. "I just wanted to apologize face to face."

He just looked at me, expressionless, so I went on.

"I didn't realize what was going on. I had no idea. Now, I don't know what to do. I'm being used, I realize."

Still frozen, but eyes narrowed.

"I wonder if I could get your advice. I mean . . ."

He slid his chair up to the desk and stopped looking at me. Looked down at his desk and listened.

"I also wondered, if you are in agreement, if you would consider going public with me. If two of us . . ."

He looked up from his desk, eyes squinting now, like he was aiming a gun. "This is about what I expected from you." He slowly shook his head. "No, I don't want to give you any advice. I certainly would not go public with you, whatever that means. I wouldn't go to lunch with you, for that matter."

I just sat there and took it like a bunny rabbit about to get eaten by the wolf.

He went on: "No, I don't want to be a part of your stunt. Your lame grandstanding. Setting yourself up as a whistle blower. What a laugh. You were hired to be the whore, and you've been a splendid one, haven't you? Now, you want me to turn into a Judas, too. I wish I could say I was surprised."

I was stunned and immobilized at his tirade at first, but by the time he told me to quit the second time, I was heading for the door. Just before I went through it, I turned to him, ready to challenge him, make some major insult, some profound dig. But all I could think about was how right he was.

Out on the sidewalk in front of his building, it looked like it was going to rain. I started walking back to the White House. I had hoped Crane would know what to do. So if he wouldn't help, I'd have to do it myself. I didn't know what else to do. I wasn't going to give up.

I stopped at a drugstore and bought some plain envelopes. After everyone in the press office left, I could get a SECRET cable from Lixubistan and copy it. A big no-no. Jail time if I get caught. I could type out a note to go with it, about the President's health. I wanted something on Cunningham, but I had nothing in writing. No proof of the investigation. I could see myself sending it to the home addresses of the two most aggressive reporters I knew. They would know it was a leak by the Secret cable and that they should check it out. I could drive the envelopes down to the post office at the corner of North Capitol Street, away from the White House but just a few blocks from the Capitol. The postmark would suggest the leak had come from somebody on the Hill.

But with only a few days left until the election, would they be able to corroborate this? Some press wouldn't wait to corroborate it. They would take it at face value and let someone else verify it. And that would lead straight back to me. Instead of doing the right thing, I would be portrayed as a turncoat. That would be the story. My motives would be questioned.

So by the time I got back to the OEOB, I gave up that idea. But I was still determined to find a way. Then I remembered something Bob had said about respecting my creativity. That was the answer. I was going to have to get creative.

Chapter Twenty-four

About ten days before the debate, I called Roger Castleton. I had known Roger from way back, from when I worked for John. He was as balanced as any reporter, and his Sunday interview show was top rated most weeks. I told Roger I might have some news for him and that it would be exclusive. It was always tricky to give something to only one outlet. That was just insurance so he didn't bump me if something interesting happened before Sunday.

I had an idea that might work, but I still had my doubts. I could say that I had misgivings about my plans, that I needed to talk them over with trusted friends, but maybe I was just scared. I already knew what Bob thought. If he found out what I was planning, he would probably try to lock me in a closet or something. I wanted to see Evan. Evan and I thought more alike. I didn't really want the whole world to know what I was up to, but I trusted Evan. And I wanted to talk to John Cook. Without John, I wouldn't be in the White House. He vouched for me. I owed him. And, I knew I could count on John to tell me the truth.

It was Saturday morning, the day before I was scheduled for Castleton's show. Evan was hunched over his desk, the afternoon sun streaming in behind him, reading a stack of papers. He didn't even look up when I stood in the doorway, so I knocked on the door jamb and startled him.

"God, what are you doing sneaking around here? Are you helping the CIA now?"

"I see you are attempting to earn your salary for a change. Very commendable."

He leaned way back in his chair and reached his arms up over his head in a long stretch. "You missed John. He's on a run. Why don't we go in his office."

I would have suggested it myself if he hadn't, because Evan's office didn't have the kind of privacy I wanted. It didn't matter that there was nobody else there. "Got any Diet Cokes?" I knew that was all he had, and I was thirsty.

"Sure. I'll give you some of my private stock."

I followed him to the refrigerator and then to John's office where he sat on the couch, put his feet on the coffee table and cracked open his soda. "So what's the latest? I'm afraid to ask."

"Okay." I sighed. Where to begin? "Okay, just between us, right?"

"Of course, Jack." He sounded a little indignant.

"I mean I haven't told Bob a lot of this. You know how Bob thinks . . ."

"Sometimes he has a point."

"Right. But you won't share any of this."

"That's what I said." Evan fixed his eyes on me. "I have to admit I thought about what you said. I think Bob was pretty hard on you . . ." Then he caught himself. "Go on . . ."

"Okay. Well, first I went to Crane. He essentially threw me out of his office and spat on me."

"Bastard."

"Right. I know I shouldn't have been surprised, but I thought, you know, we were after the same thing . . ." I shrugged. "So, then, well . . . I thought about leaking. Big, major leaks." I hated saying it out loud. I wasn't above leaks, of course, but never to the detriment of my own boss.

Evan pulled his feet in and leaned up. "And?"

"Nothing. I chickened out. There was no way to do it that didn't lead back to me. And no way for them to corroborate the story before the election."

Evan relaxed into the sofa and propped up his feet again.

"I guess that's right."

"So where does that leave me?"

Evan took a long breath, sipped his Diet Coke. "I don't know. Press Secretary to the leader of the Free World, I guess."

"Coasting along in my dream job . . ."

"Yep."

"I guess I'd be an idiot to blow that, right?"

"Duh."

"Well, what would you do, Evan? Let's say the President has a heart condition. A serious one."

Evan nodded, closed his eyes. "Shit."

"Exactly. And, I bring up Lixubistan only to illustrate how unfit Cunningham is to be President. His behavior has been disturbing, but what he said about Lixubistan getting nuclear weapons . . .It shows how unfit he is . . ."

"Okay, okay. Agreed."

"I didn't even tell you . . . Get this. Remember how I told you Tyler said Justice is investigating him, right? He also said they were going to dump him and name John."

"What?"

"Remember? I told you—he said Cunningham was under investigation. That he was going to have to resign? Tyler told me that John would be Dexter's choice to take his place."

"When did this happen?"

"Chill out, Evan. He made it up to appease me. Don't you see? They're trying to keep me quiet until after the election."

"Oh."

"I think that's why I got to go to the baseball game . . ." I stopped when I noticed the hallway door open. John pushed through, back from his run, big circles of sweat on his shirt, his hair wet.

He waved, stepped into his bathroom and came out wiping his head and neck with a towel. "Jack, how are you?"

"Senator." We shook hands.

"I need some water." He went toward the office

refrigerator. "You guys need anything?"

"No," Evan called back.

John sat with us, perched on the edge of the chair seat so his damp skin wouldn't stick to the leather. "So, Jack. Looks like you're cruising to an easy victory."

Evan and I looked at each other. "Looks like." I said, perhaps sounding a little sullen.

"Jack is worried about the President, Senator."

"And my immortal soul."

John looked at me quizzically.

Evan said. "He thinks he's been lying. They've been lying to him, and he's been lying."

John looked at the floor, thinking. "About Dexter's cancer?"

I nodded. "His cancer is gone, at least for now. But he has a heart condition. Remember when he fainted at the Convention? I just found out—he actually had an angioplasty at Walter Reed."

"Are you serious?"

"That's why Crane quit. He wanted him to pull out of the election. But Dexter thought, so close to the election . . ."

"Cunningham would have been the nominee . . ." Evan finished my sentence.

"Not just the nominee. You know he would have won."

"I'm not so sure."

"Oh yeah. His favorables are way up. He was seen as so supportive of the President during the cancer announcement. At least that's what everybody thought. But can you stand the idea of his being President?"

John looked doubtful, crossed his arms. Evan shook his head. But they didn't say anything.

"Neither can I. But I'm the guy telling everybody it's okay. A couple of weeks ago, Cunningham had to be *told* not to talk about how he thinks it would be great if the thugs in Lixubistan had nuclear weapons. Think about that one. Of course, Dexter says it's all going to change after the election. But he's going to be in the hospital. Or worse."

Evan crossed his arms. "So what are you going to do, Jack? Are you going to leave after the election?" He looked at John and added, "I forgot to tell you, they already told him they want him to stay."

I didn't answer at first. "I'm on Roger Castleton's show tomorrow." I glanced at both of them but that's all I said. I let it sink in.

"You're on Castleton's show? Oh my God, you're not going to quit on the show?" Evan looked at John.

John added, "Or announce you're leaving?"

"Sort of." I was trying not to cringe because I could already see what their reaction would be. "I was going to—you know—straighten things out."

Evan rolled his eyes and slumped back in his chair. "Oh Christ, Jack. Can you hear yourself? What the hell has gotten into you?"

John was more measured, as usual. "I'm all for the truth, Jack. But do you think that's wise?"

"No, not really."

"Get the truth out." Evan snorted. "Is that what you think would happen? Jeezus."

John nodded. "What do you want the outcome to be, Jack? The President resigns? Loses the election? What?"

"I don't know. I just can't go on lying. I'm not just spinning, I'm saying things, crucial things, that I know are lies."

John shifted on the seat. "What about some well-placed leaks?"

"Too late."

John looked at Evan. "Can't we generate something up here?"

Evan shrugged.

"Even if you could, it would take too long." I took a deep breath. "I have to do something. Now, when it counts."

Evan raised both hands, like I was the choir. "Okay, Jack, then here's what you do. You go on Castleton and say, 'I'm announcing that I'll be stepping down after the election. I want to return to private life.'"

I stared back at him.

John leaned forward again, pressed his hands together. "The thing is, Jack, I'm sympathetic to what you're saying. But think about it. What would actually happen? Christ, listen to me—I sound like you." John smiled. "Come on, you tell me—what would happen?"

Evan interrupted again. "They would be on every network, every schlocky cable channel telling what a moron you are. How you are unstable, how you were about to be fired. What would the story be Jack?"

I closed my eyes.

"You're fucking delusional if you think it would do any good." Evan's voice was becoming disgusted and angry. "John is right. Forget what they would say about you. Do you think it would change anything?"

I didn't answer.

Evan answered his own question. "No, of course it wouldn't. It's too late for that. You said it yourself."

John said in a gentle voice, "Jack, I don't know all the facts, of course. But I know that if you said anything misleading, it was to serve a higher purpose."

Like keeping my job, I wanted to say. "It seemed like the right thing at the time."

John nodded sympathetically.

Evan was rolling his eyes so much you might think they would get stuck. "What the fuck is wrong with you, Jack?"

John ignored Evan and went on: "As I see it, you have three choices. You can resign immediately, you can announce your resignation, or you can wait. But it makes no sense to self-destruct on the way out."

"A book deal. Is that it?" Evan sat back and crossed his arms. Looking smug. "Are you thinking this will get you on TV? Get you a book deal?"

"No. Of course not."

"I guess it could happen." Evan went on, ignoring me. "But the odds are you will be marginalized . . . and then, what do you do for a living?"

"I guess we don't have to ask what Bob thinks," John mused.

"You can guess. He thinks I'm a complete idiot for even questioning my role." I looked to John. "So you're saying, Senator, there really isn't any way to get right with this? I have to admit, that surprises me, John." I forgot myself. Although he didn't care if the formalities were observed.

"I don't know, Jack. I can't think how you do it. It's like the defense attorney who has somebody on the stand who has changed their story. They ask, were you lying then or are you lying now? Once you admit you lied, don't they stop listening to you?"

"Right. You're done." Evan added. "What about that good looking blonde woman from the State Department. Sandy, Sally . . ."

"Sarah?"

"Yeah. What will she think?" Evan smirked. "It might even hurt her career, right? After all, it's been in the papers—you two are an item and all."

"That's past tense, Evan." I hated to answer him. But I did think about Linda. She was supportive of me now, but if I went public, it would be over before it started.

"Past tense? God, you move fast. You don't happen to have her number still, do you?"

He was trying lighten up. That was better. Evan had dated, if you want to call it that, the same woman for at least five years. I relaxed a little. There was a long silence where we glanced back and forth at each other, not sure what to say. I looked at John. "I haven't forgotten who got me this job. You vouched for my loyalty. I remember. It means a lot to me."

John waved his hand. "Listen, Jack. I never thought . . . Let's just say, if you can use that devious brain of yours to figure out a way to make things right, as you say, without just falling on your sword, don't worry about me. But don't sacrifice yourself for nothing . . . What's the point of that?"

We shook hands and they wished me luck.

I couldn't sleep. Had no trouble getting up obscenely early for the show. The sun was just coming up as I drove to the studio. The streets were empty. I got there in time to eat a muffin in the Green Room, which I realized was a mistake as soon as it reached my stomach. Roger and I had about five minutes in his office before the show. I have been nervous before, but never like this. My hands quivered. I thought my knees would buckle when I walked on the set. I waited for them to hook up my microphone, then I sat at the table and waited.

A few minutes later, I saw Roger. They wired up his microphone and he sat across from me, placing his notes on the table in front of him. "Are you okay?" he said, hand over his mike.

People bustled around us, rushing around. I don't know what the hell they were doing. I spotted a trash can on the floor by Roger's feet and resolved to dive for it if my nausea got worse. I wasn't the only guest, but thank God I was the first one.

I managed to swallow and grin nonchalantly. Gave him the thumbs up. He stared at me, "Okay. Here we go . . ."

He did his intro then turned to me. He had the kindest voice—he sounded really nice, caring. But his questions invariably had daggers at the end. He began with the economy and the President's program. I smacked the answers back at him with humor and, if I may say, wit. I started to worry we would run out of time. It seemed like I had been there forever.

"Lixubistan has been in the news recently. There are reports Vice President Cunningham believes we should send in some troops to help the government maintain order. Is the President waiting until after the election to send in troops?"

"Come on, Roger, you know the Vice President's advice to the President is always private."

"But you aren't ruling that out?"

"We are very reluctant to take any option off the table."

"Given our concerns about nuclear proliferation, isn't the administration concerned about their plans to build a nuclear power plant?"

"They are a sovereign nation. They don't take orders from us, Roger."

"But couldn't they divert the nuclear materials and use them for military purposes, as other countries have done?"

"They have reassured us they need power, and have no intention of diverting anything . . . You worry too much, Roger."

"Is the Vice President calling the shots in the State Department, since President Dexter's illness? Are we beginning to see the reigns being turned over to him?"

"President Dexter has the highest confidence in the Vice President, Roger, but the President is fully in charge of his administration and his foreign policy."

He began, "Jack, there are only a few weeks left in the election. I know you lost your own father to cancer a little over a year ago. Did you ever have doubts about how President Dexter would do with the treatments and whether it was wise to maintain such a rigorous campaign schedule?"

"Why do you ask that? What have you heard?"

Roger looked at me, clearly puzzled. "I'm just asking how the President is doing, Jack. How's his health?"

I shot out of my chair, pointed at Roger: "Shame on you. You have no right to bring up questions like that. That's irresponsible. You are listening to idle rumors."

Roger blinked, then shrugged, "Jack, I don't think it is unreasonable to ask for his medical records."

"Really. So the President doesn't get to have any privacy? I told you what the President's condition is. I tell everyone every day."

Then I snatched my microphone out of my lapel, unhooked the wire behind my neck and threw it down on the table. And stormed off the set.

From the side, I could see Roger look into the camera, "Well, I guess we will leave it there. My guest today has been

Jack Abbott, Press Secretary to the President."

The broadcast went off the air and Roger sidled over and whispered, "You okay?"

"Sure," I whispered, offered a little smile. "How'd I do?" I said quietly, without moving my mouth.

His face told it all. Eyes a bit wide, the way he was looking at me. "Good." He nodded. "Good, I think. We'll see."

I nodded, realizing as I turned to go, that my stomach was betraying me. I knew where the bathroom was and I went for it.

Chapter Twenty-five

My cell phone started to ring as soon as the show went off the air. It was Linda. "Jack, are you alright?"

I exhaled. "Yes. I think so."

"What the hell just happened? Did you have a stroke or something?"

"No. I'm sorry. I just couldn't stop myself. When he started badgering me, hitting me with all those rumors."

"Jack. He wasn't . . ." I could hear another phone ringing. "Hold on, Jack. Don't hang up. It's Tyler"

After a moment she came back on the line. "Jack. Tyler thinks you did that on purpose."

"Are you serious?"

"You know I am. So how are you going to fix this, Jack? Are we going to put out a statement? Are you going over to the press room to resign? Or what?"

That stung. "I honestly don't know. I'm still in shock myself."

"Right. Keep holding." After another moment, she came back on the line. "Tyler asks if you know how to disappear."

"Yes. I guess so."

"Do it. Don't talk to any press. Keep this phone turned on and charged up. Just let the press calls go to voicemail. Then delete them."

I knew a place to go where the press couldn't find me. I was about halfway to the cabin when Evan called.

"Jack. Where are you?"

"I'm on my way to the cabin."

"Okay. I'm coming over."

"Really? That's great, but, don't you have to work?"

"It's Sunday."

"Oh, that's right."

As I drove in the lane, I saw a car was already there. Evan's. He and Bob were sitting on the front steps, clutching grandé coffees. I parked and got out of the car. I was exhausted but relatively calm. "How did you do that?"

They moved out of the way while I unlocked the front door. "We saw the show."

I pushed the door open and they followed me inside to the kitchen. Bob straddled a chair and Evan leaned in the doorway. I put on some tea.

Neither of them said anything. For a long time. Finally I couldn't stand it. "So, you saw the show."

Still nothing. I looked back and forth.

Evan drew a breath. "Why the fuck did you do that, Jack? Now all of Washington thinks you lost it."

I was working on an answer when he went on, "Did you? Did you lose it, Jack?"

I started to answer, looked at Bob.

"Brilliant."

"What do you mean?"

"You know what I mean. You know exactly." He chuckled. "I have to hand it to you."

Evan looked at Bob. "What are you talking about? He ralphed on himself. He messed his pants. Hell, he committed suicide on TV. On national TV."

"That's right."

"And here he sits. Like nothing happened." Evan squinted at me. "I was worried about you. After that—what was it Bob? A stunt?"

Bob smiled. A creepy, cynical smile.

"Oh shit, and here I thought he might hurt himself."

"You thought I was going to, what did you call it, 'hurt myself?' Oh Christ." It never dawned on me that they might

~ 267 ~

think I was suicidal.

"Fucking brilliant. And at the same time, stupid. You probably took down Dexter, as you well know. At least you didn't sacrifice your career for nothing. At least you can be smug about how you took down the best president we've had in fifty years, how you put our country in the hands of a . . ." Bob closed his eyes for a moment. Trying to recompose himself I guess.

"So that's all you two have to say? I was used. I was manipulated. I was managed. And I let them do it to me. Then, when I woke up, couldn't let them go on . . . Well? What do you think I should have done?"

"Okay. That's fine. I just hope you can afford your scruples. The only possible way to save you is to take you to rehab. Or to a hospital. And I'm not sure that would work. I don't know who in Washington is going to hire you after this. Your career is over."

After a long pause, Evan sighed. "I don't know about that."

Bob switched on the TV. At least I wasn't on the networks. He flipped to cable news. There I was, almost in slow motion. The anchor cut in, sympathetic tone, "The White House has issued a statement: 'Jack Abbott has asked the President for some time off after the grueling pace of the campaign. While he is gone, Scott Goodington will act as Press Secretary.'"

"I'm surprised. I thought for sure you would have offered your resignation and the President accepted it with appreciation for your service."

Bob shook his head. "No. No way. That would just send them scurrying in all directions to try to find out if there is anything really behind his breakdown."

"Shh." Evan held his finger to his lips, then pointed at the TV. The commercial was over and they had convened a panel to consider what it all meant. "Privately, White House officials are saying that Abbott has been acting increasingly strangely the last few days, showing unusual concern for the

President. They suspect he somehow has gotten him confused with his own father." And so on, debating my mental health, or lack thereof.

"So what good did it do? Just like I told you, Jack. All you have done is marginalize yourself."

"Not so fast, Evan." Bob crossed his arms. "Wait until this sinks in. They are going to bore with the deranged staff angle and explore the 'maybe he knew something' angle. By tomorrow. They won't be able to corroborate it, but people will start to talk about how Dexter looks. About how sick he looks."

"But they won't find anything, and Jack is left banging his head against the wall."

"I don't think so. He pulled the loose string. Now it is going to unravel until election day."

Chapter Twenty-six

The President was at Camp David for the weekend, practicing for the debate, resting up for the final push of the campaign. Tyler was up there with him.

Bob and Evan went back to Washington. Bob advised me to go to the office like nothing happened, so I would stay on the payroll. At least for now. Not a bad idea.

I went in early the next day. I skipped the staff meeting and hid in my office.

Goodington saw me unlocking the door, hurried to my side and patted me on the shoulder. "I'm sorry, Jack. Truly sorry."

Yeah, right.

The campaign had already faxed a new release to Goodington, and he sheepishly showed me a copy:

"Daily briefings are suspended until after the election. Please direct all policy and scheduling questions to the campaign staff."

Linda came over later in the morning. She plopped on my couch. "I hope nobody saw me come in here." That was a joke. There were no secrets. "I'm surprised to see you."

I nodded. "No doubt." I asked her, "Why didn't they fire me? I mean, accept my resignation?"

She sighed. "Dexter. He wouldn't let them." She tilted her head, like she was too tired to hold it up. "And Tyler decided it would make it seem too important. Better to shrug it off."

I didn't know what to say—that I hoped I hit my mark?

She looked me in the eye, unsmiling. "Did you really do it, Jack?"

"Do what?"

"You bastard."

I shrugged. "Not newsworthy. Also, I might be a bastard, but at least I can look myself in the mirror now."

She frowned. "You seemed so smart, in some ways . . ." Then she shook her head, like I was hopeless. " . . . but you still don't understand."

"How's the President?"

"Tired. We're putting him through his paces for the debate." She stood up, crossed her arms, then uncrossed them. "I'll be glad when it's over."

"Me too." I took a step toward her and she eased away from me." I hope he wins, you know. I still do."

She held the doorknob but before she tugged open my door, she turned and said, "Take care of yourself, Jack."

I walked toward her, held the door with both hands, as she slipped through it. "You too," I whispered after her.

The debate the next Sunday night was even more important, now that the President's health was in question again. Would he look tired, was he "with it?" Who could forget his fainting spell at the Convention? Tyler had negotiated for only one debate and had, as usual, gotten his way. There would be no second chance. The week zipped by and the questions did not go away.

The debate was held just outside Washington, in Richmond, Virginia. Oakton, who had become pretty much a foreign policy scholar during his stint in the Senate, was understated and respectful. But if he had a submachine gun with him he wouldn't have been much more effective. Okay, faster maybe.

"What are the major threats to our country and what should we do to handle them?"

Oakton launched into Lixubistan. He talked

knowledgably about the politics and our role: "We have no business helping a corrupt government suppress its people. We shouldn't be encouraging our companies to rush into a very unstable area. I have grave questions about the wisdom of assisting them in building their power plant, as Vice President Cunningham has been advocating. And, he plans to take a trade delegation after the election. I think that is a huge mistake which could lead to another unstable country holding nuclear weapons."

Dexter looked like he was going to keel over right in front of us. He should have said, "The Vice President has done an excellent job and I fully agree with his statements." But what he actually said was, "I think the Vice President has done an excellent job. I fully support his *intentions* in this region." He smiled one of those million dollar grins. "However, American interests are humanitarian as well as strategic and economic. It is the policy of this administration to discourage the proliferation of nuclear weapons and nuclear capabilities throughout the world. This policy is unalterable."

The interviewer blinked, pausing an extra second to move on to the next topic. Surely that would be the headline the next day. Dissension in the Administration. President yanks chain of Vice President.

Or, that would have been the news. A few moments later, Dexter, rebutting a point Oakton had made, stopped mid-sentence and closed his eyes. He took a couple of breaths, then went on. The cameras were tight on his face.

Secret Service agents started toward him from the wings, but stopped when he resumed speaking. Dexter gave a sharp look to the Secret Service and they disappeared again.

The Secret Service insisted on taking him to Walter Reed, where he spent the night. This close to the election, there was no way to pretend to hide at Camp David. Oakton announced he would take a break from campaigning as long as Dexter was in the hospital, which turned out to be only one day.

There was an immediate gush of sympathy for the President. But in a few days, the twin images of my emotional defense of him and his tottery performance at the debate, in combination with his public rebuke of Cunningham let the air out of his support. Clearly, the President was feeble, and Cunningham? After all, even the President had problems with him. With less than a week to the election, support for the President drained away each day like a snowman melting in the sun.

I suppose it didn't help that the press figured I was muzzled because I had let the truth slip out. But I wasn't a hero or anything, because they *knew* I hadn't done it on purpose. They thought I was just another loyal stooge, whose fealty had gone over the top. Bob and Evan were barely speaking to me.

I wondered. Seeing is not always believing. I remembered how the President could go from a crumpled heap to his ebullient, smiling self in a matter of seconds. And I remember looking into his eyes in the limo and seeing the anguish when I mentioned Cunningham's name. So I wondered. The only one who really knew was the President, and I didn't expect him to share with me.

The President heard the election results in his hotel room, surrounded by friends. That, of course, did not include me. I had voted absentee, and I went to the White House to watch the show with the press office staff. We were running a little behind in the polls, but with the margin of error, who knew? But this time, the polls were right: Dexter lost.

It was close. A hundred thousand votes would have turned around the popular vote, and the electoral vote hung on two close states. The President didn't concede until after three. I had gone to sleep on my desk, quite unintentionally. I woke up and there he was, conceding. I cried, right along with all the other Dexter staff.

After the election, Tyler seemed to lose the will to castrate me. In a way, I was protected from Tyler by his own spin. To explain what I had done, to pull my White House pass, he would have had to explain why I was disloyal and what I had done. Linda didn't speak to me. She looked through me like I was a ghost, never making eye contact. I steered clear of Linda and Tyler's office.

Bob and Evan forgave me enough to invite me to a New Year's party at Evan's house. After some preliminary insults, we were back in form. Evan took me aside and said he was thinking of getting married. Bob acted even nuttier than usual, but I noticed he was drinking 7up. Maybe he could drive me home for a change.

On Inauguration Day, I waited with the other staff on the East Front of the Capitol, as Dexter got in the helicopter with Tyler. It wasn't as sad as you might have expected. Not like a funeral. Very dignified, actually. To me, it looked like relief on their faces, especially Dexter's. Or maybe that was what I wanted to see.

After, I got in my car and drove back across the bridge to the cabin. It was unusually warm, almost fifty degrees, but a little windy. I pushed the dinghy in the water and tied it up to the dock. The wind picked up and I decided to get the small outboard from the shed. I got the bottle of Jack Daniels from the dresser and powered the boat out to the mouth of the cove. Close to home but far enough to see the big water. The wind was stronger there, cold and hard. I unscrewed the top of the bottle and held it over the side, so the wind wouldn't blow Dad's ashes up in my face. The wind whipped them sideways as they trickled out—a wild ride. He would have liked that. I almost could smile. It took a while to empty. Then, I pushed the bottle under the chilly water, watched the bubbles rush to the surface. When it was heavy with water, I let go and it dropped out of my numb fingers toward the bottom of the bay.

I sat in the boat for a few minutes and just drifted. The wind pushed me steadily toward the other shore. But that wasn't where I wanted to go, so I cranked up the little engine and headed home.

Acknowledgements

Spin Doctor is entirely a work of fiction. It may be tempting for those who know me to try to match up my past life in politics with the characters in this book. As for my former employers, without exception, I owe them my thanks for their generosity in hiring me, for their patience and kindness towards me. My former employers and associates were truly public servants and I am proud to have worked with them.

This novel has been in progress for a long time. During that time, Paula Aaronson, Randy Fisher, Dorothy Fisher and J.C. Carter have given me many invaluable comments and edits. My editor, Evan Roe, is first-rate and a pleasure to work with. I owe a special thanks to Cassandra Lewis, award winning playwright and niece, for her insights and inspiration. This novel would never have been begun, let alone finished, without the ongoing encouragement and support of my family: Dorothy and Charles, Charles, Pamela and Gabriel, Randy, Dorrie and Tom.

A Note to My Readers

Thank you for reading *Spin Doctor*. As an indie author, I especially appreciate your support and am helped tremendously by your word of mouth recommendations and reviews on Goodreads, Shelfari, Amazon and other booksellers. Please visit my website, mclewisbooks.com, for more information, including a reading group guide. My blog, NovelPolitics.com, follows the great drama found in every election. I love to hear from my readers. You can reach me via my website and on Twitter, @NovelPolitics.

Coming soon: *Potomac Lights.*

What was life like before *Spin Doctor*? How did Jack get to know Bob, Evan and Senator John Cook? What compelled John Cook to run for office in the first place? And what about the scandal that almost ended his political career?

Printed in Poland
by Amazon Fulfillment
Poland Sp. z o.o., Wrocław